C000229140

ROPE'S END

ROPE'S END

Seneca Drewe

Universe Press

Universe Press
an imprint of Unicorn Publishing Group
101 Wardour Street
London W1F 0UG

www.unicornpublishing.org

All rights reserved. No part of this publication may be
reproduced, stored in a retrieval system or transmitted,
in any form or by any means, electronic, mechanical,
photocopying, recording or otherwise, without prior
permission in writing from the publisher.

© Seneca Drewe, 2016

The moral right of Seneca Drewe to be identified
as the author of this work has been asserted by him
in accordance with the Copyright, Design and
Patents Act of 1988.

A catalogue record for this book is available from
the British Library

First published 2016

ISBN 978-0-9932424-5-8

Cover design by Ryan Gearing
Typeset by Vivian@Bookscribe

Printed and bound in Great Britain

CHAPTER ONE

Twenty-eight feet under water, in utter silence and darkness, James Huwes waited, immobile in his breathing apparatus. During the next five minutes he would either kill or be killed. All other options had vanished. And his enemy was extremely close, perhaps six feet away.

He was surprised to find that he did not fear death itself, but the manner of dying, knifed and drowned at the bottom of a muddy river in Santa Rosa, would be highly disagreeable while it lasted.

He knew what he had to do and his mind was super-alert to do it, but his memory kept reverting to the terrifying tangle of circumstances that had put him in this deadly position.

* * * * *

It had all started in the hot summer of 1967. An overnight telegram had arrived as he was having breakfast with his mother. It was a moment that changed his life:

> HUWES UPTON HOUSE CHURBRIDGE ARE YOU
> INTERESTED TAKING LADY STEYNES YACHT TO WEST
> INDIES LEAVING SEPTEMBER DURATION UNKNOWN
> RING STONHAM MAGNA 372 SIGNED HODGES

He read it, and his mother watched him, curious.

"Who's Lady Steyne?" he asked her, handing her the telegram.

"I don't know," she replied, reading it slowly. "Try *Who's Who*."

He got up and went to the study. His father's old copy of *Who's Who*, dated the year of his death, contained no entry under Steyne. He went back to the breakfast room and his mother's probing.

"Any luck, dear?" she asked.

"Not a word."

"Who is this Hodges?"

"He was my captain in the *Wilton*." James remembered his time in the Navy with a touch of wistfulness. He had had a modest success there. Those minesweepers in the Mediterranean had given him perhaps the best and most fulfilling time of his life. Since then there had been failures – all sorts of failures.

"I remember, dear," his mother said. "He was the one you always liked, not like that other dreadful man. I wonder why he's taking this yacht to the West Indies."

James said nothing. His mother was desperately interested in his reaction to this surprise, but he did not know his own mind yet. He had a good deal to think about. Recently he had felt the millstone of his family home and estate becoming more and more oppressive. When his father died his mother had run the estate, which had always been legally hers, and although James had become more and more involved in its management his mother never released her hold over any important decision. James was fond of his mother, but he found the situation stifling. There was just not enough money to run the place properly, and this fact made them both edgy in their endless discussions of what should be done. Several ideas of his to make the estate more profitable had foundered because of his mother's reluctance to experiment. His latest enterprise, which he had at last managed to persuade her to agree to, was to breed Shetland ponies in the park. It seemed that failure was not very far away there either because although Shetlands looked attractive from a distance, people did not seem particularly interested in buying them.

"Well, dear," said his mother, totally predictable as always, "I don't know whether you are taking this mysterious offer seriously. Of course whether you go or not is your decision. I dare say I could manage to get along without you, so don't feel obliged to stay here on my account, although it is the most important time of the year. But if you ask me ..."

James felt spontaneous annoyance making him uncomfortable. Why should his mother always intrude on his decisions?

"... you'll run into endless complications," she continued. "As an employee of Lady Steyne, whoever she may be, you'll be subject to her every whim and fancy. You may find yourself thrown off in some unknown part of the world and have to pay your own way back home."

"I doubt that."

"James, you really ought to settle down to one thing and stick to it. If you go flitting from job to job like your cousin Freddy ..."

"I haven't decided for or against this business yet."

He was irritated. The gibe about Freddy, who was always taking on unexpected jobs, was unfair. He excused himself and went back into the study. It was good of Oz Hodges to telegram rather than telephone this offer; it gave him time to turn it over unhurriedly. Clearly there were many things that had to be sorted out before he could decide definitely, but as he dialled the number he realised that he had practically made his decision already.

Oz's voice was jovial and familiar.

"Hello old boy – how's things?"

"Fine, thank you sir – I got your telegram just now."

"Splendid – are you interested?"

"Yes indeed – what's it all about?"

"Well, I'm not entirely in the picture myself, but Lady Steyne, who was an old friend of my mother's, is having a yacht built for her to swan around the world in. She's asked me to drive it. And having been on the beach for two years now I leapt at it. I'd like you to be my First Lieutenant."

Oz sounded the same as always. He couldn't quite say his r's and he pronounced the word "built" as though it was spelt "beelt".

"Sounds just the job, sir. How long for?"

"Don't know yet. Look, I shall know more about this later today after one of Lady Steyne's henchmen has been to see me. Why don't you come down and spend the night here and I can tell you all I know about it?"

James had agreed and rung off, reminding himself that staying in the Oz household was an experience in itself anyway.

* * * * *

As he guided the old Rover along the curving roads of Wiltshire with the telegram beside him, he realised how little he knew about the whole venture. Was he crazy to contemplate abandoning the estate and his ponies just now? Could his mother really manage?

He turned off the road at the Stonham Magna signpost and the car moved easily down a hill towards the village. It was ages since he had been here. It looked more built-up and vaguely unfamiliar. He stopped alongside a woman pushing a pram.

"Could you tell me where Down Hill Farm is, please?"

"Down Hill Farm? Couldn't say at all. Sorry." A local though.

"Commander Hodges?" he tried.

"Ah, Hodges's – straight on past Big Tree and first left."

James thanked her and drove on. He remembered Big Tree; it was an enormous chestnut growing more or less out of the middle of a crossroads, with a shabby wooden sign that had once invited you to

"Keep Left". As he kept left and encountered the savage turns required for this manoeuvre, he remembered five years ago a hazy-hot Saturday afternoon when Oz had invited him up from Portland for a game of golf. That had been when he first discovered Stonham Magna, sleepy and nestling deep in unkempt winding lanes. He felt quite separated from the self he remembered of those days, recalling his slightly disreputable sports car, hood back, bare elbow resting on the window ledge and golf clubs tossed into the seat beside him. He had scarcely played golf since then. How had he managed to get into such a rut?

Suddenly he was driving up to the front door. He got out, stretched his back, and extricated his grip from the boot. The front door was open, and as the various noises coming out of it seemed in no way connected with his knocks, he walked in.

Two enormous Old-English sheepdogs bounded up, growled, interrogated him briefly, and bounded off. James, by now covered with dog hairs, picked his way carefully between two pianos, side by side, round a Chinese urn, and past an ancient barrel of cider dripping into a jug. Two clocks started striking. A girl aged about ten rushed in at a door, said "Hello-they're-all-in-there," and rushed out again. He had a vague feeling that something was happening and realised he had been counting the chimes. Fourteen, fifteen, sixteen – one of the clocks had dropped out but still the other struck and struck again. He paused in the hall, counting to himself, as the house seemed quieter.

Twenty-four, twenty-five – could a clock strike forever? Thirty-two, thirty-three, click! Suddenly it stopped. The drawing-room door burst open and people streamed out into the hall, laughing, hooraying, congratulating each other. He found himself surrounded by the entire family, which seemed to consist largely of dogs and small girls, and towering above them all was the basset-like face of Oz Hodges, welcoming and explaining.

"My dear James, how very nice to see you again. Please forgive this display of family hysteria, but your arrival has precipitated a horological jackpot. These American clocks – a hobby of mine, you may remember – this particular one is a great favourite and it's just achieved a *triple* – ten plus eleven plus twelve – the theoretical maximum for this kind of mechanism. It's never happened before. We were all in there counting breathlessly. This is a great moment. Come on in. Have a glass of cider."

James received the warmest of smiles from Mrs Hodges and a heavy cut-glass goblet of cider from Oz.

"We haven't seen you, James, for far too long," she said with her rather attractive trace of a French accent. She was an Alsatian.

"What an omen, you coming and Matilda striking thirty-three," said the eldest daughter, wearing red slacks and sitting cross-legged on the floor by the fire. "You must come more often, James."

She looked a sophisticated thirteen, tall and leggy, like her mother but not yet so pretty. He would have to find out all their names. No one was likely to do much introducing.

"It was a glorious summer's day," said James, "and we played golf, last time I was here. And you gave us a fine dinner of mussels with pearls in them, Mrs Hodges, if you remember."

"I remember it well, but you seem to have forgotten to call me Marie-Claire." A flashing smile.

"Thank you, Marie-Claire."

Someone dashed off shouting, "I remember, I remember," to find the matchbox with the tiny seed pearls she had collected from the grown-ups on that memorable evening.

"Have we got time to, before tea?" asked one of the girls in a stage whisper to her mother, with conspiratorial glances towards the others.

"I suppose so," said Marie-Claire, "if James can bear it."

James looked suitably mystified and intrigued.

"Could you bear to witness a ..."

"Oh, Maman, don't tell, you beast."

"Well," said Oz, "let's talk turkey. You know when they promoted me to the 'dry' list after all my faithful work driving *Wilton* around the oceans ..."

"Damn shame," said James.

"... and I was pretty disappointed, naturally, and I suppose somewhat resentful of all those twerps who got on to the 'wet' list ..."

"Particularly Angus Swallow?"

"Among others, Angus Swallow. Anyway, I resigned to run this creaking family farm and I also got a two-days-a-week job as a local salesman for a firm of fertiliser distributors, of all things."

"I didn't know that," said James. "I thought you were just a gentleman farmer."

"Didn't bring in enough to keep my large team of women happy," said Oz. "You must know some of the difficulties farmers are in at the moment."

"I do indeed." The number of people in the room seemed, on balance, to be diminishing.

"So. That's the uninteresting life history of O. Hodges, until a week ago when I got a letter from a certain Mr Winter, who seems to be a sort of accountant-lawyer-Flag-Lieutenant to Lady Steyne."

"Who *is* Lady Steyne?"

"The widow of Sir Joseph Steyne, late recluse, miser and chain-store millionaire, or probably billionaire. My mother used to know her ages ago in Malta, before either of them was married. She was quite a gal: dark, half-Spanish in fact, attractive, and on the fringes of the so-called International Jet Set. Apparently, when she married Joe Steyne, who was already quite well known for meanness and money, everyone hoped she would be able to bring him out of his shell."

"She didn't succeed?"

"No. The old boy became quite eccentric as he got older – they say he used to keep most of his vast wealth in emeralds secreted about the house and make his wife wash up with Lifebuoy soap. He hated publicity and wouldn't go out at all. Anyway, last year he died, and was hardly cold before her ladyship decided to make up for lost time."

"So she bought a yacht," said James, not forgetting his telephone conversation but trying to provoke Oz into saying "built" in his own peculiar way.

"Well, she's having one beelt," he replied. "At Cowes. It's due to be completed in September. And that's where I come in. Lady S. thought of me in a brainstorm, and I found myself invited to be captain of this yacht, man her, and take her out to the West Indies to await my lady's pleasure. This chap Winter was here this morning to iron out the details."

"And what are the details, sir?"

Oz outlined them. They were remarkably generous. A salary rather more than James had thought possible, all expenses paid, and a free flight back to England twice a year for a fortnight's leave – more if the programme allowed. Oz had a contract for a year; the rest of the ship's company were to be at one month's notice.

"So you see, James, I jumped at it. Although I shall hate leaving my family, it will be a great joy to be back at sea again, and financially of course I shall be able to put this farm back on its feet."

James's thoughts were following similar lines, but without the family ties.

"This yacht – how big is she?" he asked.

"Large motor yacht, eight hundred tons, a hundred and ninety feet long, twin screws. Looks very pretty. She's called *Mozart*. Apparently Lady Steyne has just discovered music."

"Have you seen her?"

"The ship or the lady? Anyway, neither. I'm going down to Cowes this week to see the builders and how they are getting on. Later I shall have to stay at Cowes until she is completed, and I would like you to do so too. As for the lady, she is somewhere in the Middle East at the moment. I doubt if we shall meet her till she flies out to the West Indies to join us."

Suddenly the door burst open and four creatures minced in, moving in step and howling. It took James a moment or two to realise that these were the four Hodges girls performing a burlesque of a well-known pop group. Their heads were covered with fantastic wigs, they strummed imaginary guitars, and they weaved their hips around in a lithe and seductive way. Their grotesque noises filled the room, unmelodious, harsh and yet surprisingly rhythmic. James was completely astounded. It was a dreadful row.

They finished as abruptly as they had started, and were duly clapped out of the room. Comment seemed superfluous, and it became very quiet. Oz rose from his tattered armchair and strolled to the window to look out over the farm – his ewes with their lambs, his small herd of cows, his beehives, his cider-apple trees. James wondered whether it was deliberately arranged that they should all be visible from this window. Without looking down Oz picked up a pipe with his right hand and with his left opened a Chinese casket containing homemade tobacco. He filled his pipe, thoughtfully, knowing James would be guessing most of his thoughts – how much it would trouble him to leave his wife, his four children, his farm, his clocks, his collection of Chinese oddities. And how much Marie-Claire would have avoided dissuading him, if he really thought he must go back to sea and earn a small fortune. A Chinnery portrait of a Chinese, all benevolence and composure, smiled down from the wall.

Oz turned: "Are you on, old friend?"

"Of course I'm on, sir. When do we start?"

CHAPTER TWO

James had much to occupy him during the next few weeks. Oz had asked him to come down to Cowes a month before the yacht commissioned, which gave him four weeks to organise his affairs. It had seemed just about enough at the time; three weeks later it seemed absurdly little. First his mother had to be coped with, and he remembered driving back from Stonham Magna wondering how difficult that would be. But she had made no difficulties over his decision, and seemed calmer about it than he had expected. In fact he found that they could discuss the arrangements for the estate without exasperating each other – almost the first time this had been possible since his father's death. Of course, she had had time to think it over during his absence, and seemed to have realised that his mind had been nearly made up anyway. Surprisingly she was even encouraging him and taking an interest in his arrangements. James reflected sadly how little they now knew each other. They had once been so alike that when he was a boy people would mistake their voices on the telephone, and their conversation would be almost unintelligible to outsiders. The estrangement had been mostly his fault, he decided, because he had been unable or unwilling to cut the apron strings delicately enough and she remained subconsciously resentful. Not an unusual situation perhaps. As he struggled to do all he could to make his absence easy for her, his mind leaned, as it often did, on a favourite truism: he had his own life to lead. She refrained from saying so too, and for that he was grateful.

There was also the question of Alice. Alice Cullerby had become a tall, dark girl – little more than a childhood friend really, he thought, but they had known each other for years, and he suspected she might be becoming fond of him lately. He would have to say goodbye to her in a way that would not leave her guessing. She worked in London for a music agency, but her family lived nearby. Her father was a businessman of some sort and kingpin of the local Conservative party; her mother was an opera singer, more or less retired. It was common talk that James and Alice would make a very suitable match – common, that is, with everyone except James and Alice. He found her likeable, and very pretty, and her letters were literate and entertaining, but her outlook and conversation lacked sparkle. Being in her company did not inspire him with any kind of restless enthusiasm.

He mused, as he drove up to London to say goodbye to her, that if ever he wanted a conventional wife Alice would provide one *par excellence*. Strikingly good looks, a family he could certainly get on with – but a trifle dull perhaps? – No, it simply would not do. But at her little basement flat she greeted him on the doorstep with a most stimulating smile.

"James – you are most welcome." She did speak beautifully.

"Alice, my dear." He kissed her lightly. She was a little too tall for him.

"How are you?"

"Fine. And you?"

"Oh fine!"

It would require a good deal of perseverance to keep the evening's conversation alive. A charming, devoted girl, without much originality in her sleek, dark head.

The evening itself was to start on conventional lines. As they took their places in the theatre he remembered how he had looked through the theatre guide and wondered how it was possible for such a large list to provide so little choice. He was jaded, he told himself, as the curtain rose on some upper-class drawing-room of fifty years ago. He should have stayed at the flat and discovered if Alice wanted to be seduced. He suddenly found the possibility quite enlivening.

The play ended, they agreed it was not bad, and went off to a small restaurant for dinner. They sat at the miniature bar and James found his spirits revive with the second gin. Count your blessings, said the old song. After all, he had just landed a job full of interest and money, a job that would be envied by all these dark-suited characters sitting around with their London girls. While they continued their common tasks, he would be buccaneering off to the West Indies. Another gin. Alice was as charming as ever and listened to what he was saying, which was much more than most people ever did. In fact he found her raptness encouraged him, and his sentences were becoming longer and better formed, and his amusing arguments proceeding logically to unanswerable conclusions. They took their places at a table, and he saw his companion with new, kindly eyes – saw her measure up to the severe glamour-pussies at the neighbouring tables, and perhaps exceed them in every aspect of their art. She had become infinitely more amiable and desirable, and he was a blithe deceiver with an intimate manner. After all, they had known each other for years and years. Had they not, as children, once had a forbidden bathe together in the nude? He reminded her of it, and she blushed and laughed but did not look away.

"This wine is excellent," he found himself saying.

"Yes, isn't it," she said. "I do like a really good fruity wine."

"I thought you'd like it."

"Well chosen."

"It's Chilean."

"Of course it's Chilean."

"I'm getting hints of ..."

"Me too."

That was a surprise, and she gave him a lovely wild burst of laughter.

"I love your laugh," he said.

"So do I. I'd be miserable without it."

They both laughed.

He raised a finger. Normally raising a finger does not summon a waiter, but it did in this case.

"Waiter, another one of these superb bottles of wine, if you please."

As he drove very carefully back to her flat, he realised that whatever the outcome of the rest of the evening he was not making his long-term intentions any clearer. This was only a tiny irritation of conscience, and like an oyster he overlaid it with a covering vastly more attractive. Anyway, he thought, perhaps it did no harm after all to keep a girl guessing for a bit. Anyway, here was the flat.

She was all lightness and pliancy in his arms, and he knew with a surge of excitement that he could succeed. She had conformed for too long. She made some coffee while he sprawled on the sofa, basking in his great good fortune. Was it not astonishing to spend the night with dear conventional Alice? Was this not a memorable evening after all? Surely here, tonight, he had the world at his fingertips.

She sat beside him and they talked and kissed and she smiled, most beguilingly, and the coffee became cold on the table beside them. And then he led her into the bedroom, she apologising for its untidiness and he earnestly brushing her apologies aside. Outside it was beginning to rain.

"Shall I turn the light off now?" he said. "Or don't you mind?"

"I don't think I know," she said, bounding into bed like a frightened hare.

She was sweet and ladylike and required no excuses to be made for her; she had made up her mind. James was courteous with her, and successful because he liked her very much; and at the last moment she tossed her head back with a startling gesture of total abandonment, and he loved her utterly. Then she nuzzled the hair on his chest, sighed, and smiled remotely, and he wished he could purr. Then she cried a little with joy, and they made love again. She looked absurdly young when they made love. How old was she? He could not remember. Cradle-snatcher.

Afterwards, in the sullen London dawn, he left the flat and started the long drive home. The streets were shiny-grey and empty. He felt triumphant but tired, and his mind refused to face the changed relationships this surprising night might be expected to bring. Sex does change things.

But he had a job to do, he told himself, starting tomorrow, and he would be gone in a month. Perhaps he had created problems, but Alice had been very loving, and surely there was an obligation somewhere to live one's life to the full. His mind was a confusion of Don Juan clichés and lurking accusations. Cad, it told him. Gallant. Buccaneer.

* * * * *

James headed for Cowes with his car full of baggage. There seemed to be a sense of expectancy in the air as the ferry left the jetty and headed down Southampton Water towards the Isle of Wight. It was a sunny morning, but a stiff breeze over the deck made it pleasantly cool. Great cumulus clouds billowed all round the horizon. Good gliding weather, he thought. And the fishing season will be over soon. Pity to have missed it. Not many trout in the West Indies, and I haven't fished this year.

As the ferry passed Netley, the largest liner ever built came into view, rounding Calshot Spit light vessel in a smooth curve, heeling just perceptibly in the turn. Then she steadied on to her course like a faultless gymnast on a high bar. The ferry was keeping well clear, but *Queen Elizabeth* seemed to tower above them as she glided up Southampton Water to her home. With the wind full in his face, James was stirred by the sight of this enormous complex of humans and machinery. Ships and the sea held a great fascination for him. It seemed a good omen for a seagoing venture.

The ferry entered Cowes harbour and he had half a glimpse of a large motor yacht behind the floating dock: light grey hull with a blue band round it, white superstructure. No other yacht of that size in the yard – it must be *Mozart*. Once off the ferry he drove through the narrow Cowes streets, crowded with shoppers and anoraked yachtsmen. He parked outside the arch that marked the entrance to the old shipyard. Oz met him as he walked underneath it, going in the opposite direction.

"The gateway to adventure. Morning, James. Welcome aboard." He was in a hurry.

"Morning, sir. All well?"

"No. Moderate crisis. See you lunchtime in the bar of The Bull. Must fly." And Oz was gone.

James went into the grey hangar-like collection of buildings, which were echoing with shipbuilding noises. Few things disturbed Oz's equanimity, but something had.

This time yesterday, he thought, I was driving back from Alice's flat. I wonder what she thinks of me now. But enough of women. On with the job!

CHAPTER THREE

The little office which the shipbuilders had put at the disposal of the master of the *Mozart* was crowded with people, and James could see through the glass door that they were all arguing with each other. There was some kind of a flap on. Being reluctant to get embroiled just at that moment, he walked past the door and found his way down to the yacht. She was secured alongside the cluttered disorderly jetty, and was indeed the one he had seen from the ferry. She looked sleek and beautiful, with a shimmering coat of grey paint, so light in colour that it seemed almost white until the eye compared it to the stark white of the superstructure. A few feet below the unbroken sweeping line of her main deck ran a band of the brightest blue, interrupted only at the bow with a space for her name. A man suspended on a plank was painting in the name, and for some reason he had started at the end. ART it read, and she did seem to James a work of art as she lay there, almost finished, gleaming in the sun. Both bow and stern were raked, not excessively so, and the sloping lines of bridge, mast and ensign staff all matched each other, giving her a sturdy air of surging forward into the sea. He wondered how true it was that what looks good to a seaman's eye behaves well at sea. Certainly she gave an impression of grace and compactness that was entirely pleasing. ZART she was now called, as he stepped up the brow and went aboard.

Between decks the ship was a mess, but there was a hint of system in the chaos of panelling, electric leads and ventilation trunking that were strewn along the passageways. He picked his way round carefully, gradually becoming familiar with the layout of the ship. Clearly no expense had been spared in the fitting out of this splendid vessel. She was air-conditioned throughout of course. Her finishings were luxurious, but not gaudy. The officers' quarters were extremely comfortable and made James remember his year sharing one of the tiny cabins of a coastal minesweeper, cheek by jowl in almost intolerable sweaty heat. Dockyard workmen were all over the place, and occasionally a muffled roar of welding came from another part of the ship.

He went aft and came to what were obviously Lady Steyne's staterooms. They were sumptuously furnished. He noticed polished wood, deep carpets, a faint expensive smell of new leather, and some elaborate tape recording equipment discreetly built in. There was something missing from the traditional decor; he couldn't determine what it was at first. A man in brown overalls was standing on a cocktail cabinet doing something to the panelling, almost hidden by chintz drapery.

"Morning," said James.

"Good morning to you," said the dockyard joiner, jumping nimbly down from the cocktail cabinet. He was wearing felt shoes to avoid scratching the French polish.

"So these are the royal apartments," said James. He felt inclined to talk to this man.

"Proper job, isn't it?" said the joiner, lighting a cigarette. "Do you see what's missing?"

James was aware of an incongruity. Part of his mind had been nagging away at this problem ever since he had entered the room. Another part took refuge in a rather feeble bit of repartee.

"If it's missing how can I see it?"

"Ha! Wise guy."

"I'll buy it. What's missing?"

"No lights," said the joiner. "Photo-luminescent panels. First ever at sea."

There were indeed no lights in the cabin. The joiner explained the principles of the electrically charged panelling on the bulkheads that provided flat, heat-less sources of light.

"All this lot's coming out again though," he said. "Lady Whatnot wants this berloody great five-wheel safe in here. Why she couldn't've thought of it before beats me. *And* another cabin for her nephew they tell me. A lot of the officers' accommodation's got to be reorganised. Flipping breaks your heart. There's a right panic going on about it."

"Will it put the completion date out?"

"Bound to." The joiner then considered it for a moment. "Well, we might just get it done on double overtime, *if* they want to pay for it. *I* don't mind – I enjoy starting early on a sunny morning at this time of year. All depends on money."

James left him and went ashore. It did indeed mostly depend on money. But the yacht was also built with good sense and good taste, and he warmed to her and felt protective. MOZART was now painted bravely on her bow and it seemed the final touch that gave a personality to a beautiful ship, as the Chinese, when painting a ceremonial dragon, brush in the eye last to bring it to life. He found he had taken to her in a way he had almost forgotten that seamen take to their ships, and then usually only in retrospect. He retraced his steps delighted.

Back in the little office the throng had subsided a bit and James went in. A number of people round a desk were taking instructions from a very dark young man who was giving orders with remarkable self-assurance. They caught each other's eye and at the same instant recognised each other.

Peter Moraes, of all people.

But what was he doing here? Why was he giving orders to the builders? James remembered him as Black Pedro, a schoolboy in a straw hat, slightly an outsider, not quite liking the nickname by which everyone knew him. Did his family not live in South America? What was going on?

"Thank you, gentlemen," Moraes said to the dockyard officials round him, and ignored them completely as they collected up papers and drawings and left. "James, my dear chap, good to see you after all these years."

James's slight bewilderment did not show above the well-worn social ritual. They exchanged pleasantries and the situation unfolded. Peter Moraes was Lady Steyne's nephew, and had arrived the day before with her new instructions which were now spreading alarm and despondency among those responsible for the nearly finished yacht. Apart from the requirement for a large safe, which entailed refurbishing much of the main saloon, Moraes was to come with them in some undefined capacity, and an extra cabin had to be fitted up to accommodate him. As the joiner had surmised, this was going to cost a fearful amount of money, but no one seemed less concerned about it than Moraes himself.

James had never liked Black Pedro much at school. Now he felt that he was already casting a blight over the proceedings, and that his supremely confident manner might well become irritating. Then James remembered an old maxim of his father's: nothing is ever as good or as bad as it first seems. Dull, depressing, usually right.

He escaped from Black Pedro to keep his rendezvous in the bar of The Bull. Oz was in rather less than his usual high spirits, and it was not difficult to guess why.

"Good to have you here, James. I need an ally. For the past three weeks I've been battling with the builders to make sure Lady Steyne gets a ship worthy of the colossal amount of money she is spending. The firm is absolutely first-class but naturally they see all things in terms of profit and loss, and they need a bit of chivvying. Just as I was beginning to see daylight and *Mozart* moving to a grand finale, this character Moraes arrives acting like the god from the machine and turns the place upside down. Of course if Grandma wants to rehash her yacht at the eleventh hour at enormous expense, that's up to her. But this nephew of hers is going to require my utmost resources of self-restraint. Ah, well, the best laid schemes ..."

"And he's coming with us, he tells me," said James.

"Yes. Perish the thought."

"What's he going to do on board?"

"Dunno. Self-appointed political commissar, I suppose."

James smiled. Oz was resilient and would soon come to terms with the imposition of Black Pedro. He ordered another couple of pints. In *Wilton*, he remembered, his captain had never drunk spirits, not even duty-free gin at tuppence a tot.

"Will the ship be ready in time?"

"Well, we don't quite know yet, but I think they may just about be able to make our completion date. We've got to be in Bermuda by the middle of October to pick up our alma mater."

"Grandma?"

"Grandma."

"What then?"

"Quite a nice programme ahead. It seems we shall do a quick tour round some of the Caribbean islands, through the canal about Christmas, then Acapulco, Monterey, San Francisco, Vancouver. Then all the way south to Santa Rosa, where we've got to be in the summer."

"Why Santa Rosa?"

"Grandma has relations there. In fact Moraes is half Ecuadorian and there's a family firm in Santa Rosa."

"I knew he had some connection with South America," said James. "Forgive my lamentable ignorance, but where *is* Santa Rosa?"

"Three quarters of the way up the left hand side, you heathen. How did you know about Moraes?"

"Went to school with him."

"Copulating cats!" Oz sometimes came out with odd interjections, often more distracting than illuminating. "Well, James, you are hereby appointed Moraes Liaison Officer, short title MLO, main duty to keep him away from me and maintain my good temper. Now, to a more interesting subject. I'd like to give a commissioning party just before we leave – a dance perhaps on board. I think we ought to get weaving about this now – when to have it, invitations, arrangements, etc. – over to you. Let's eat."

They had lunch and Oz explained all kinds of other problems that needed dealing with. For a start, the yacht had to be manned. She had been built with all the most modern labour-saving devices in her machinery, and needed no more than a crew of twelve. One other officer was required and Oz had already made contact with an Australian who had recently left the RAN and was to join them as Navigator just before they commissioned. Provisioning and supplying the yacht before she sailed was another major concern, and required detailed arrangements with builders and ship chandlers. Charts and navigational instruments had to be obtained, and the various pieces of electrical equipment tested and tuned – which included some recording equipment remarkable for its high fidelity and high price. As Oz outlined what had to be done, explaining with great enthusiasm just how he wanted it and giving an inkling of his subtle relationship with the builders, James remembered how much his captain had enjoyed the running of ships and all the organisation it entailed. He pondered a little on the sense of purpose which he had noticed before with men and their ships; it was more than conscientiousness in doing a job well, or devotion to duty, or even the desire to serve one's employer faithfully; it seemed that the driving imperative was a sense of service to the ship herself and the function for which she was built. That men should feel this way towards a collection of iron plates and rivets put together by other men, and moreover think themselves rather ennobled by such feelings, was quaint but true.

He checked into the hotel, which was nearly full – the yachting world had not yet departed. The rest of the day passed busily. He had plenty to do.

The next day woke him with the early morning sun streaming in at his window. He got up feeling invigorated and his mind thinking about orange blossom. It was a little while before he could recollect why; the vivid orange blossom at his windowsill in the Jerusalem YMCA had swung gently on just such a morning as this. His mind brought back to him his feelings of that awakening – a sense of confidence, awareness of beauty, excitement and a brave new world – emotions that had somehow eluded him for so long. But on this splendid sunny morning he felt the spring in his bones, and he dressed quickly and stepped out into the deserted streets of Cowes. It was going to be a scorcher and as he walked along the front towards the shipyard he was pleased to find himself the first to appreciate such a glorious day.

Even the grey shipyard looked rejuvenated. He stepped lightly under the archway, spurred on by a wish to see his ship again. *Mozart* would be just round the next shed – and there she was. As bright as a new toy, she gleamed in the low red sun, and he loved her.

He went up the brow and on board the soundless ship. It was scarcely 6.30 and there was not a soul about. He sensed a slightly eerie atmosphere in the strange emptiness, for it is uncharacteristic of any ship to be completely silent.

On an impulse, he opened the door of Lady Steyne's saloon. It was dark inside and he paused, leaning in, with his hand on the doorknob.

As his eyes became accustomed to the light, he could just make out what looked like a pair of legs; legs with felt shoes, suspended in space. He backed out and closed the door.

He leant against the bulkhead, his brain labouring thickly. A great shudder made him hunch his shoulders. He looked at his watch: 6.32.

His brain fastened on to the time as the one definite certainty: 6.32. Just after half past six a.m. and there's a body in there, a suicide, hanging from the deckhead, swinging in space. The joiner in his felt shoes. And I'm the first to find him.

No, I'm not, I never found him. I shall go back to the hotel, and when I get there I shall have breakfast and this thing may never have happened. Somebody else can be the first to find him.

But I can't possibly do that. I've got to be the first to find him, because I'm here and I did find him. I've got to go in there and see if it really is a body, and then get some help. I've only seen the legs so far. He might not even be dead.

That thought was even more alarming. In desperation he looked again at his watch. Still 6.32. The bloody thing must have stopped. He put it to his ear. It was working perfectly.

Courage, man. Go in there and face it. And he opened the door.

He stood there once more, leaning in, his eyes getting accustomed to the light. It was clearly a pair of felt shoes and there seemed to be some sort of bundled-up figure hanging from a rope. Having recovered his courage, he put his hand round the door frame and switched on the photo-luminescent panels.

It was indeed the joiner, and he seemed completely lifeless. James's enforced courage had numbed his senses and he looked at his first dead body with no reluctance. Here was an obvious crisis for him to deal with, and it is not too difficult to behave properly in a real crisis; it is the half-crisis that makes cowards of us all. The joiner had sat on a chair on top of another chair on top of the table and secured a stout rope to one of the deckhead fittings. He had then tied his neck to the rope with a complete round turn and two half hitches – an unlikely knot but efficient for the purpose, James thought without any cynicism. He had then passed the free end of the rope under his knees and trussed himself up before toppling off his chair. He had therefore had a fall of about eight feet, and it had been ample. He swung just perceptibly at the end of his plumb line, hunched up and staring, head on one side, eyes and tongue swollen and protruding, with large discoloured blotches on his cheeks. He was recognizable enough, and James remembered his conversation of the previous day and felt sorry for him. But it all seemed a little unreal.

He felt he ought to cut the body down, if only because it obviously had to be done some time, and there did not seem to be much else to be done at that moment. It would be difficult to untie the knots, so he looked around for something to cut the rope with. In the pantry next door he found an ordinary kitchen knife. Not sharp but serviceable. He started sawing away at the rope just above the man's head. This joiner had had dandruff, like most people. Why did he kill himself? What dreadful agonies of mind had he suffered, poised on his perch with his knees under his chin? The knife was blunt and getting more so. And then we shall need an ambulance, he thought, and the police. Or perhaps you get an undertaker instead of an ambulance? The police anyway; they should know.

A noise outside made him pause. He went, knife in hand, to the door. It was Oz, always an early riser, looking for once slightly startled.

"Hell's teeth, James, what on earth are you up to?"

"I'm trying to cut this poor fellow down, sir. Can you give me a hand?"

* * * * *

James's sense of unreality lasted into the coroner's court, where he sat remembering his conversation with the sprightly joiner while the legal mummery went on round him. In due course he was told to get to his feet while certain legal answers were extracted from him, and then he sat down again feeling that none of the right questions had been asked. He felt unhappy about it all, and he could trace his disquiet back through the shock and ugliness of finding the body to his five-minute conversation with the joiner. Surely men who jumped down so nimbly from cocktail cabinets would not hang themselves the same night? But the world thought otherwise.

"Death by asphyxiation," said the medical expert.

"Suicide while the balance of the mind was disturbed," said the coroner.

"He had been having difficulty in meeting his Hire Purchase Agreements," said the local newspaper.

CHAPTER FOUR

If the suicide drama wreathed *Mozart* in a thin mist of uneasiness, it did nothing to impede her headlong progress towards completion. Oz declared he had never seen a dockyard work so hard. Perhaps they wished to be rid of a ship that had harboured death, for dockyard men are not immune to the superstitions that ships can so easily acquire. Or perhaps it was simply the apparently unlimited money being poured out to enable her to be finished on time. It became clear that she would certainly meet her completion date, and all plans went ahead accordingly.

The Australian, a large genial character called Rod Trumper, arrived and stayed at The Bull. Aged about twenty-four, he had recently been invalided out of the Royal Australian Navy because of a car accident, which had left him with a small, but permanent, disability of the spine. He had been discharged at his own request in England and had been only too pleased to take up the offer of Navigator of the *Mozart*, a job he was sure his back injury would not prevent him doing perfectly well. He was frank in his conversation, talked loudly, and was quick to roar with laughter. He obviously enjoyed being thought a typical Australian, well practised in provoking the usual ruderies and skilful at returning them. But as James came to know him better he found him considerably less brash than he pretended, and careful and conscientious in his job. In fact, James reflected, he probably *was* a typical Australian, if there is such a thing.

Oz continued to have cause for irritation with the high-handedness of Peter Moraes, whose self-confidence seemed impervious to any kind of tactful manoeuvring by James's peace-keeping endeavours. The subject was sometimes discussed by the three officers in the bar of The Bull. It was a gathering into which Moraes seldom intruded.

"What beats me," said Rod Trumper, "is what Black Pedro thinks he's up to. He sits behind that desk nauseating every bastard from the Ship Manager downwards. What's his game?"

"He's Lady Steyne's personal representative, or so he told me this morning," said Oz. "Fortunately he doesn't directly interfere very much because his manners might be capable of bringing the entire shipyard to a standstill, and he contents himself with some annoying and time-wasting demands for information on progress."

"Tried to tell me how to stow my charts this morning," said Rod. "I played the blustering Aussie card and told him to put his advice where the monkey put the nuts. He didn't seem that pleased."

"And who's that female I keep seeing him with?" said Oz. "The smart-looking blonde, forty-ish, who collects him in that enormous car sometimes?"

"That's Ishbel," said James, who had been introduced to her. "She joined the family about twenty years ago as his nanny, and seems to have stayed on."

This fascinating piece of news caused something of a sensation amongst the other two. Rod spluttered into his beer, and Oz threw back his head and guffawed. Others around the bar looked up, wondering if they could share the joke.

"Nanny my eye," said Rod. "I bet she's more than a nanny to him. He dominates her completely. I wouldn't be surprised ..."

"The trouble with Moraes," said Oz, "is that he hasn't had the benefit of a naval upbringing."

The three ex-naval officers took a drink of their beer and James thought: it's true. He's an outsider. He hasn't got the good sense and good manners to stay on the same side as the captain.

"All the same," said James, who realised that they would have to get on with him somehow, "he's quite civilised in some ways. Anyway, he went to a good school! I think he'll be a reasonable messmate once we get going and he stops seeing himself as Grandma's man-on-the-spot. I'm sure he's quite a good chap really."

"I'm glad to hear it," said Oz in a voice that managed to convey hope, scepticism, and I-trust-this-subject-is-now-closed. He had obviously come to his own conclusions about Moraes.

* * * * *

Completion day approached and James was busy with many things, not least with all the arrangements for the party they were to hold on board on their last weekend. It was to be a cocktail party in the staterooms followed by a buffet and dance, and some of the dockyard officials were coming, plus the chairman of the company. Moraes of course was going to be there, although whether as host or guest had never actually been determined. Oz was having Marie-Claire to stay in Cowes for a couple of days, and also inviting some people he had got to know locally. Rod had asked a sheila to come down from London. James had some misgivings about asking Alice to come. It would mean her spending a weekend with him unchaperoned, which for someone like Alice meant fairly serious involvement. Did he want to be part of a serious involvement at that moment? No; but he recalled the way she had tossed her head back and telephoned her office.

"Miss Cullerby is out," said Alice's voice. "This is a recorded message answering system. Please leave your message, which will be recorded."

James was disconcerted. Alice's voice, but no Alice. Of all the ghastly inventions ...

"Miss Cullerby is out," said the voice again. "This is a recorded message answering system. Please leave your message, which will be recorded."

How could you ask a machine to spend a weekend with you? James was not often caught at a loss for words, but he was rendered speechless by the impersonality of Alice's clear soprano on the tape. Here it came again: "Miss Cullerby is out ..."

"Come down to Cowes next weekend, Alice," he blurted. "For a party. You can stay at The Bull. It's our farewell party. Ring me when you can."

And he rang off, annoyed with himself for being stampeded by a perfectly ordinary answering machine.

Luckily, she did ring back at lunchtime, rather amused, and teased James about the way he had been intimidated by her taped message. But she seemed delighted to be asked and accepted with only the slightest of hesitations. He booked her into the hotel. Well, that's fixed, he thought. I've got myself a girl-friend.

Relax, he told himself, relax. Enjoy the pleasures of the double bed while you can – they don't come that often. Lie back and bask. You're a lucky fellow.

* * * * *

It was party night, and the guests would be arriving soon. James and Alice were sitting in the after cabin of the staterooms, which opened through large glass doors onto the quarterdeck. It had been decorated for the party with coloured lights and signal flags, and there was a long trestle table on which the steward was arranging drinks. James had brought Alice on board early to check all was well and be in good time to welcome the other guests. It was clear and quiet, and the light was beginning to fade.

"It's a beautiful, sad evening," she said after a pause, looking beautiful and sad herself.

"Sad – nonsense!" said James, startled by such a thought. "How can you say such a thing?"

"There's sadness in the air."

"I don't understand. Why?"

"I ... I don't know, quite."

"I know why," he said, without really thinking what he was saying. "You're sad because you feel you are committing yourself." Good heavens, he thought, who's committing whom? Well, plunge in. "You're unhappy because you're not quite sure whether you're doing the Right Thing. And you feel that every passing moment increases your involvement, and you have doubts about what our grandparents would call 'my intentions'. So you're naturally somewhat thoughtful. Well, I'm sorry, Alice, it's really my fault. And I'll be truthful for once and say that I don't really know what my intentions are – which doesn't help much – but honestly ..."

He took a sip of his cocktail. She was looking ceaselessly lovely.

"... I can say I feel very strongly that we ought to live our lives as we find ourselves, to the full, not trying to be anyone else or live up to anyone else's standards – life's not long enough. 'Had we but world enough, and time ...'"

"Oh James!" She cut him short, but seemed unable to continue. Just as well, he thought. I was floundering.

"What is it, Alice? What's the matter?"

She smoothed her hair, which had surely been coiffured that morning. "I agree with what you say, more or less. But it's the everyday details that are so disheartening. I mean, Jane asked me where I was going this weekend, and I lied to her – which I hate doing. And when I asked for my ticket at the station I thought the booking clerk looked at me in a rather sinister way, as though he knew about us! Ridiculous, I know, but still. And I dreaded booking into the hotel. It was lucky there was no one around."

James felt kindly and protective. The Bull had been deserted when they arrived. Alice had signed in and they had taken the key and gone upstairs without anyone seeing them. She had been nervous.

His feelings towards her seemed to grow stronger as they talked. He thought she was more articulate than he had ever given her credit for, but still a little shy, and unsure of herself in an unfamiliar role.

"Don't worry," he found himself saying. "My intentions become more honourable every minute. Meanwhile, let's enjoy ourselves."

They rose, hand in hand, and walked out onto the quarterdeck. He smiled at her with the comforting thought of a new tentative understanding between them. And what did she think? You could never tell. But she was tall and elegant, and moved well. He undressed her mentally, and thought how lucky would be the man who would sleep with her every night of the week. And then the others started arriving.

It promised to be a good party. Marie-Claire was looking splendid, and a couple called Harford appeared to be a genial and interesting pair. They had brought their daughter, a dimpled eighteen-year-old, who was perky and seemed undeterred by the fact that all the men were already paired off. Even Peter Moraes was going out of his way to be pleasant. He had brought with him a most striking girl, obviously attractive in a rather aggressive way, and dressed to kill. She was the kind of girl who turns all eyes at first sight but not perhaps at second, and frightens off as many men as she attracts, while women grudgingly admit that she dresses well, "if you like that kind of thing."

James had a whiff of the heavy and expensive smells that followed her around, and thought she was just right for Black Pedro. But Black Pedro seemed to be taking no notice of her at all.

The management of the shipyard were all in good spirits, and the chairman, a tall, knighted tycoon, steel-grey round the temples and in a conspicuously well-cut dinner jacket, was all poise and affability. He approached James, obviously doing his rounds.

"So you must be the Chief Officer?"

"James Huwes." They shook hands. "First Lieutenant."

"Ha, First Lieutenant – so *Mozart* is being run on naval lines, is she?"

"Commander Hodges runs everything on naval lines. I served with him during my time in the Navy, and I can't imagine ships being run any other way."

"I see." He twinkled down at James from a considerable height. "And how long do you envisage being First Lieutenant?"

"I don't really know. We are engaged at one month's notice."

The chairman smiled. He was presumably at about ten years' notice, thought James, remembering the chauffeur-driven Rolls Royce that had brought him. These city men certainly looked after themselves pretty well.

"In this capricious world," said the chairman dogmatically, "almost anything can happen in a month." He was about to move on. "Look after *Mozart* won't you?"

A steward was discreetly filling up their glasses. The cocktail was excellent.

"We will indeed look after her. She's worth it."

The chairman looked around at the varnish and polish and resplendent fittings of what was surely one of the finest private yachts afloat.

"Yes," he said musingly, "I think she's probably worth it. Good luck." And he was gone.

James started talking to the Harford girl, who he discovered was an amusing, lively creature. Across the quarterdeck he saw Peter Moraes having a serious conversation with Alice. He was quite pleased when Moraes was called away; the presentations were about to begin.

The chairman then made a graceful speech, which managed to say all the right things effortlessly. They all drank "To the good ship *Mozart* and all who sail in her", and James thought that perhaps the chairman deserved his chauffeur-driven Rolls Royce after all. Then a marble bust of Mozart was produced and handed to Oz as a present from the yard to the ship. Oz made a suitable brief reply and called upon Moraes to reply on behalf of Lady Steyne. If the yard officers hoped to hear something that would confirm or justify their dislike of Black Pedro, they were disappointed; his speech was as fluent and courteous as it could be, and he finished it with a showman's gesture. At his signal a trolley carrying a draped object was wheeled up, and he removed the cloth with a flourish. Glistening in the coloured lights was a magnificent silver replica of the ship, perfect in every detail, a present from Lady Steyne to the builders. Everyone was astonished and delighted, and the chairman's poise was momentarily shaken. But he recovered himself quickly, made a most appreciative expression of gratitude, and everyone looked mighty pleased. More healths were drunk, and James thought that when he'd finished this drink, perhaps he wouldn't have any more.

* * * * *

It was later, when all the guests had left except a small number of the ship's officers' personal friends, that James suddenly noticed the absence of Alice. He had been dancing with Sue Harford and had not seen her go. He then noticed Moraes was not present either, and was at once suspicious and annoyed.

"Sue, I've lost Alice. Be an angel and see if she's in the ladies, would you?"

"Sure. But I don't think she is."

"Just check for me, would you mind?"

But it worried him. It was inconceivable that Alice should abandon him – at least he hoped it was inconceivable. Perhaps that swine Moraes had inveigled her off and was at that very moment importuning her in the yard, if nothing worse. Hell.

"No, she's not there, James. I do hope there's nothing wrong. Is there anything I can do?"

"No, nothing wrong, thank you, no."

It took him five minutes to be decently rid of Sue, chafing at his own reluctance to make a drama of it. But finally he was free, and he straightened out his cummerbund and strode off the ship, feeling defiant and revengeful. Moraes's car was still in its place; he couldn't have gone far. The yard looked gloomy and foreboding in the dark. Large areas of blackness were perforated by single unshaded lamps that cast deep shadows behind sheds and along alleys. James's heels hit the concrete with a hollow sound as he forced his way round the coils, drums and timber that clutter all dockyards, cursing angrily as he splashed into a puddle of oily water. No part of his mind considered what he would do with Moraes when he found him; it was by now too full of fury.

When he reflected afterwards on his futile search of the shipyard, he thought he must have been away from the ship for about half an hour. At all events, when he returned, wet, heavy-footed, and no less angry, Moraes's car had gone. The party had also gone. Apart from a night watchman, the ship was deserted and seemed silent and sinister.

Any man feels miserable when he loses his girl, particularly when she has come down specially to spend the weekend with him, and in addition James now felt utterly inadequate as Alice's host and protector. Why had he been so foolish as to allow that bastard to get near her? Why had he let them escape while he was trudging round the yard? And what was going on anyway?

He slowly got into his car and stared at the dashboard, floundering in indecision. Where could they have got to? Was it possible that he had merely taken her back to the hotel? He could soon find that out anyway. Better to do something than nothing at all.

He pulled the starter, but the car refused to start. Odd. Again – nothing. Odder still. Again and again he tried and cursed. He got out and lifted the bonnet, but of course could not see a thing. No torch – there was nothing for it; he must walk.

The walk between the yard and The Bull seemed a long way, but eventually he reached the hotel dog-tired, and he took his key from the rack. Perhaps she was in the room and all was well. After the disappointments and disasters of the past hour, as he groped his way upstairs, his mind held up a tempting slogan: *she may be there, and all is well.*

But she was not there.

There seemed nothing more to be done.

His mind, heavy with a great weariness, rejected the uncertainties that remained. He undressed quickly and went to bed.

CHAPTER FIVE

He woke feeling uneasy and unwell. In a flash he remembered the disasters of the previous evening, and realised with a dull clutch of anxiety in his stomach that the whereabouts of Alice was still uncertain. How could he have abandoned the search like that? His head ached, and he checked his watch to discover how late it was. His limbs responded lethargically as he got up and surveyed himself in the glass: all the symptoms of a slight hangover. Those cocktails must have been quite strong. He shaved and dressed, cursing the time-wasting essentials that intervene between getting up and appearing before the outside world, and then left his room.

He went downstairs, and the first thing he saw was an envelope addressed to him in Alice's handwriting. He tore it open.

"Please don't worry," it said. "We can't go on like this. Don't write. Alice."

The large manageress was sitting at her reception desk, smiling and, in her own estimation, understanding everything.

"Miss Cullerby left quite early this morning," she said. "Said she had to go in a hurry as she'd heard her sister wasn't well." The manageress contrived to show that she knew Alice had not got a sister. "Caught the early ferry. Wouldn't even stop for some breakfast. Of course, we're used to *yachtsmen* leaving early so we can always *do* an early breakfast …"

James, disheartened and fearing the worst, left without a word.

* * * * *

Normally the yard would be deserted on Sundays, but on this occasion things were going on busily, and there was a carefree, shirt-sleeved atmosphere about the place. *Mozart* was sailing for Bermuda the following morning, so it was everybody's last chance to get the finishing touches done. Peter Moraes, surprisingly, was at his desk; he looked as disarmingly bland and self-assured as ever.

"Good morning, James, how are you this morning? I feel ghastly – splendid party, wasn't it? My blonde bit got as tight as a tick. But then, didn't we all?"

"Where's Alice?" said James severely.

"Alice Cullerby – charming girl of yours, charming, but I've no idea where she is – how could I? Presumably in her hotel."

"She's not at the hotel. Did you go off with her last night?"

"My dear fellow! Really, James, what do you take me for? No, we just went for a quick drive round to see the sights of Cowes – it was her idea – and then she said she was tired and would I take her back to the hotel. Which of course I did …"

"What time?"

"About two or three I suppose – look, James, I'd like to be helpful but this aggressive tone of yours doesn't make it any easier. Alice and I were conducting ourselves perfectly properly last night, and even if we hadn't been that's her business and mine. It's nothing to do with me if she's not in the hotel now. She can't be far away."

"She left by the early ferry, telling the hotel staff she had to attend to a fictitious sister."

"James, I *am* sorry. Leaving without a word. Something must have gone terribly wrong between you. Women are contrary creatures. No, really, I had no hint of this during my brief acquaintance with her last night. I wish I could help you more. Now listen, I've got a couple of rods on a nice stretch of the Itchen and I'm going off about midday – why don't you join me?"

"I haven't any gear with me."

"All tackle and trim provided, old boy."

Really, the man was quite skilful. He knew an afternoon's fishing would be hard to resist. And "tackle and trim" – the quotation instantly took James back to his schooldays, recalled the intensity of emotion which some poets had been able to evoke, and reminded him of the common background they had between them. Black Pedro was certainly trying hard to fraternise. James, thinking that he might be able to extract something more from him on the journey, accepted the invitation. He would try to contact Alice in the evening. She perhaps hardly deserved it, but he wanted to be reassured.

He walked down to the ship. She was lying patiently at her berth alongside, just as she had the previous day, shapely, gleaming-smart, complete. Her clean outline was in striking contrast to the shambles of clobber that he had tramped over in the pitch black, only a few hours ago. How different her character now seemed from the time he had first seen her, innocent looking, with her name just being painted in. She had had a different personality again on the occasion of the suicide: unobtrusive, witnessing tragedy without comment. And last night? James recalled the deserted ship with a shudder. She had seemed almost malignant. Yet now he felt protective and kindly towards her. Seagulls hovered and dived round her superstructure, balancing on the wind eddies, knowing nothing of the hopes and anxieties of the man who watched them and contemplated their unconcern. But he suddenly stopped his thoughts wandering, and reproached himself for attributing to ship and gulls such asinine feelings, so obviously a piece of self-indulgent anthropomorphosis. Come back to earth, he told himself; it would not do to be a seagull; and as for *Mozart*, they would do their best to look after her. And he must drive himself to do a couple of important things that morning.

Surprisingly, his car started perfectly easily. There seemed nothing wrong with it at all.

* * * * *

At midday the large blue and grey Jaguar was waiting for them at the office. Ishbel Fergus was at the wheel, and it seemed as though she had instructions to stay there. James was pleased to have a chance of interrogating Moraes, as they sat side by side in the back seats, but found the task hopeless. He could get nowhere beyond the original story, and eventually stopped trying. He comforted himself with the thought that there might be some explanation for Alice's behaviour which a telephone call would reveal in the evening. But he did not feel hopeful. Clearly his host was going to give nothing away.

They stopped at a pub for a quick lunch. Moraes, with an irritating air of command, determined what everyone would like to drink, and Ishbel collected the drinks from the bar. James watched her and pondered on the odd arrangement he was watching: an alleged ex-nanny buying drinks for her ex-protégé. She seemed naturally devoted to Moraes without any of the maternal peevishness one associates with nannies. He treated her not quite as an equal, but familiarly. She was certainly a good-looking woman, slim and fair, neat and well dressed. When she spoke, which was not often, she had a Scottish lilt that was altogether becoming.

Moraes took the wheel after lunch, and insisted on James sitting beside him in the front. He drove, predictably, very fast and very well. It was a glorious day. The valley of the Itchen was looking superbly green and pleasant, and James felt his heart bound in spite of his troubles. They reached the place and parked the car in a field. Over a stile and round a little wood – and there the stately chalk-stream was gliding clear before them. Fish were rising in all directions in a business-like way, which means a good hatch. It was a fly-fisherman's paradise.

They went into a little hut and selected some gear from the profusion of rods, reels, lines and fly-boxes neatly laid out inside. Then they set off in different directions. Ishbel sat on a bench outside the hut and took up a book.

James walked downstream cautiously, keeping about ten yards from the bank. A determined rise in mid-stream made him decide to start just there. It looked like a good-sized fish; what was it feeding on? He edged towards the bank and a position from which he could cover the fish. Sherry Spinner? He looked at a spinner struggling on the water, its duty done: it looked as much like a Sherry Spinner as anything else. He took one out of his fly-box and tied it on, the sound of more rises disconcerting him as he did so. At last the fly was firmly on and he began to cast. The first was short; the second short; the third just on his nose; the fourth a foot above him. Watch it, James told himself, as the fly floated beautifully over the fish; don't strike too soon.

There was a most gratifying plop as the fish took the fly, and with a slight tightening the line and cast went taut, straight to the centre of the ring of ripples. It was on! And, furious, it streaked away to the other bank, shaking its head, and made a prodigious leap into the air. It seemed absurd to have two pounds of fighting brown trout at the end of such delicate equipment. The fish bored towards a bed of weeds and still, incredibly, the hook held.

It was ten minutes before James brought the fish to his net, and during that time he had passed through excitements and anxieties that he had forgotten fishing was capable of arousing. It was a fine trout, sturdy, bright, and gloriously spotted. He delivered the *coup de grâce* with the twinge of regret that even the most predatory fisherman feels.

He sat back on the bank and breathed in the scents of an ancient water meadow. What a magnificent battle! What a lovely day!

For the next three hours Alice and Moraes, ships and suspicions, all were well in the background of his mind, and he kept them there resolutely. There was nothing to be done about them at present, and meanwhile his creel was becoming of that weight known only to fishermen, when it is pleasant to relieve one's back of the load, but even more pleasant to feel its weight again. Four fat trout came to his net, and he retraced his steps back to the hut with a great sense of satisfaction – partly the satisfaction of the hunter in obtaining food from the natural resources of the earth, and partly the craftsman's pride in having acquired a subtle and difficult skill and put it to good use.

He came to a small wooded hillock and looked down at the river, a well-ordered band of silver-smooth water cutting the greenness into two halves. Certainly England, by anyone's standard, was the most beautiful country in the world.

And then Moraes came into view and began casting below him. There were two fish rising within reach of where he was standing, and he started, quite properly, with the downstream fish. His first cast was not straight and fell short. His second, straight enough, was taken, and there followed an exciting five minutes while a good fish was brought to the net. James continued to watch. Moraes unhooked the fish, tossed it on the ground behind him and went on fishing. It flapped frantically for a minute or two.

James turned away in disgust. The man was obviously a blackguard. Unlike the final denouement of detective stories, he felt that the villain of the piece was already exposed. There could be nothing pleasant in a man who could not be bothered to dispatch his fish promptly and decently. The thing was as clear as a chalk-stream.

＊ ＊ ＊ ＊ ＊

That evening James started by ringing Alice's flat: no reply. He then rang her parents' house and spoke to her father. No, Alice wasn't at home, she was at her flat in London, its number was such-and-such, kind of James to ring to say goodbye, good luck. Hopelessly, he then rang her office, and of course only heard that infernal recording machine, to which he wisely said nothing. Then he got through to Jane Thompson, Alice's friend and neighbour whom he knew slightly. She believed Alice was spending the weekend with an aunt in Colchester.

James knew it was useless to continue. Alice had gone, and because she had covered her tracks in coming to Cowes, no one could possibly know where she was. He felt helpless. If there was any real reason to suspect anything he would be able to go to the police, but he had nothing definite in the eyes of officialdom. In fact, all he had was her note: "Please don't worry. We can't go on like this. Don't write. Alice." Undoubtedly her handwriting, but undoubtedly odd. It was just possible that she had run off with sudden guilty feelings. He could do nothing, and his suspicions of Moraes mocked his inaction.

He rang his mother, who told him of a number of problems that were worrying her, and which she would certainly know would worry him, and suggested that he should have come to say goodbye. He knew so well that she was right. He should have made time to see her during this last hectic weekend. It was impossible to explain or attempt to justify the fact that he had had vital and perplexing problems, which had taken precedence over everything else. All his mother would remember of their conversation was that he had been fishing all day.

Finally, driving to the garage where he had arranged to leave his car, he came to the following notices, in large writing:

ROAD WORKS AHEAD
DANGER
SLOW
NO WAITING
DIVERSION

So it was perhaps not surprising that he went the wrong side of a small *Keep Left* sign. A policeman emerged out of the shadows and flashed him down.

"Excuse me, *sir*, you have just committed an offence."

"What offence?"

"Failing to conform to a road traffic sign namely a keep left sign contrary to section …"

"But officer, all those signs … unlit … it was very confusing … I thought …"

"I shall have to report the circumstances to the Chief Constable who will take whatever action he considers necessary."

James fumed. Foreigners may find our policemen wonderful, he thought, but they can also be the most tiresome, pernickety, bone-headed …

"Please show me your licence, *sir*?"

James hadn't got it with him. Nor his Certificate of Insurance or his Test Certificate.

"I must ask you to produce them at your nearest police station within the next five days."

"But I'm going to the West Indies tomorrow."

"I can't help that. You have in my opinion just committed an offence and that's the law."

It was about half an hour before they came to terms. James would get the necessary documents into the post and the policeman would say no more about it. But his temper had been roughened.

Not a very satisfactory last night.

* * * * *

They left the following day, sun shining, miraculously on time after a number of crises that threatened to delay them. The bosun, a red-faced sailor called Framley, who stood six foot three and looked every inch a bosun, was nowhere to be seen; at the last minute he arrived on a pink child's bicycle, hungover and still half asleep. It was lucky for him that the Captain was talking to some reporters and did not see him. James gave him an imitation of a naval "bottle" he had once received from Angus Swallow, and felt better for it. Dreadful man, Swallow, but he was certainly good at giving words to his wrath. The bosun took it meekly and went below. Then the Engineer reported that the telemotor system was losing pressure. Oz, pacing up and down the bridge, was calm, with the result that an unflustered Engineer was able to put the fault right quickly. Finally, the mobile crane, which had been expected to remove the gangway, was nowhere to be seen. Frantic exchanges between James and the builder's men on the jetty produced no sensible answer, so James gathered all available hands together and just managed to shift the gangway over the side without damaging the paintwork.

"Ready to proceed," he reported to his Captain, and as the berthing wires were slipped from the bollards and *Mozart* drew away from the crowd of shipbuilders who were waving them goodbye, they turned up a recording of the overture to *Figaro* on the ship's loud-hailing equipment. The sleek grey yacht, splendid in the sunshine, slid from her birthplace and headed for the open sea.

CHAPTER SIX

James placed both hands on the varnished wooden rail that enclosed the bridge top, leant his weight on his arms, and mused. It was half past three in the afternoon watch. Below him *Mozart's* bow cut into a gentle swell that made the Atlantic look like a strip-farmed field long since ploughed over. Away from the sun it was the colour of an expensive sapphire; towards the sun the silver reflections were so bright that if you looked at it steadily everything else went black when you looked away. The sun glared out of the sky, pouring itself down on teak decks and white paintwork, on bare arms and knees, giving the scene almost the vividness of a colour-slide. The bridge top was the highest deck in the ship, and he could see the whole of her from where he stood. She seemed to surge forward into the sapphire, trailing her creamy wake astern far away almost to the horizon.

He filled in the deck log. Course 255 true. Speed 12. Wind – calm. Waves – nil. Remarks – low southerly swell, vis 98. Signed JH. And he felt like adding: "All is well. The sun is shining and all is well."

Below him, Rod Trumper would be rousing himself from his afternoon caulk before having a cup of tea and coming up to take over the watch at eight bells. Oz would be sitting in a deck chair just outside his cabin, reading, or writing a letter to Marie-Claire. Moraes would be in his cabin – he seldom left it, much to everyone's relief. Amongst the crew there were probably only three men who were not asleep in the mess-deck or dozing in the sun: the helmsman on the wheel, the watch keeper in the engine room, and the steward who would be taking Mr Trumper his cup of tea.

Bermuda was five hours' steaming away; they were to anchor off shore that evening and go up harbour the following day. James peered through his binoculars right ahead. Nothing in sight. A verse by that incomparable landlubber Arthur Hugh Clough came into his mind, its rhythms first, then the words:

Where lies the land to which the ship would go?
Far, far ahead is all her seamen know.
And where the land she travels from? Away,
Far, far behind is all that they can say.

But they could say a bit more than that. He looked at the chart. Bermuda was thirty miles WSW of their present position. He looked again through his binoculars, straining his eyes along the horizon. A tiny cloud materialised, dead ahead, at the absolute limit of visibility, and a cloud in a cloudless sky could mean land. Was this the land to which the ship would go?

Rod clattered up the ladder to the bridge top, hearty and efficient.

"What a beaut of a sea. Never seen the Atlantic so calm. What gives then, matey?"

"Course 255, speed 12. And I think that a microscopic cloud ahead on the horizon might be the first sign of Bermuda."

"Magic. Just where she should be. Did you get a sun-sight?"

"Position line on the chart. Ties in nicely with our DR. Got the watch, Rod?"

"Got it. Thanks mate."

And James went below to a most welcome cup of tea.

* * * * *

Their arrival the following day caused something of a stir. Bermuda is used to millionaires' yachts, but seldom had anyone seen anything as sleek and trim as *Mozart*. Lady Steyne was in fact not due to arrive for a week, so everyone had time to look around. They gave a small party on board and went to several ashore. James found the island full of generous people anxious to make them welcome. Being welcomed was a full-time occupation, and most congenial. A little of the island's atmosphere seeped through the parties, as he talked to people, all, like himself, smiling, polite, and having a glass of whisky permanently fixed in their left hands. It was an atmosphere of tidy opulence and cautious tax-avoidance, of unscrupulous tourist-milking, of cocktail-party-permissible topics and some unmentionable ones; of blue seas and pink beaches, rocks and little bridges, flowering oleanders and winding roads walled with coral; and a society bounded by money and a few important rules. The inhabitants split themselves up into well-defined and almost party-tight groups, depending on colour, income and proportion of lifetime spent in Bermuda. In all, a functional sort of community; and it is practically impossible, he discovered, not to be delighted with its welcome.

A British frigate was in harbour and James went over in the *Mozart's* boat to invite some officers on board. He was pleased to find that an old friend, Mark Hillier, was the Navigator. They arranged a rendezvous for dinner in the Prince George Hotel, and that evening as they sat out in the hotel garden drinking rum punches and watching the sun set over the white roofs of Hamilton, James heard the recent history of HMS *Fowey*.

"The Captain had always been pretty erratic," Mark was saying, "and soon after we got out here things started getting worse."

"What sort of things?"

"Well, for one thing, he drank like a fish. He was sometimes pickled for days on end. His routine was fairly consistent – up late in the morning, about ten, sit in his cabin with a sore head till eleven, then out with the gin bottle. He would often come down to the wardroom about midday, and the lunchtime session might go on till half past three. Then of course he'd stagger into his pit till the evening, when the serious drinking would start."

"Did anyone know how much he actually drank a day?"

"I was the wine caterer and I knew very well – never less than two bottles of spirits."

"And how did the ship run without a sober captain?"

"Pretty badly. The First Lieutenant was an old woman, or he would have done something about it. But that wasn't all."

"What else, for heaven's sake?"

"The Captain disregarded one of the most sacred rules of the navy."

"Never under the white ensign?"

"Precisely. One Sunday morning the Admiral came aboard unexpectedly – I think he must have had got some inkling of what was going on from somewhere. Imagine the panic when the Captain was found to be locked in his cabin with his girl-friend – *in flagrante!*"

"Imagination boggles. So what happened?"

"No end of nausea. Board of Inquiry, then Court Martial, and he was dismissed his ship and his resignation from the Service accepted."

"Not surprised. What reaction from the ship's company?"

"Well, as my Yeoman said: 'We didn't mind the Captain fornicating, sir, but we thought it a bit much, fornicating on board before church on a Sunday morning.'"

"Well put. Who was this fellow anyway?"

"A chap called Commander Swallow."

Good God! Angus Swallow, James's first captain in the *Wilton*.

Lieutenant-Commander Swallow, as he was then, was well known in the Navy as a hard living playboy and rebel. Endowed with plenty of money, sandy-red hair, and an irascible disposition, he and his nickname of "the Red Terror" were well known in the Fleet. But if some people admired from afar the swashbuckling exterior, those who served with him found him boorish and a bully, and he gave James none of the direction and support that a brand-new Sub-Lieutenant needs. He had been a heavy drinker then, and James recalled some near-disastrous incidents that they had had to cover up for the good of the ship. Life had become more and more unbearable, and then, suddenly and certainly unexpectedly, Swallow had been promoted to Commander and was relieved by Oz Hodges, who had quickly restored James's faith in the system.

So now the sins of Angus Swallow had found him out at last. James could not suppress a feeling of *schadenfreude* that naval justice, sometimes seemingly so circuitous and slow moving, had eventually hit its mark.

Mark Hillier noticed his interest. "You knew him?"

"Served with him. He was Captain of my first ship. Quite a baptism by fire for me, really. What's the Red Terror doing now?"

"Well, that's the irony of the situation. He's stayed on in Bermuda – in fact he's bought himself a fine residence on the shore by Spanish Point, where he continues to lead a life of unbridled licence, unencumbered by the traditions of the Royal Navy. We see him about the place quite a lot. His large house is supposed to be full of totties. They're known as 'the Swallow-tails.'"

"What a fellow! I wonder if I shall meet him."

"He still goes to all the parties, so you may well see him around.

* * * * *

Mozart was now preparing herself for the arrival of her *raison d'être*, Lady Steyne. This meant different things to different people, and at various times they said so.

Oz said, "So she is arriving at the airport at midday tomorrow, and at last Grandma will assume earthly form. There've been moments during the past three months when I've been tempted to doubt her reality. It will be interesting to see whether she likes living in the yacht her money has created, and indeed how she takes to the bunch of characters who already live there, drawing their fat salaries. I think if she is reasonable she can find little fault with the ship or the way we run her, but it is extremely unlikely that she will be reasonable. In fact, we rather expect her to be eccentric and she probably knows it. And if she doesn't have any eccentricities, we shall soon manage to invent some for her, poor woman. They make life more amusing. James, I'd like you to meet her at the airport tomorrow and bring her and her possessions on board – best Flag Lieutenant stuff, please, all arrangements like a well-oiled Seth-Thomas. I shall stay here to welcome her aboard. You'd better hire a large car and be at the airport in plenty of time."

Rod said, "I don't know what a Seth-Thomas is but I do know that you won't find a large car anywhere in Bermuda – they have a size limit. I wonder what the old girl will be like. I hope her activities don't affect ours too much, but I'm afraid they will – this life is too good to last. If I were as loaded as she is I'd stay here a hell of a lot longer. It's a great place for the good life, but it's so bloody Yankified – just like Sydney. We were in this club last night, nice place with a great view over the reefs, although the beer's not worth drinking – anyway along comes the bill, quite a sum by the way, and it's all in US dollars. So I said, 'How's about the bill in pounds, mate?' to this waiter, and he said, 'Our customers usually prefer their checks in dollars.' So I said,

'Don't come the raw prawn, laddie, I'm not paying until you change it.' Blow me if the cunning old bastard didn't come back with the bill in Australian dollars, and we parted best of friends. I'll be going back there, if Grandma lets us stay. The longer the better as far as I'm concerned."

Moraes said, "I believe my Aunt will want to stay here about a fortnight, to settle herself in and see a few old friends on the Island. I shall certainly want to stay for some time, as I'm buying a speedboat and also some aqualung gear, and I intend to do some more water-skiing and skin-diving. Incidentally, James, I hope you'll be able to find somewhere to stow the boat on board; we badly need a speedboat and I can't think why it wasn't thought of before. I understand you will be going to meet her tomorrow. Well, you don't have to bring her back on board – I shall of course be at the airport and if you would see the luggage through customs I will deal with Aunt Mercy. Incidentally, there's a picnic tomorrow on the private beach of a friend of mine, to which you are all invited – we shall see who can water-ski. And now, if you'll excuse me, I must leave you."

James said, "I think a Seth-Thomas must be a kind of clock."

* * * * *

Lady Steyne arrived at the airport, a tall greyish woman of strikingly gaunt features, rather drawn and unbecoming, but carrying herself with a lively bearing which belied her age. Her clothes, too, were young; the only things that typified her seventy years were her many rings, which were entirely emeralds of great size. She was greeted by her nephew, who kissed her on both cheeks, then James, who shook hands, then two newspapermen, to whom she promised an interview. She was all courtesy and slightly distant charm, and everyone seemed pleased. James had smoothed her way through the immigration and health people, and within ten minutes she and Moraes were being handed into the car by the airport manager. The car moved off a few yards and then stopped. The departure-smile on the face of the airport manager lost a little of its spontaneity, and Lady Steyne got out. "Those reporters," she exclaimed. "I'd forgotten all about those reporters. I promised I'd talk to them."

Moraes followed her reluctantly. It was clear he had lost an argument.

As James tried to explain to the customs that the baggage was destined for the high seas and therefore presumably exempt duty, he reflected that his employer had shown that she would keep her word and could be stronger-willed than her nephew. Which was no bad thing.

* * * * *

People's plans for the following day became apparent by breakfast time. Lady Steyne was going to have a quiet day on board. Oz too had decided not to go ashore. The others were to leave for the water-skiing picnic at ten o'clock. James found life satisfactorily busy between breakfast and ten. His open and thoughtful way of dealing with the crew had made him a successful First Lieutenant, and the domestic organisation of the ship was now running smoothly. He felt particularly confident that morning as he dealt with a few minor matters that were referred to him, and walked round the ship talking to the men as they went about their various tasks. He had a good memory for details and remembered that Framley had once mentioned that he was an aqualung enthusiast. He asked him if he had brought his gear on board. Framley replied that he had, and was in fact using it that afternoon spear fishing inside the reef. He seemed happy in his work; indeed, the whole ship's company seemed to be happy with the very well-paid job they were doing. It is always pleasant to be confidently in charge of an efficient organisation, and James felt pleased with himself. A tiny part of his mind still reiterated that something was wrong with his congenial world, but only occasionally did he worry about Alice.

* * * * *

Peter Moraes brought his boat alongside at 0945. It was full of shiny water-skiing equipment, and there was also an aqualung. The boat took them across Grassy Bay, and as they looked back *Mozart* swung slowly at her anchor against the low skyline of Bermuda. This is the life, thought James. "Beauty," said Rod from time to time, meaning exactly the same thing. But as for Moraes, he was not over-generous with his innermost thoughts, and was making conversation with his usual well-chosen words.

The shores of Bermuda are speckled with pastel-coloured houses, and most of them carefully guard their piece of waterfront and keep a boat or two at a little jetty. They headed for one of these, and as the boat came closer you could see there was a fine house set back slightly from the beach, with well-trimmed lawns surrounded by a forest of hibiscus and oleander. There was a party gathered round a swimming pool, where elegant garden furniture supported tall glasses of expensive-looking drinks. As they secured to the jetty, two pretty girls in bikinis, young and boyish in their movements, bounced down to greet them, long bronzed thighs and sleek waists gladdening everyone's heart. And clearly there were more to come. A playboy paradise, thought James. This is how these people really do live.

He heard his host before he saw him. That loud, aggressive laugh was startlingly evocative, bringing back the noises, resentments and triumphs of his first ship. It was a laugh that set out to dominate the conversation, and usually succeeded by sheer persistence. And then he saw the large figure wearing a magnificent silk shirt, and the smile broadened in the tanned round face as it recognised him.

"This is James Huwes," said Moraes. "James – Captain Angus Swallow. But you seem to know each other."

James could not help smiling also. Swallow, dismissed his ship and publicly disgraced, had promoted himself to captain. There were no rules in this bright playboy world.

CHAPTER SEVEN

There were several boats, including a big cabin cruiser called, rather quaintly, *Peccavi*, and people started going off water-skiing and diving, or remained lazing by the pool. The party was now getting under way. It was large enough for James not to have to spend too long talking to his host; having discussed old times in the *Wilton* for five minutes or so he felt free to concentrate on the pretty girls and the bronzed thighs. He saw one particularly beautiful slim girl in a white bikini, and the bugle-call of feminine attraction, soundlessly but compelling, called to him across the swimming pool. He sat down beside her at the edge of the pool, legs luxuriating in the warm water. She introduced herself as La Rue Fafoux, which she was then good enough to spell. She was, apparently, a local playgirl of indeterminate background – undetermined, that is, by James, who was trying to show interest without curiosity. She had a sweet, slow voice, almost a drawl, and a tendency to split words in two. Their conversation developed, and the party looked like being a success.

It had, of course, the best possible assistance from its surroundings and amenities. The garden was superb in sunlight that was not quite too strong. The view of Bermuda and the wide bay it encloses has a powerful effect on most people; on newcomers it can be almost hypnotic. The boats were spacious and the engines always seemed to work first time. Food was plentiful and good, and fine drinks invariably to hand on land or sea. James, after three long rum punches, thought he observed that some people relied on alcohol more than others at parties. He, *of course*, did not rely on it at all, but it did bring a frankness and sparkle to his conversation that otherwise, perhaps, he had to try a bit harder for. For instance, it made him wish to confide in this slim La Rue. He began to talk as he had always known he could, but so seldom had the chance to. He was cheerful, cultured, and funny. She seemed to be really amused, and unobtrusively revealed her I.Q. and education and interests to be stratospheric. Arts, religions, love – the world's great subjects were probed, analysed powerfully, and then tossed away as being worth no more than a glance from these two super-humans. He knew for sure he was being happy and spontaneous and perfectly controlled; he could feel the control flowing through him like a faith healer. He sensed their conversation enveloping each other; in a large party that was fragmenting they seemed to be in a world of their own. And his mind, made somewhat detached by another cool rum punch, considered this to be a very remarkable thing.

She had another cool rum punch too, and would no doubt be thinking just the same.

They went down to the jetty, he in his own estimation walking as straight as a tightrope, and climbed into a little speedboat that some of the others had been using. The engine started at a touch. They were away, out into the blueness of the bay, free and alone with the slapping of the waves on the thin fibreglass hull. The girl stretched out her long legs in front of her, golden as a cornfield, smooth as ivory, and James heard himself saying:

"I love you, lady."

"Non-sense," she drawled.

"I do. I love you, Alice."

"Who's Alice?"

Idiot.

"James, you are a goose, but quite a funny goose. Can you water-ski?"

"I love your size and shape and colour and conversation."

"I can, superb-ly." And she leapt over the side with a single ski.

Crass, drunken idiot, thought James to himself. Suddenly the situation had become harsh and prosaic. He had been bemused by her attractiveness and confused by the rum. She was now a brilliant water-skier, curving effortlessly over the blueness like a seagull. Driving the boat rather less than competently, he felt a complete fool.

As for Alice, how did she come into it?

He circled the bay until La Rue signalled she had had enough. She released the line and sank gracefully into the sea. He came round, cut the engine, and helped her aboard, dripping and exhilarated. She sat down, breathless.

"I'm exhau-sted."

"You were fabulous."

"If only one could live as one can ski."

"La Rue, I'm a little confused – this sun ..."

"It doesn't matter," she said prettily, putting a hand on his arm.

"The trouble is, we're too much ... alike."

"How alike?"

"As alike as two peas, two pins, two potatoes?"

"Two cherries, two cherubs ..."

"As the two halves of a bro-ken marble?"

"I do love you, dearly. I'd like to sleep with you some time, if you'll excuse my saying so."

"This year, next year, sometime, never?"

The magic was back again. It seemed both subtler and more primitive than before, or perhaps less alcoholic. She was certainly a remarkably good-looking girl, and it was still a lovely day.

"Perhaps we ought to be getting back to the party," he said. "Or where shall we go?"

"Over there … to the island."

"To the island then." He swung the boat round. "What happens on the island?"

"There's a grand piano there. And I want to play."

"Remarkable woman," he said, and she smiled.

They reached the island, which was about a quarter of an acre in extent and was part of the Swallow property. It was used as a water-picnic base for barbecues. There was a small hut with a rough dance floor outside. Inside, the piano filled over half the space. The hut must have been built round it.

"I love this place," she said. "It's my favourite refuge. I close the door and thun-der to myself, and it rever-berates … like a cathedral?"

"So Angus has given you a free run?"

"Of course."

"Are you his girl-friend?"

"In a way."

"But why? *Why?* You're the very last person in the world …"

"It's a long story."

She began to play something, rolling great arpeggios at prodigious speed, and the hut was filled with sound. Her back was brown and straight. James put his hands on her shoulders; the skin was hot and he could feel her muscles whisking about their astonishingly intricate tasks. His hands strayed. Her bikini top was warm and, with a lunge of happiness, he slipped his hand inside and felt one breast, trim and soft and truly beautiful. She was not surprised and went on playing.

"Do you like it?" she asked.

"Vastly. The Chopin too."

"Liszt. Sex before or after?"

"Before, after and during."

"Undress me then. I a-dore Liszt in the nude."

* * * * *

"Where do you come from, La Rue?"

"Adven-ta."

"Where's that?"

"West Indies. It's one of the Grenadine Islands ... very small and remote. My father died there three years ago. That made me an orphan, and so I came to Bermuda to see the world a bit."

"And have you?"

"A bit. But I've kept my family house in Adventa. I love it. It stands empty at the moment. My aunt, who's the island's doctor, keeps an eye on it for me. If ever you want to borrow it, let me know. It's a lovely place."

"Thank you, my love. How long are you going to stay here then?"

"Till he lets me go, or things change."

"Is this a typical day in the life of a Bermuda playgirl?"

"Not partic-ularly."

"How many times do you ...?"

"Often. I don't nor-mally take sex too seriously, I'm afraid."

"Normally?"

"Normally, I'm not really ... all that interested?"

Suddenly she seemed to be on the point of tears and looked quite old. Could she be thirty?

"Come on La Rue, La Rue, do. We must show our faces back with the rest of the party."

"Who's Alice?" she said.

"I'll tell you some other time."

"But you love her … do you?"

"Yes, my love, perhaps I do."

"Gentle James."

"Come on now."

He had mismanaged things, but she had more than forgiven him.

* * * * *

The party broke up as the sun was lowering itself over the bay in colours that would have made a travel poster jealous. People went off talking loudly to each other, Rod with a girl he had found, Moraes to do some more diving on a wreck in the harbour. James refused all company, feeling disinclined either to go back to the ship or to have dinner with any of the jovial people who invited him. He walked along the road, his mind a confusion of triumph and tragedy.

Certainly it was good to have made love to that nimble girl, good for the ego anyway. It was a great victory, perhaps. She was the best looking lass of the lot, and he had made it first time. Had that ever happened to him before? He considered. No, never. You great big lady-killer, you.

The sun caught the tops of a row of hibiscus. The low walls beside the road were coral blocks, now black one side, red the other.

And yet she seemed much more than just a goodtime girl and obviously unhappy in that Swallow set-up. What a strange quirk of fate had blown them together.

That startling declaration of love for Alice – how did that fit in? They were superficially rather alike, those two, but Alice was lighter-skinned, darker-haired, firmer, more innocent of course. Did he really love her?

"Yes, my love," he had said, "perhaps I do."

Quite alone on an empty Bermuda road, he blushed hotly. Sudden guilty questions leapt at him out of the shadows. Where was Alice now? Could she have been abducted by that fiend Moraes? And whose fault would that be? And what had he done about it?

A telephone box came into view at the bottom of the hill, and he remembered his telephone card was valid throughout the Commonwealth. He was approaching Hamilton. His rubber soles made a little padding noise on the road. He reached the telephone box and opened the door. It was very smelly and a pane of glass was missing. No, he really couldn't ring up London now, nor Alice's father. If Alice really had disappeared, her father would surely have raised a hue and cry by now. What more could one do? She was probably all right, anyway. There was probably a letter from her waiting for him on board.

He continued down the road into Hamilton, by now reflecting that it was most unlikely that there would be a letter from her on board.

He consulted his watch. He could either go straight back to the jetty, where a boat would be waiting for him, or else to a bar, where the third gin would eradicate his indecisiveness and enable him to bask in the memory of his triumph. He chose the bar.

I'm a rotten fellow, he thought – a most inadequate hero for this extraordinary work of true-life fiction I seem to be living through. Perhaps I may be able to sort everything out in the morning.

But the chance was denied him, because he was woken in the morning with the news that the ship was to sail at nine. Their whimsical employer had decided she wanted to leave, and James, cursing his folly in having had too much to drink the day before, had to bend all his energies to fight a hangover and get the ship ready for sea.

CHAPTER EIGHT

Yacht *Mozart*
at sea
Sunday 10th Jan 1968

Dearest Ma,

I'm sorry it's been so long since my last letter, but things have been as busy as ever. Never a dull moment, at sea or ashore! I do hope all is well at Churbridge, and that you are organising everything with your usual skill. It must be reasonably quiet now the winter is in mid-career and no doubt the Christmas parties have tailed off. We haven't seen many English papers lately, but one dated 23rd talked of a possible white Christmas. Out here, it's difficult to imagine snow.

Well, we've had a varied time. Our stay in Bermuda was abruptly terminated by Lady Steyne, who suddenly decided after one day she wanted off. So we left in a big hurry. Pity – I was just beginning to enjoy Bermuda. Big surprise when we'd got to sea after all the panic of leaving – Peter Moraes (nephew) wasn't on board!

We thought (hoped?) he'd jumped over the side, but Lady S. was approached and said, "I believe my nephew has decided to stay behind – I imagine you will have no objection." No indeed. Funny thing, no one likes that man, not even, it seems, his aunt. We think he met some girl at a party. There were certainly plenty around.

So we get on very well without him. Oz Hodges is a splendid captain

– he always was – and the other officer, an Australian called Rod Trumper, keeps us amused. With only three of us we can do little at sea except watch-keep, but we are training up one of the seamen, Jenkin, to keep a day watch, and he'll be able to carry some of the load soon.

Lady Steyne is a grande dame but there's sometimes a touch of wistfulness about her that makes you wonder. She's certainly devoted to her Mozart – the music – and plays it almost constantly at sea on her hi-fi-issimo equipment back aft. I think she's lonely. We don't see her all that much, as a matter of fact.

All known plans have gone by the board (it was to have been Vancouver at one time) and all we know now is Santa Rosa by next month. Her ladyship often changes her mind – and why not, it's her yacht? I rather like an air of mystery about our movements. One thing though, it does make our mail erratic. I haven't heard from you for eight weeks now, I do hope there are no ghastly crises. I sent you a postcard from St. Kitts but I gave it to the victualling contractor just as we were leaving, so there's no knowing what's happened to it. St. Kitts was great fun. There was a very nice fellow there who runs a sort of boatel who took us in hand and made us most welcome. It's quite a small island but very pretty. Then we spent a week in Antigua, where Nelson's dockyard in English Harbour is being restored to something like its former glory – fascinating.

We went to Nevis too, and Montserrat, and St. Thomas (the American one), all very much with their own identities and characteristics. I always wish we could stay longer, but the wanderlust gets Grandma and off we go. As you know we spent Christmas in Jamaica (hope you got my telegram?) and boisterous times were had by all. Not difficult to enjoy yourself in Kingston – particularly at Christmas. I thought of you and hoped you were also enjoying things as we all drank to "the Absent".

I love being back at sea again and often feel I should have stayed in the Navy, even though the fact that the Navy is usually not like this was really why I came out. Of course we live like kings on board. There can be few ships afloat so well appointed. The work is congenial and not too demanding, and the sun keeps shining. We went through Panama yesterday and I'm pretty sure I saw an alligator in the fresh-water lake. The canal's a remarkable feat of engineering. Everyone comments on that.

So we're off to Santa Rosa now, and heaven knows what happens there. Lady S's relations come from there and Peter Moraes threatens to re-join us. It's sure to be hot and sticky. Apart from that we have very hazy ideas of what to expect. I do hope there's a letter from you waiting for me; I feel rather out of touch and even now it feels as though I'm writing into thin air. If you see Alice please give her my love. I hope the estate is thriving. My pay should be mounting up in the bank. When I get back there should be enough to start something really profitable. This could be the break we've always hoped for.

Best love

James

* * * * *

Yacht *Mozart*
bound S. Rosa
10th January

La Rue, La Rue,

Once upon a time there was a lovelorn swain whom the winds of fate blew across the seas to Ariel's paradise island, a place of sunshine, hibiscus and grand pianos. And there he found a slim lady who was all lightness and gaiety and golden hair. And Ariel manoeuvred them into a boat and away on their own, and the lovelorn swain wasn't so lovelorn after all. And his lady was kind and intelligent and had the gift (if it is one) of unmasking him, so that he found himself delighted but confused. She was kept by a bold bad baron in a castle, and the swain didn't quite know how much she stayed there of her own accord. And while he was wondering what to do next (slay the baron and free the lady?) suddenly the winds blew him away again. And he is still wondering.

I have been pondering life in Ariel's Isle. In many ways it's not much different from Prospero's time. One arrives, by sea, of someone else's volition, makes fatuous conversation, gets drunk and wears trumpery. Mysterious affairs are conducted by all-powerful agencies quite beyond one's control; strange and wonderful noises can still be heard. And yet the differences are glaring: no trusted old counsellor, no plots hatched in black and white, but oceans of indeterminate grey; if less of Caliban's wickedness, more of Ariel's mischievous uncertainty. You can take it at several levels. I can't get rid of juvenile clichés like unrelenting destiny and the jealous gods and the rolling rivers of time. Sometimes I just think sex is best. Ours is/was certainly not a cliché, my love! And I can vaguely hear my mother's voice, back home with her cronies over morning coffee: "But, my dear, he's having a simply fabulous time."

She's right. It's all fabulous, a fable. Dogs and cats and horses and foxes, disguised as humans, wander across the stage to say their piece and contribute to the story. And the moral? – all fables must have a moral. (I open my Shakespeare at random.) "Be cheerful, sir!" – as good a moral as any.

We've had some cheerful times lately, but I've been mostly thinking of you and me-and-you. There are all sorts of things about you that intrigue and puzzle me. In 1910 one might have said, "I don't quite manage La Rue." Indeed I don't. But I have optimistic, part-selfish, part-conceited, totally affectionate hopes of being allowed to puzzle her out one day. Puzzles are supposed to be solved. Roll on that day!

We went invitingly close to Adventa. It lies much where you left it, green and mountainous. I hinted to Grandma that it might be a good place to stop, but she only smiled sadly. She's an inscrutable old bird. But I haven't forgotten your offer to stay there one day. I'd like to. May I borrow it for my honeymoon? Or perhaps if that doesn't happen, and if you can escape from your castle, and if I ever get some leave or throw over this extraordinary job, we could rendezvous there and play Desert Islands. You see, I have discovered a taste for this playboy life, and before long I shall have plenty of money and be able to carry it off for a while. We could work on that puzzle together.

But nothing happens as you expect it. Nothing turns out as planned. I had vague (ominous word) plans about my Alice, but she has simply disappeared. And it's not really cost-effective to keep building on hopes of memories of imaginings of symptoms of love – as I don't need to tell you. It seems absurdly easy, now, to assure myself that I was really smitten the whole time. This is a well-documented phenomenon known as 'absence making the heart grow fonder', and has got to be watched carefully.

So the days go round and round. I get up at ten to four, and spend four hours driving this painted ship across the great wide painted ocean. Big lazy breakfast at eight. See the men working, make myself human to them, check everything's swinging along, cups of coffee and discussions with my splendid Captain (Oz has bottom, *in the eighteenth-century usage), gin and tonic before lunch – the days slip agreeably by. She's a good ship, satisfying to run properly, and we're a cheerful crowd. Of course, we haven't got Peter Moraes with us now. Is he still staying with you? How is that strange household of yours?*

If ever, ever, you need any possible kind of help or support or affection, dear La Rue, you have only to ask

Your loving

James

* * * * *

Yacht *Mozart*
at sea off Panama
10 Jan 1968

Darling Alice,

I hope you got my last letter and Christmas card. I haven't heard from you, but our mail has been most erratic. When this reaches you do drop me a line and tell me all is well. I'm a bit mystified by everything as you must surely know. Write c/o British Consul, Santa Rosa. We expect to be there till March.

Love *from*
James

CHAPTER NINE

Mozart felt her way upstream towards Santa Rosa on a huge brown river, moving slowly and carefully because of its well-deserved reputation for rapid silting. It swirled downstream with a strange flotsam of trees, dead cows and matted rafts of greenery with blue hyacinths growing on them. Low mud banks. Sparse hot horizons. Buildings of crumbling plaster with advertisements for unfamiliar cigarettes. The ship slid between these surroundings, breasting the murky current and more powerful than it, a clean thing from another dimension that spurned the excreta of the land. And the sun beat down on clean and unclean with astonishing vehemence, for they were within a few miles of the equator and it was nearly midday.

James felt elated and surprisingly energetic. After all, a man of twenty-five, sound in wind and limb, fingernails neatly trimmed, bowels easy, hormones working correctly, fit and fancy-free – more or less – ought to have a firm grasp on the ropes of life. He had plenty of money, too. His ship was as smart as a ship can be, his friends worth knowing, and his non-friends comfortably despicable. Surely all was well in the world of James Huwes. Here before him was a new port of call where anything might happen. He felt unreasonably confident in himself.

As the ship lined up for her allocated berth, she dipped her blue ensign as she passed the four old destroyers of the Ecuadorean navy that were anchored near the centre of the town. Some streets seemed to be quite full and others quite empty. There were very few women to be seen. Bad sign. They let go the anchor opposite a large grey wharf with the word "MORAES" written all over it in black letters ten feet high. Another bad sign, perhaps.

Peter Moraes was the first aboard. He was followed by a swarm of people, including the British consul dressed up as a creditable imitation of Lord Jim. James tried to sort out the local officials from the ship's agents, the newspapermen, the touts and the missioner to seamen; the remainder seemed to be members of the Moraes clan, including a cousin of about the same age. They were all quickly syphoned off by Peter Moraes himself and taken into the staterooms, where Lady Steyne appeared to be "At Home". James thought they were a shifty-looking bunch. It was easy to see how easily Black Pedro fitted into the same pattern: dark hair, plausible smile, confident manner, and not to be trusted further than you could throw a flick-knife.

Down in the cool of the wardroom Oz was talking to the consul.

"Thank you for calling," said Oz. "It's good to have such a friendly welcome. Gin and tonic?"

"Thank you. It is indeed good to see such a superb yacht. We had heard all about you but I could hardly have expected such magnificence." He leaned back in his chair, cooling off. His white duck suit was beautifully pressed, and he would have looked every inch a British consul, complete with pith helmet and MCC tie, apart from an aura of trying too hard.

"Bless us all," said Oz, earning clerical looks from the missioner who was also present. "So you've heard all about us, have you? Is that because of Lady Steyne's connection with Moraes & Co?"

"Chiefly. As you will of course know ..."

What a very distinctive consular phrase, thought James; but somehow this fellow doesn't quite ring true.

"... as you will of course know, her sister married the Moraes who founded the whole concern, and young Peter is quite well known here. They are a large and prominent family, one might say *the* most prominent."

"And what does the firm do?"

"Shipping, import-export, wharves, storehouses, refrigeration. A very big concern."

"Yes, yes, a very big concern," echoed the missioner suddenly. It was his first contribution to the conversation, and for some reason he did not speak again.

"Is there a thriving British community?" said Oz.

"I think I can say we thrive," said the consul while the missioner nodded. "My job consists largely in endeavouring to safeguard our security and business interests against the ever-shifting political background, which at this moment appears particularly confused."

"Fill me in," said Oz archly.

"I beg your pardon?"

"Put me wise."

"The situation is such that an annual revolution has become a normal part of the political life of this country. It is expected at about this time every year, when the recruits finish their initial training. Last year the Army achieved a *putsch* in about two hours – a really remarkable feat even for such habitual revolutioneers. This year all eyes are turned towards the Navy, who are widely tipped as favourites for the next race. I have been here some fifteen years, and encountered eleven revolutions during that time."

The consul's well-rehearsed sentences rolled forth glibly, and James wondered how many times he had used them. Had fifteen years blurred his distinction between a foreigner's version of an English gentleman and an Englishman's idea of the same? And that slightly pretentious pronunciation of the word *putsch* – definitely trying a bit too hard.

* * * * *

That afternoon James had an impulse to climb to the highest point of the city and look down. He filled his pockets with money, equipped himself with binoculars and walking stick, and went ashore. Santa Rosa was having its siesta, and not a mouse was stirring. He walked lithely and lightly through the town, where the shops were empty but still had their wares hanging up – enormous wickerwork dog-baskets for great danes, whole bunches of bananas, and stuffed alligators swinging lazily in the heat. His impression of a rather faded and crumbling city reinforced itself. The buildings were in bad repair, and the only people visible were the very young or the very old. The sun was absurdly hot and he soon felt his shirt darkening on his back. He started walking up the hill, his stick a-swing to his stride; he felt confidently ridiculous, unhatted in the great heat, the mad Englishman out for an afternoon constitutional.

The hill was larger than he had supposed, but he gained the top at last and found a small café, apparently empty, but providing shade and a magnificent view of the town and its thick brown river. He dropped into a chair, pleasantly tired by his walk and sweating like a racehorse. A small boy appeared noiselessly at his table. What could one drink?

"Coca-Cola please." It was easiest.

The small boy slipped away without a sound. Indeed, this was a fantastic view. He was glad of his binoculars, for the whole shambling town was spread out before him, coloured like a child's drawing – yellow for buildings, brown for river, blue for sky, and spattered with those moth-eaten advertisements. There in the river were the rusty destroyers, and near them the trim lines of his own ship. He could see through his binoculars every detail on board: the ship's bell, the white guardrails, the awning aft that shaded the veranda deck where Lady

Steyne was still presumably holding court in her photo-luminescent cabin. What a curious set-up it all was! Enormous wealth had legally descended on an old widow. She had said: "Do this" – and men had built her a magnificent yacht for other men to carry her about the world in. He felt in his pocket and searched for a note small enough to give the small boy; some of the inherited wealth had leaked out in his direction. Pleasant. Lucky. But it was a strange business.

And of the lady herself? They had seen little of her, but her personality had affected everything they did. As Oz had guessed, there was no need to invent peculiarities for her: she had plenty. She had little sense of time and place, and would cast all their arrangements into confusion with courteous requests for a change of plan. She would suddenly insist on meals at odd hours, or would require to be taken in a boat a little way from the ship in the middle of the night, saying nothing, looking around her. But when she did speak there was no doubt at all as to what she wanted or whom she wanted to do it, and she had the gift of throwing herself entirely into a conversation, not necessarily with a dramatic gush but so as to exclude everything else from a mind which would concentrate with extraordinary precision on the subject. When listening to music she was at her most endearing, for she would be lost inside the workings of the composer, sometimes for hours on end. It surprised no one that her collection of tapes should be almost entirely Mozart and Haydn. But the strength of her concentration, when she could be seen motionless on the veranda deck, from perhaps five to eight o'clock in the morning, surprised everyone. They were fond of her by now, being used to her absentmindedness and eccentricity. And she kept her nephew tolerable; they must always be grateful for that.

James had another drink and his gaze wandered to the main street below him. It was almost empty, but a lone policeman motorcyclist in gorgeous uniform was riding down the middle, sounding his horn aggressively. Other road users would have been disconcerted, but there were no other road users. The policeman disappeared and a dog that managed to look both hungry and lazy strayed across the road.

Suddenly a true spectacle was in full view: a vast black car with flags flapping on the bonnet, preceded by resplendent outriders on motorcycles – about two dozen of them. These motorcycles had six-foot aerials with some kind of flag on them that whipped about madly like drunken fishing rods. It was an impressive display, and James with his binoculars had a grandstand view of the cavalcade as it came quite slowly down the main street in his direction. As it approached the crossroads the lights went red against it, and he thought it impossible for mere traffic lights to be able to halt the progress of such a very important personage. But the leading outrider waved a gauntlet; a succession of waving gauntlets vied with a forest of careering flags; and incredibly the whole procession came to a stop at the deserted crossroads.

He looked at the figure lounging on the back seat of the car in his shirtsleeves, his arm resting on the open window. The Mayor? The President?

All at once a small boy ran into his field of vision, darted towards the car, and – while James could see every detail – wrenched the watch off the great man's wrist. Several things then occurred simultaneously. There was a convulsion visible in the back of the car, which shot forward. The outriders broke into disarray, and started firing their revolvers. He had an impression of men and dogs scattering in the street, which had just now seemed deserted. The car hit an outrider and jack-knifed him into the gutter, and as the noise of the shots began to reach James so did the strident note of a siren. He could only watch the scene, thunderstruck. There was no sign of the small boy.

People then were running for cover, and the car disappeared round a corner, siren shrieking. A Land Rover full of khaki uniforms hurtled past the crossroads, collided with a motorcycle, and turned over. More shots were fired and crouching soldiers appeared. The Land Rover started billowing smoke into the air. Confusion was complete.

James was hustled out of the café as its owner and his son hastily started to board it up. He offered to pay for his drinks but they were in too much of a hurry. He walked away feeling rather less than confident. It seemed that this year's revolution had started.

There was nowhere to go but down the hill, so he went down. This is it, he thought, as a single shot rang out, definitely close. Help ... damn. An inglorious end to all my hopes and fears – shot like a rabbit in a woodland ride. The Churbridge parish magazine will briefly note the fact "... in the recent revolution in Santa Rosa." "Somewhere in South America, I believe," the remoter cousins will tell each other. And Alice? She at least will weep for me. I love her.

Can none of these doors give me a hiding place? They are all bolted and boarded. Then I must put a bold face on it and die like a gentleman. How does a gentleman die? Confident step, head up, swinging walking stick – try that. And think the words of that absurd song: "Whenever I feel afraid ..."

It seemed to work fairly well. Gradually the spring in his step became less artificial and drove some of the fright out of his belly. The road down the hill was flanked with shabby plaster arcades that overhung the pavements; he tapped his stick on them as he passed, gaining confidence with each tap. A figure scuffled into a doorway ahead of him, but he bounced by heedless, not even turning his head. Who the hell were these people anyway?

A man was crouched down by a parked car ahead of him, pointing what looked like a light machine gun away down the hill. Suddenly he fired, a neat burst of three or four, so loud and near and quick that afterwards James wondered if he had heard anything at all. He was firing into the arcade ahead. What should one do?

James's mind was drunk with its newfound power – the conquest of fear. It reasoned that if the man was firing parallel with the pavement, the best place would be away from the pavement, along the road. So he stepped out into the road, into the sunshine, and walked on.

There was probably ten seconds in time between doing this outstandingly stupid thing and reaching the parked car and the man with the gun. During that time the old sense of self-preservation was able to assert itself over his crazy power-drunk confidence, and his mind went through every agonising stage in between. But there was no going back. He had chosen to walk down the middle of a road in the middle of a South American revolution. No going back.

It so happened that the machine gunner, intent on aiming and firing, did not notice or hear James until he was almost on top of him. He turned from his gun with such a shock of terror and surprise that James knew he was at least safe from this one, for the look in his eye was that of a leveret that you nearly tread on: too frightened to move or squeal or think. So he walked past him and on down the hill. There seemed to be nothing else to be done.

There was now quite a lot of firing going on, but he was too sick with fright to know where it was coming from. He just kept walking – *don't look back*. And the stick was a help, because it is impossible to walk with a stick unless you get into a rhythm, and the rhythm kept him going. Down the hill. On. Keep walking. Brain's not functioning very well, so must keep walking.

At that moment there were in fact about six guns pointing at him, but for some reason the six men behind those guns did not fire. He was to ponder the reason afterwards. Perhaps they were nonplussed by the strange-looking foreigner with binoculars over one shoulder, striding down the middle of the road through the cross-fire. Perhaps they recognised him as outside their game. But more likely they were bemused by the colossal idiocy happening before their eyes. At any rate, they held their fire. Of those who were alive to talk about the incident later, half described a miracle and half some kind of an unfathomable trap.

One of the first half was Rod Trumper. "A bloody miracle," he was muttering to himself, high up in the bar of the Hotel Supremo where he had retired with a grandstand view to watch the fighting. He had heard the shots and seen some of the confusion which followed, for the hotel overlooked the crossroads. He was astounded to see James walk into view like the hero in a Western, and could count some of the guns that followed him down the road. Rod's first reaction was to think that his First Lieutenant had gone off his head, touched by the sun; his second was to rush for the lift and discover it had been immobilised. He started down the stairs, three at a time, but it was a long way down, and he reached the bottom in an unfamiliar part of the hotel, breathless and disorientated. He burst out of a back door into the street, and practically fell over James, who seemed to take his arrival calmly.

"Hello Rod, and what are you dashing out of the hotel kitchen for?" he asked.

"James, you crazy bastard, don't you know there's a shooting match going on? You've been covered by a dozen rifles for the past hundred yards. Didn't you know that? Why the hell are you wandering round like this, or are you out of your sodding mind?"

But James's answers to these questions, which would have been difficult to make convincing just then, were obviated by the sudden intrusion of a third voice.

"Come over to here, both, *now*," said the voice. It was authoritative, and they obeyed. "Don't try any of the tricks, I think. I have you in my pistol-aim."

So James and Rod were arrested by a Santa Rosa paramilitary official of some kind and thrown rather roughly into what looked unpleasantly like a Santa Rosa jail.

CHAPTER TEN

Prison, to begin with, is only a thing of the body, and the first thing that James felt as the cell door closed on his isolation was a sense of relief, verging on elation. He had, after all, defied a riot and emerged unscathed, and that was something to be thankful for. He was presumably safe in his cell, and Rod was somewhere in the building and presumably safe also. So there was little to worry about, except how to pass the time until officialdom discovered who they were and released them. It would probably only take an hour or two. He lay down on the narrow bunk. It was damnably hard.

He looked around him. It was laughably just as a prison should be: six by eight, bare walls covered with graffiti, mostly unintelligible and undoubtedly obscene; cement floor; open window high up with heavy bars; heavy iron door with a peep-hole through which he could see nothing. In all, not much of a place to spend too long.

His mind retraced the events of their arrest: how the official had crushed handcuffs over their wrists, rather unnecessarily roughly; how his demeanour and weaponry had brooked no argument and they had offered none; how they had been bundled into a jeep and jolted off, saving up their explanations or protests till they should arrive at the police station. They had driven very fast, and shots were still cracking round the walls from unseen guns. But when they did arrive their captor immediately dumped them and drove away, and the guard who took over did not understand a single word of their explanations, while protests only provoked rougher treatment as they were searched. He and Rod were separated, and James was manhandled into his cell, resentful, but safe from the bullets … at last safe.

The first thing he wanted to do was to have a pee. How did one arrange that in prisons? He hadn't had one for some time. He glanced at his wrist where his watch should have been. It had of course been removed with all his other possessions. Well, he could last for a bit longer. Then he would have to call the guard.

His mind wandered easily over the events of the afternoon. He had been foolish, but possibly a little splendid as well; certainly lucky. He recalled his feelings when confronted with those random bullets: fear, self-pity, self-conscious dramatising, and the wish to behave properly. And one further half-remembered element – Alice? In a flash of insight that bordered on revelation he saw his life from end to end, a clear pattern, and he discovered that Alice was part of it. Astonishing! This was *love*, which some idiot had defined as an insane preference for one other human to the mystification of the rest of mankind. He must find her and marry her, the sooner the better. He had never felt more completely certain of anything.

He looked again for his non-existent watch. A pity he could not fix the exact time this inspiration had come to him, but he owed it to history to record the event somehow. On the wall? He searched around for something hard and sharp and eventually decided the only thing was the zip-fastener tab of his trousers. So he took them off, and began scratching on the cold concrete:

J. H. LOVES A. C.

Not very original, but a clear statement of fact, for all who cared to read. It stood out well on the wall. He filled the letters in, proud of his skill and the evenness of the lettering. He was about to add the date and an estimate of the time – it must be about 6 p.m. by the light – when the door swung open and an unpleasant-looking man came in, small and squat with dirty clothes and the local look of having shaved the day before yesterday. He was carrying a plastic bowl with some measly kind of soup in it, but seeing James against the wall without any trousers the man smiled; and James knew unequivocally from that smile that the man was a predatory homosexual. He felt inclined to jump on him and beat his way out of prison, trousers or no, but decided not to. If he didn't make it, they would surely detain him forever. Beating up a warder is a crime in any country. So he stood there while the man put the bowl of soup down on the bunk and continued to smile at him.

"Look," said James, "I must have a pee." The man smiled. "Do you understand? I must use lavatory, water-closet, toilet – urgent. Please. I must go soon or there'll be a disaster."

Smile.

"Do you understand me? I'm desperate. Pee, piss, psss …" and in an effort to convey his meaning James pointed to that part of himself that was in need.

The man smiled broadly, a nasty suggestive leer, and went out of the door chuckling to himself. The key turned. And I fear that's not the last I see of him, thought James.

Well, there's a fine thing, he thought. Here am I, locked up in a sinister prison, dying to "go", and all I've managed to do is encourage that little queer. I can probably cope with him, unless he drugs me or assaults me in the dark, but it bodes ill. Now they've brought me food, which means I won't get out tonight, I'm afraid. It's getting dark already. Meanwhile, there is simply no alternative …

So he chose the corner furthest from his bunk – about four feet away. And he relieved himself gloriously, marvelling at how much there was. It spread out all over the floor. He found himself being cut off from the bunk, his only island in an encroaching sea of sewage. He leapt for it, and upset the bowl of soup on the coarse blanket that would be his only covering for the night. *Foul.* He sat on the bed, hunched up away from the mess, utterly miserable, and could have howled like a whipped child.

There was an explosion outside, but he didn't care. There were men's shouts, a clattering noise, and a scuffle of running feet outside his very door. Then quietness. Then three deliberate cracks from a well-aimed rifle. Then complete silence.

The light faded out of the cell until J. H. could no longer be seen to love A. C. amongst the crude scribblings of earlier convicts. Somehow he fell asleep.

* * * * *

He was suddenly awake and sloughing off fantastic dreams, conscious of the darkness, the smell, and his own stiff limbs. Why had he woken? His instincts told him to alert his senses and keep quiet.

It was a low-pitched rustling, so regular that he scarcely noticed it. It reminded him of the ilex tree back home at Churbridge that used to swish its dry leaves gently on summer evenings. Once distinguished, the noise became obvious. Or was it getting louder?

A fluttering at the window of his cell made him immediately wide-awake and watchful. Something fell lightly from the window on to the floor. More rustling.

My God, he thought, it's alive.

More things came fluttering through the bars, things like bats only smaller, and the rustle became a loud swish. Several flapped him in the face, and he lashed out wildly. What were these horrors that had come to torment him in the dark? He put up a hand to shield his face. One of them flew into his palm, squirmed, and was gone.

James had never heard of grillos, those locust-like creatures with an incredible hunger for organic matter that sometimes swarm through the towns of South America. If he had, his fears would have been somewhat allayed, because a grillo has the uncanny knack of not attacking anything that can defend itself. But alone in his miserable cell, not knowing, abandoned, defenceless, he found them frightening enough.

They were streaming through the window now in hundreds, attracted by the smell of urine and spilled soup. The air seemed completely full of them. They swarmed round him as flies swarm round a dead horse, settling briefly and then escaping. He got off the bed, close to panic, and crunched over a carpet of grillos to the other side of his cell. With his back to the wall and his arms free he was just able to keep down the urge to scream and go mad. It was like fighting seasickness, and he only just won. Help me, he thought. If I survive this hideous night I will give thanks. I haven't said my prayers for years, but please, something or someone, please help me. I'm at the end of my tether. If I survive I shall devote my life to something great and noble and selfless. I will marry that wonderful girl and with total spiritual dedication we'll live simply but beautifully with our family. I will adore her. Help me!

He slapped away some grillos from his body. They seemed quieter now, concentrating on the bed.

He remembered his revelation of a few hours ago, when he had had a visionary sense of his life from end to end. So he would survive! It was written! He took some comfort, and the grillos were suddenly cut down to size.

But was the revelation true, or had he dreamed it?

Then the growing light began to reveal the outline of the letters he had scratched on the wall. So his survival was assured, and his prayers had perhaps been answered. He gave thanks wholeheartedly, anyway. It was true: there are no atheists in foxholes.

* * * * *

An hour later, most of them had gone. As the edibles in the cell were consumed he had been able to drive some of them out of the window. Others he smashed with his hands and feet against walls and floor. Gradually the day came, and showed him his tiny cell: it was a battlefield. The grillos had eaten every square inch of fabric on his bunk. The blanket had simply disappeared. The mattress was now bare horsehair, and where it had rested on the iron bars of the bed there was a neatly trimmed line of mattress cover. His clothes were full of holes, and spattered with squashed grillo. And pervading everything, sticking to his throat and inside his nostrils, was the harsh reek of stale urine.

The last grillo was whizzing around, and eventually he succeeded in chasing it out of the window – the very last of them. He sat on the ruins of his bunk and took stock.

Well, well ...

It was quite a night, but I survived. They attacked me mentally and physically, but I just managed to beat them. I'll never forget that ghastly nightmare moment when they started coming in – unspeakably awful! I remember appealing to all sorts of metaphysical ideas, which is consistent with my upbringing, and was certainly a comfort. Thanks due to someone for that. Now I must get myself out of here and cleaned up, and somehow I've got to find Alice and tell her how much I love her. Truth moves in mysterious places. I'm hungry. Certainly my fortunes can never be lower than last night.

He was wrong, but he would look back and feel that his night in prison had somehow matured him, filled out some parts of his character and made them stronger. It was as though all the rough edges of growing up had been polished smooth, and he had emerged with a more complete personality. He dated from that night a new ability to worry less about trivialities, and to see major decisions more in perspective. After all, he had been through hell, and it seemed to have purged him of the irrelevancies of life. And he had had something close to a vision, and that does not happen to everyone, or to anyone very often. He now felt certain about some important things, and most especially his love for Alice was enamel-clear in his mind. It was a kind of love at *second* sight, every bit as surprising and delightful as the other kind.

Footsteps in the corridor made him jump like a startled animal. They approached as he looked round his shameful cell. The door swung open. It was Oz.

James had never seen Oz look so haggard. He must have been up all night, although this for a seaman is not particularly unusual.

"James, you look a fearful wreck, what the hell's been going on?"

"We were arrested and locked up. They wouldn't let me pee, and then I was attacked by these … these …"

"These what?"

"Things."

"Where's Rod?"

"I don't know. They separated us. In this building somewhere."

"Come along. We must find him."

"What's happening? Where are the guards?"

"Fled. The revolution has taken over."

"How did you get the keys?"

"I didn't. The door was open."

So. The door had been open.

James followed him round the deserted prison, pushing open cell doors and calling. The place was clearly empty and echoed their calls. Outside there were distant sounds of sporadic rifle fire.

"No luck," said Oz. "Must try that consul's office again. I've got a car waiting."

"Perhaps it could drop you there and take me back to the ship. I can't face the world until I've cleaned myself up a bit."

Oz looked at him gravely. "There is no ship," he said. "*Mozart* caught fire and sank in the harbour last night. Lady Steyne was drowned." And Oz burst into tears – deep, masculine, actual tears shaking his whole frame.

James again felt that his fortunes could never sink lower. This time he was right.

CHAPTER ELEVEN

"Take a seat," said the missioner to seamen, the Reverend Joshua Barking. He beamed. "It's a real pleasure to be able to rescue a seaman in distress, especially as it's my duty to do so. You'll have lots to talk to each other about, and I have to go to the hospital. The revolution seems to be dying out a bit. So here is a bottle of whisky and see you later."

Oz and James exchanged glances.

"There's an ally," said Oz, "and don't we need one. He has fixed up all the crew. They call him Holy Joe of course. Funny, when he came on board I hardly noticed him."

James looked down at himself, now fed and clothed in some of Holy Joe's off-duty garments. Not quite what he would have chosen, but entirely serviceable. It had been a great joy to drop his prison clothes into the dustbin. It was midday.

"Tell me about it, sir."

"It will be a relief to be able to discuss it with someone. Things have moved so fast, so irrevocably, that I need to put my own thoughts in order too.

"Now … fairly late yesterday afternoon I went ashore for a look around. By that time all Lady Steyne's guests had gone and she was apparently resting in her quarters. Moraes was tinkering with his boat at the stern-boom. There were five men aboard, including Framley. I hailed a local boat, and went off to the silver market to buy some things for my girls. Framley says that about half an hour later he saw smoke coming out of the after ventilation exhaust. He dashed aft and heard crackling noises of fire coming out of the cowl. He got to the ladder leading down to the generator room, and found dense smoke coming up through the access hatch. There's a hose connection at the bottom of that ladder, and in trying to reach it he lost his grip on the hot handrail and fell. He bruised his back and got some nasty burns on his hands. By the time he'd reached the deck again, choking with the fumes, smoke was curling out of all openings aft, and the teak was beginning to scorch.

"He was badly shaken, but he had the presence of mind to think of Lady Steyne. He ran for the main door of her stateroom, but the fire was by this time – to use his own description – 'exploding' all around him, and he couldn't reach it. He then made for the galley door, which as you know is the only other way in. He found the steward banging on it with an empty fire extinguisher. 'She's had it,' shouted the steward. 'Door's locked.' 'Where's the key?' said Framley. 'The cook must've got it, and I think he's ashore.' They put their weight against the door, but it wouldn't budge.

"Framley was now on the point of collapse, and Moraes appeared and did a lot of shouting. There was by this time no pressure on the firemain, and the fire was much too extensive for anything less. The entire after end of the ship was blazing. The large after port burst open, and she began to sink by the stern.

"I was in the market when I heard the shots which I'm told sparked off the expected revolution. I made for the jetty to get back aboard as soon as possible, in case anyone tried to requisition the ship or something. I saw smoke coming from aft and tried to get a boat but a naval launch was not permitting any boat traffic ..."

"Why on earth not?"

"The Navy had been tipped off that the Army was planning to take over their four ships, boarding them in small craft. The destroyers were busy weighing anchor and putting to sea. So I could only plead ineffectually with the launch and the local boatmen and watch frantically while our poor *Mozart* slowly sank into the river. If you only knew …"

James did know something of what his late Captain must have felt, and he hurried him on.

"So what happened to Moraes, Framley and the rest?"

"Moraes got his speedboat away, and took them off. I saw them as they came ashore: Framley in pretty bad shape, the others dazed and shocked, Moraes grim as death."

"So what's happening now?"

"Several things. First our patron is certainly drowned; there can be no possible doubt. Secondly, I believe *Mozart* will be unsalvable. I've spoken to the Harbourmaster and he says that the soft mud here on the river bottom is of unknown thickness, and is famous for swallowing up wrecks mighty quickly. In a week you won't be able to find the ship, let alone salvage her, and the chances of getting salvage operations going in this country so soon are simply nil. Thirdly, I've established that the cook did have the galley key on him, but 'doesn't remember' locking the galley door. I have it now, incidentally. Finally, I've worked out that *Mozart* sank in about eighteen minutes – and I don't believe ships on fire normally sink as fast as that."

"You mean someone …"

"I do. James, you will know whom I suspect. Listen. Moraes sent word this morning that he was too distressed to come and see me, and would be staying with his relations for a while. Then when I was in the consul's office this morning enquiring about Rod Trumper I just caught sight of a note scribbled on the consul's blotter: 'B'da visa 813471.' I have now looked up Moraes in the local directory –

813471 is their office number. I think the fellow's about to do a bunk to Bermuda."

"And the consul's in on it?"

"Up to the neck. I must admit when he came on board I thought he was too good to be true, and I wondered why he should be playing such an obvious part."

"I thought so too. Why don't we see if Moraes is still here – through the office?"

"Tried it. A competent secretary tells me that Mr Peter Moraes is not in town. Home address not available. In three languages."

"What do you think he's up to?"

"I darkly suspect the following: Lady Steyne had a lot of money, much of it in emeralds which she kept in that safe on board. If she died intestate Moraes would get the lot. If she had made a will, Moraes is probably in it anyway, being her nearest relation, but she might have lived for twenty years – too long for him and his expensive tastes. So I believe he may have set fire to *Mozart* and opened the main discharges at the same time, knowing that the ship would be unsalvable in Santa Rosa harbour. Not difficult to do. But first he immobilises his unfortunate aunt somehow, and ..."

"The safe?"

"I'm not sure about the safe. He would have wanted to clean it out if possible, but I don't see how even he could have broken into it – unless he'd got hold of the combination somehow."

"He is the most utterly despicable man."

"Remember all this, James, is only suspicion so far. But the Santa Rosa police won't help us – they've got enough on their hands at the moment, even if they were immune from persuasion by the Moraes gang. In any case, the senior police officers lost their jobs yesterday, and as you know all the prisoners have been released by the revolutionary council. So no help from the police. And I see no way of proving our suspicions without more evidence."

"I'll go down there," said James, "and have a look."

He surprised himself by not properly considering this gruesome task before volunteering. His only difficulty was persuading Oz that it was feasible. He had done some diving in the Navy. Framley was out of action but could lend him the gear. Furthermore, there was no time to be lost. In the extreme silting conditions of Santa Rosa the wreck would be burying itself further and further into the mud every hour. Eventually he persuaded Oz to let him try it at slack water that night. They would take a seaman to help with the boat, and be ready to go by two-thirty.

"And now," said Oz, "both of us are going to get some sleep."

* * * * *

They had a boat and the necessary diving equipment. They had the galley key. They knew exactly where *Mozart* sank. Their problem was to do the job discreetly. Fortunately the opposite bank had a number of bare stretches, and one of these became their diving base. It was very dark and quiet as James, helped by Jenkin, put on the Mistral scuba set and tested it. They talked in whispers, partly because the ambience was so furtive and ghostly. He felt like a smuggler, but not so brave.

"You have an hour of slack water," said Oz quietly into his ear. "Don't be longer. If you aren't back in an hour and ten minutes I shall start initiating a major flap. Which would be awkward for all of us. Have you got a watch?"

"No. Lost it in prison."

"Take mine. It's luminous and watertight. And don't be more than sixty minutes from now."

James strapped his sharp knife on one side and an underwater torch on the other. "I'll be back, sir. Shouldn't take all that long. Quite safe."

He slipped into the cool water. This is it, Jim-me-lad, you're on your own.

He had two transit marks – a street lamp and a neon sign – and he swam out steadily, keeping them in line. *Mozart* is certainly somewhere on this line, he told himself. The river looked large and black and unfriendly, but he held to his transit, swimming crabwise against a slight stream. The wreck of the good ship *Mozart*, in which so much human endeavour had been invested, must be somewhere on the line, about halfway along.

The hopelessness of his task suddenly struck him, and he felt very alone. He had a weight and a length of cordage, and the plan was to drop the weight in the most likely position, and then swim in a circle, keeping the line tight and hoping it would snag on the wreck. He had done this before, but in totally different conditions, and he had no idea if the weight would hold in the exceptionally soft mud of the tidal river. At that moment it began to seem fairly absurd to try to find a wreck this way, without a boat to dive from, or at least a marker buoy. Needle in a haystack; chance in a hundred. But he held to his transit. Quite safe, he had said. Those might be his last words to a fellow human, quite safe.

About here, perhaps? It seemed more or less half way. He put his feet together and dropped down like a stone. It was quite black. He tried his torch. It was working all right, but illuminated nothing in the murky water.

At thirty feet he grounded in very soft mud. It was impossible to see more than a yard. Which way should he go? God, this was all madness.

He felt something hard at his back and whipped round. It was a rail. A guard rail. He had found her first time.

He then realised that he must be actually on the deck of the *Mozart*, and the soft mud he was walking on had collected in a day and a half. The wreck would indeed soon be buried. It was a relief to ditch the weight and the cordage, no longer needed.

He pulled himself along the guardrail towards the stern. He came to a for'ard awning stanchion and the gap where the ladder must be. This fixed his position precisely. It was an eerie feeling, floating around his ship in the pitch-black water, and for a moment he thought again of all the careful craftsmanship, money and affection that had been lavished on that lifeless hulk. But only for a moment. He had a crucial job to do.

And what a job, he thought, pulling himself steadily along the side of the ship, hand over hand. What a dreadful job. He was to enter a locked compartment with a dead woman inside, and grope around to see if she had been murdered. And how he was supposed to do that when everything would be covered with a layer of mud and visibility was practically zero, God alone knew. And it was frighteningly quiet.

The background of his hearing rang with a just-perceptible high-pitched whine – the sound of complete silence.

But courage, he thought again. Breathing apparatus going well, lucky to find her first time. I do at least know my way around. It's not the first dead body I've dealt with in there. The mud may not have permeated inside yet. Besides, I have my secret love, he thought, strengthening himself as he reached the galley door.

It was open. *Open.* It should have been shut. But perhaps the heat had burst it open. He felt the edge of the door, and the tongue of the lock was withdrawn. Inescapable fact: the door had been unlocked.

He went in. He remembered a basic rule of diving: when entering a wreck under water, unreel a line, like Ariadne's silk, to help you find your way out if you get disorientated. But he knew the place well, and (he looked at Oz's watch) this was no time for rules.

It was totally without light, and he could only move around by feeling his way. He found it helped to close his eyes, and soon he accustomed himself to slow groping movements, using the back of the hand to sweep ahead. Keep close to the starboard side and there should be a clear passage through to the cabin. Mud's not too bad. Feel along the bulkhead – frying pan, galley range, mixing machine. The fire seems to have done very little damage inside. Presumably the ship sank too quickly. He got to the cabin door. It was also open and he floated through into the utter blackness within, fins waving gently, just keeping him moving.

His eyes were shut, but he had a clear picture of the staterooms in his mind.

Where to begin this horrible search? The bed must be somewhere on my right hand; better see if she's there, poor old woman. That swine may have drugged her or strangled her first. Move slowly. There's the French sofa – damn shame it's ruined. Chair next. No, the chair was never bolted to the deck, so it must be floating on the deckhead somewhere. Everything's odd. Bed must be next – there.

He groped on the bed. His fingers felt a rope, and followed it across the bed to a smooth knob of human skin. He recoiled. She had been tied down.

Horrible. Poor old girl. Swine.

He felt along the rope again, sensing carefully with his fingertips. It was knotted round the bed with a round turn and two half hitches. Then came a hip bone. Then a hand holding a knife.

Christ! He convulsed hideously as the hand jerked away. Fear, like an electric shock, collapsed all his muscles uncontrollably, and he fell into a heap on the deck. Some creature lunged over his head, and he could feel the vibrations through the water as it hit the French sofa.

That lunge did much to restore him. Here is no nightmare corpse, he thought, but a live and vicious enemy. Furthermore it is certainly trying to kill me, and I must kill it first.

It must be human because I felt it holding a knife. So as it's a diver (he was thinking a bit faster now) that simplifies the problem, because he will be subject to the same difficulties as I am now. He no more knows where I am than I know where he is. He has a knife and presumably a torch, but so have I.

Switching on one's torch would be crazy. It would give away one's position. Which is why we are both not switching on our torches.

God though, I must get away from here. It won't take him long to deduce where I am now.

James drew his knife and started worming along the deck, his free hand keeping him a few inches off the sodden carpet. Just in time. He felt the swirl of another attack miss his fins by a foot or two. This heartened him. Having deduced his opponent's intentions correctly the first time, he thought he might be able to again.

But how? To swim around blindly would be putting oneself at a disadvantage, for a moving underwater swimmer can be detected by a stationary one through the water eddies and vibrations he must make. Realising this, he stopped and crouched with his back to a bulkhead, and waited motionless. Nothing.

But the other fellow would presumably have come to the same conclusion and be doing the same thing. In fact he probably had a longer endurance, and might well be lying in ambush near the door. The situation seemed more desperate the more he thought of it.

And yet …

Switching on a torch would undoubtedly be crazy. So if James switched his on he would be suspected of laying a trap. But his opponent had moved very fast when he had first touched him. A man of quick reactions. So he might just possibly think it worthwhile to attack immediately the torch was switched on. After all, it is impossible to switch on a torch without being there. If James could sidestep quickly enough, he might have the chance of a decisive counter-attack. It seemed the best hope, perhaps the only possible hope. Die fighting, anyway, die honourably even if nobody would ever know. A day less or more, at sea or ashore ... at least fighting.

On his left must be the cocktail cabinet. He stood up carefully and groped for it. There it was. He laid the torch very gently on top, unlit, pointing out into the room. Then he backed away till it was just within arm's reach, and held his knife ready in his right hand. Will he take the bait, he thought. It's now or never.

Switch on!

He never expected such a sudden reaction from the man who must have been incredibly close. There was a wild confused flailing of arms and knives, and a lunging attack which seemed to miss James by a hair's breadth. His attacker had impaled his knife in the door of the cocktail cabinet, and as he attempted to remove it James could see in silhouette the shape of the aqualung on his back. It was easy to reach forward and slice through the soft rubber hose that connected the air supply to the mouth piece.

In the murky torchlight he saw the atrocious panic of a desperate man fighting for air, tearing off his mask and clawing his way, instinctively but uselessly, upwards to the deckhead. Then James with horror had to watch how a man drowns, a grotesque dance of death, convulsive, violent, then diminuendo.

Did I do right? he thought. No, he told himself, but there was no alternative.

The man's struggles became weaker, and stopped, and the corpse gently dropped through the muddy water to the deck. James suddenly felt very weak too. He retrieved the torch and looked at his watch. Hell, only twelve minutes before Oz goes to panic-stations. He must make a mighty quick search of this god-forsaken place and scram.

First, the man. He shone the torch full into his dead staring face. It was Moraes. No it wasn't, it was that damned Moraes cousin.

Secondly, Lady Steyne. He swam to the bed. It was her all right. She had been firmly gagged and tied down with thick ropes. Drowned rather than burnt. And that bastard had been hacking away at her sodden fingers, trying to get her rings off. Horrible.

Thirdly, the safe. He went over to it. It was shut but not locked. Inside was a massive empty space. They had cleared it out. From inside he could see the solid mechanism of the safe, with its brass wheels with slots cut in them. He wondered briefly how they could have obtained the combination. There was presumably no way in without it.

And now – *out*. He was nearly spent. He swam to the door, hitting into things from sheer exhaustion. Perhaps Ariadne's silk would have been helpful after all. Through the galley and out into the river again. He left the door open; let the mud of the Santa Rosa river settle on the grisly scene inside.

He jettisoned some weights to give himself a slight positive buoyancy, relaxed and breathed out as he rose slowly to the surface, dog tired but victorious. He had after all established beyond doubt that Lady Steyne had been murdered, and the yacht deliberately destroyed. And the case against the Moraes party would almost certainly be proved in an English court of law, if it could ever be brought to one. He would be able to tell Oz "mission accomplished".

He broke surface. Coca-Cola and Raleigh cigarettes in neon

lighting told him that the world was still going on. God, the joy of being back and breathing fresh air.

He made for the shore, swimming as fast as he could, which was not very fast. The stream was no longer slack, and he was swept a long way downstream. Damn, he thought, I'm probably late already. I hope Oz doesn't start raising the alarm. That Moraes fellow must have some supporters not far away.

His knees touched soft mud. He had only just enough energy left to crawl and squelch his way ashore. Before exhaustion simply overwhelmed him he had the presence of mind to switch the torch on. And then he collapsed, spreadeagled on the shore like a seabird with oil on its feathers.

It was there that Jenkin, anxiously searching downstream, found him a few minutes later. Somehow they got him back to the Mission House and put him to bed. Only then did they discover the long clean slash along his left shoulder. James, weak from loss of blood and nervous shock, slept like a child, and his story slept with him.

CHAPTER TWELVE

He woke, shivering, sweating and throbbing, and his back hurt like hell. He tried to sit up to reassure himself that his feverish ravings had only been foul dreams, but cool hands restrained him. They seemed to be friendly hands. A gentle voice said something soothing in no known language. Blinds flapped idly against hot sunlight. What was all this?

Hospital. Must be. They must have put him there because of his back. Oz shouldn't be far away. Oz always turned up when wanted like the god from the machine. But hell, that nightmare was dreadful; can't remember much what it was all about, but it was under water and certainly scary. Shoulder's pretty bad, better not move. Don't move a muscle, stare straight ahead. Can't face the outside world yet.

More noises in the background. An attractive dark nurse appeared on his virtual stage, said something sympathetic, and was lost to view left. But where was Oz? The throbbing began again.

Where was
Commander Oz?
Where Oz
Commander was.

You're raving, lad. Raving mad. Better drop off to sleep again.
Back to that nightmare? Not bloody likely.
Oz would save him.

Oz …

They heard him of course, and came on stage again, the pretty one and some others just as dark but not so pretty. They soothed and sympathised, but couldn't find Oz in time.

Against his will sleep overpowered him. The nightmare was waiting, and got him good and proper that time.

Underwater darkness. Horrible men fighting each other, long since dead. An octopus with eight knives somewhere groping for him. A sodden hand with missing fingers, white and rotting, cold as iron, immovable, turning off his air supply. Confusion and convulsion, no way out. Gasp and panic, James, that's all you can do now. They won't get Oz in time, this time.

Close to suffocation, he gasped himself awake.

They nearly had me that time, he thought, but fortunately Oz has arrived.

"How is it, old man?" said Oz.

"Aargh!" he shivered, still sweating. "Pretty beastly."

"What happened? Tell me about it."

"Oh, my dream, you mean."

Oz looked at him, patient but hesitating.

James suddenly felt a huge doubt rising up in front of him like an unscalable prison wall, and feverish voices whispered in his ear, *it wasn't a dream.*

"Do you mean my dream?" he asked, feeling fairly desperate.

It was real, said the voices. *It wasn't a dream.*

"It wasn't a dream," said Oz kindly. "Tell me about it. I really have to know – as soon as you can tell me."

"Where am I?"

"Santa Rosa Mission Hospital. Run by nuns. Quite safe."

"Quite safe …?"

He remembered everything. Yes, he must certainly tell Oz exactly what happened. It might take a little while.

Slowly and methodically, he told his attentive friend everything. It took twenty minutes and he felt weak at the end of it.

Oz looked thoughtful. "Did you say 'slots' in the brass wheel inside the safe?"

"Yes, slots. Two in each wheel, I think."

"Were you wearing my watch the whole time?"

"Yes."

"I think he might have had a glimpse of the luminous dial."

"Of course! What an idiot ..."

"Nonsense. Manoeuvre well executed. In fact, one of the most difficult manoeuvres I've ever heard of executed with the utmost courage and skill. Well done. We'll look after you. Get some sleep."

James settled back. God, he did feel tired. Really, Oz was one of the finest of men, a great and resourceful leader. It was good to have such praise from people like Oz. Whatever happened now no one could take that away.

He slept. The throbbing dreams had lost their terror; had been tamed; even the feverish voices were saying, *manoeuvre well executed, well done.*

Manoeuvre well execu-
Ted – well done.
Well done, well done,
Manoeuvre well done.

* * * * *

Someone was pulling at his blankets, rolling him on to a trolley.

Yow! – perhaps he had cried aloud, because his shoulder still hurt like hell. What were they doing to him? But they were friends. The pretty nurse smiled at him. Was she a nun? He smiled back.

They wheeled him off. It was dark outside and an ambulance was waiting. Really, Oz should be somewhere around to explain this latest happening.

And there he was, sitting in the ambulance. All was well.

"James, I'm sending you home. We're on our way to the airport now."

"Why, for heaven's sake? You can't send me off just when it's getting interesting."

"I can and must. Walls have ears, and in this town it's quite clear that nothing stays hidden for long from the Moraes family – family in the Sicilian sense. When they discover you've been slashed it won't take them long ..."

"My shoulder? Has it been slashed?"

"A neat cut seventeen inches long, and in places an inch deep. About forty stitches. You're very lucky it wasn't worse."

"Good grief."

"Precisely. You're in no fit state to look after yourself. I've had a fearful job getting these delightful nuns to release you, and the airline to take you. But it's simply not safe for you here. I shall stay on as long as necessary to deal with all sick and stranded, and particularly try and find out where Rod Trumper's got to. And I want to keep my eyes open here. The tides are on our side – for the next week Moraes would have to dive in daylight and I don't think he will dare do that if I am about the place. After a week the wreck may well have shifted or be quite swallowed up in the silt. So it will be very difficult for him to be certain we know of his crimes, *if* you are out of the way. I've managed to get you an exit visa – fortunately I didn't have to go through the consulate – and here it is with a thousand US dollars. I suppose we'll get paid from Lady Steyne's estate eventually. What a tragic shambles this whole business is."

"Please, can't I be a help to you here?"

"Not a chance, old man. You will be a positive hindrance. Besides, I have one or two things for you to do at home. Take my love to Marie-Claire for one."

"When will you be back?"

"Dunno. I shall probably have to go by sea with Framley, who's been quite badly burnt. They tell me his burns won't stand being subjected to an air flight. And it may be some time before I can start. So it looks like June or thereabouts. We'll have a get-together at Stonham Magna."

"I'll look forward to that. Anything else I can do?"

"Yes. Go and see my solicitor Richard Nicholson in the City. Here's the address. Tell him everything, and ask how we stand for legal prosecutions. He will have lots of ideas you can be sure. Tell him that the Santa Rosa police probably won't, can't, or daren't prosecute for barratry, and that we've done nothing yet about murder charges."

"Right."

"Also, will you try and trace that chap Winter, and see how Lady Steyne's estate stands? If possible, wire me about five thousand. Holy Joe's emergency fund won't last for ever."

"Wilco."

"Here's the airport. Best of luck, James."

"Thank you, sir. Same to you."

* * * * *

Air hostesses were everywhere. They fussed round the young man on the stretcher like hens with chicks. James found that he was to have an invalid bunk and, although his back was still painful, he had no doubt that he was going to be more comfortable than the other passengers. Very gratifying. His fellow travellers eyed him curiously, envying the sympathy and attention he was obviously going to have throughout the flight. What had he done to deserve that?

James smiled to himself, thinking that, if only they knew, he'd perhaps done a bit to deserve it. A duel with knives against a murderer's accomplice under water – it was enough to dine out on for the rest of one's life.

The aircraft, practically full, began to move.

It was splendid to be going home. Away from this tinpot country, away from those murderers, back to civilisation where people actually spoke English and a green pound note was proper money. And to return not without honour, this was good too.

A pity I haven't been able to shave recently, he thought.

Belt up, pompous old fool, he told himself. Stop bragging, even to yourself. What about peeing in prison when the door was open? What about Alice?

Yes, but not now. Must try to get some sleep. Journey'll go quickly if I get to sleep.

But he was really not well enough to travel, even lying down. The jolting and acceleration made him feel very sick, and his wound began to throb ominously. Sleep seemed out of the question. Miserable, he looked at the other passengers and envied their conspicuous good health. Time seemed to hang fire.

Fifteen hours. God! And we haven't been airborne fifteen minutes yet. What the hell to do with fifteen hours?

At Flores in the Azores Sir Richard Grenville lay …

He could always talk poetry to himself. That would last for as long as he wanted, for he would never run out of poetry. Strange that one should resort to the random selections of one's early schoolmasters in moments of stress. *The Revenge*, learnt under the flicking ruler of Old Toebang, sometimes came to his rescue when his mind turned as restless as a white mouse in a treadmill, unable to find its own diversion.

The Revenge – a glorious story of muddle, unpreparedness, mutiny and bulldog courage that surely was Tennyson at his best – yet he had seen thick collections of Tennyson's works that failed to include it. *There* was a ship that had carved her name upon history. Some ships made it, others failed. *Mozart*, for instance. What a shabby, wasted story she told now, disappearing into the black silt of Santa Rosa, photo-luminescent panels and all. And how much craftsmanship and care the human race had squandered upon her. The same amount of effort could have produced half a dozen hospitals. Now, wounded, he was flying away from the whole tragedy.

… We must fly, but follow quick …

Perhaps there was some prophetic irony in the words. Whom was he flying from or following? Moraes the murderer was in Bermuda and his evil cousin was dead.

An air hostess was offering him a steaming square of towelling, presumably to wipe his face with. He took it and she smiled.

"Where do we stop?" he asked her.

"Caracas, Miami and Bermuda. But you sleep now. We take care of you." And she brisked away, radiating efficiency, sex, but somehow motherliness too.

So it was to be Bermuda. Well, anything might happen there, in the little colony that welcomed visitors but made its own rules. Better not leave the aircraft.

And his mind turned back to the astonishing revelation of his love for Alice, reaffirmed three days ago in a prison cell and since then neglected but never questioned. It was, in fact, unquestionable; it existed; and it might be worrying because he did not know where Alice was, or because she did not know his feelings, or because he had doubts about her safety, but the old worry about one's own feelings – that at least was gone forever. He would afterwards be able to smile at the way this had happened, but would never doubt its authenticity.

How good, he thought. How good to be certain of something. At last.

But could he find her? That would be his first task once he was back in England. She must surely have reappeared soon after that last weekend, or her parents would have done something by now. He must see her soon at all costs. Seeing his mother, messages to Marie-Claire, murder enquiries could all wait. Getting fit again – that could wait as well. First things first. But her long silence was unsettling, and her last note in The Bull extremely worrying. Mails had been uncertain, but even so a few had reached the ship. Why had she not written? Perhaps when he rang her home there would be a dreadful pause. "But haven't you heard, James? Alice has been missing for seven months – we are sick with despair ..." Or perhaps: "They are off on their honeymoon, Alice and Patrick (or Ian, or David, or some creep) – no, no, I can't tell you where – it's a *secret*!" A more hideous prospect would be hard to imagine.

There were plenty of worries, but he would fight through them. He would find her; parents, friends, private detectives, advertisements in newspapers, police – he would commission the whole bleeding world to find her. For a start Freddy Baynham, his erratic cousin, might be able to help. He'd be good at that sort of thing. And if she's married? More difficult ...

... But he said, Fight on! Fight on!

That's it, he thought; that's it, "Fight on."

His favourite air hostess came running to see what he wanted. He must have said it aloud. Life was full of little jokes.

Yes, his love was strong and real, and deserved to be spoken aloud. He could sleep now.

* * * * *

They were losing height, sloping down gently into the dusk. He felt the pressure building up on his eardrums, and a voice told him to fasten his seat belt and extinguish his cigarette. Soon the lass would come along with the wide strip of canvas that she strapped over his stomach. Here she came, smiling, and bent over him. She was a happy rebel and didn't shave her armpits, and he watched them fascinated as she tucked him in. He wondered whether armpits were an orthodox minor sexual area; and how did one find out? Her breath was fresh on his face; James thought his own was probably stale from sleep, but she wouldn't mind; she was full of brisk sympathy and understood men.

"Do I have to have this corset thing?" he asked.

"Oh yes! International safety regulations ..."

"If we have a crash I'm all lashed up like a mummy."

"I will save you!" She had a slight American-foreign accent.

"Thank you. How soon London?"

"Six, seven hours."

"Where are we now?"

"Bermuda. The isles of rest. The millionaire's playground, where coral beaches and softly waving palm trees ..."

"You shouldn't believe all you read in the advertisements. Can I stay in the aircraft?"

"Oh no! I am sorry. The regulations. But there will be a stretcher and some medical attention. We have arranged it for you."

"You are very kind," he said, "but no stretcher, I think. I'll manage to walk all right. Thanks all the same."

"You're welcome." The automatic reply, but with a genuine smile.

They touched down, taxied, and came to a halt. He found himself released into the warm night, walking slowly across the tarmac on the arm of his air hostess while the other passengers hurried past them.

Bermuda again. Land of Moraes and Swallow. But he should be safe from those creatures, sealed from the outer world in the transit lounge. His back still hurt, and he couldn't possibly cope with them now.

Sundry officials were directing like sheepdogs the progress of the hundred sleepy sheep who wanted nothing but a cup of coffee and a speedy return to the air. James noticed one who looked like Freddy Baynham. Strange that he should have thought of him just now, but that often happened, one half of the mind working faster than the other, they said. The man was talking intently to some officials. Then he looked at James and grinned.

Good god, it *was* Freddy Baynham!

"Freddy, what the hell are you doing here?"

"Looking for you, old thing. You look pretty cut up."

"I am a bit. Jolly nice to see you. But how on earth …"

"Come and have a drink. I expect you need it."

"Good idea. But what's going on, for heaven's sake?"

"Drink first, old thing. This way."

CHAPTER THIRTEEN

Freddy led James to a private waiting room away from the crowds (and how did he organise that?), parked him in a comfortable chair, and went to get the drinks. James watched him, faintly envious of the way Freddy handled public situations, and how barmen responded to his approach. There had been something deftly stage-managed about his arrival. Freddy could certainly get things done. But what the blazes was he getting done now? He seemed to be in league with officialdom, but how or why would remain a mystery until he came back from the bar.

Freddy was large and fairish, and in everyone's estimation a good sport. He was in fact two years older than James, but a kind of boisterousness in his movements and an impulsive way of speaking made people uncertain of his age. He had spent some time in the Army, and since then had had numerous jobs, mostly connected with business commissions he would undertake in odd parts of the world. But he never stayed anywhere for very long, and this always aroused comment among his family and friends, to whom an "unsettled" career seemed precarious and unnecessary. To Freddy, anything else would have been a form of suicide.

As a result of his constant moving around he and James had not really seen each other much since their childhood, and it was a matter of some slight regret to both of them.

He came back with two large whiskies and a plate containing a pair of sinister-looking meat pies.

"I thought you might like something to eat, old thing. I'm ravenous."

"Couldn't manage it, thanks Freddy. You know how they try and fill you up on these flights. I'm not feeling all that hungry."

"Well, if you'll excuse me ..." said Freddy, taking a large bite out of a meat pie, which was apparently edible, despite appearances.

James took a sip of his drink. Bourbon! Freddy must have forgotten to specify scotch. That evened the score a bit.

"We have half an hour," said Freddy, "before we decide whether you are going on that plane or not, so ..."

"I shall be going on that plane all right. Wild horses won't keep me back," said James. "Whatever happens I shall be on that plane."

"Yes, well. Perhaps there are one or two things I ought to say straight away. First, I'm being employed by a firm called 'Universal Agents' as an investigator."

"You, a private eye! How absolutely splendid! What are you investigating?"

"The disappearance of Alice Cullerby."

"*What?*"

"Yes. You'd better listen, old thing, we haven't much time. The last people to see Alice in England were you and Moraes at that party in Cowes. No one since, not a soul. You haven't heard from her, no one has. Her office made a few enquiries after she'd been missing three days, and contacted a friend of hers called Jane Thompson, who said that Alice had stayed the weekend with some aunt or other, she knew not where. After another two days Jane Thompson rang the Cullerbys – had Alice turned up at home? No she had not, and you can imagine things started really humming from then on. Mr Felix Cullerby rang every aunt, uncle, friend and relation he could think of, and finally the police. The police were most energetic for a week or so, but I reckon achieved remarkably little. For one thing, they never saw the connection between Alice and you, because Jane Thompson had said that you had rung up to enquire where Alice was – so they deduced that you wouldn't know anything, and you were almost impossible to get hold of anyway. They have of course hundreds of missing persons, and soon Alice became just one more of them. At this stage Mr Cullerby got hold of Universal Agents, and they got hold of me."

Freddy started on his second meat pie. James did not say a word.

"I'd done a few small jobs for UA occasionally, and they'd always wanted me to sign on for them full time. The idea of being a private detective had a certain appeal, and the day before they took on the Alice case I had signed on for a probationary period of six months. The Chief sent for me and said, 'Your first proper job, Freddy – see what you can make of it.' I didn't of course know then that I was first cousin to one of the principal *dramatis personae*, and I haven't as yet told them – it would only add an unnecessary complication. But since then I've been quite busy. The amount a private agent can do depends entirely on the amount of money his sponsor is prepared to spend, and Pa Cullerby has recently raised his limit. Which is why I came to Bermuda."

Freddy took a sip of his drink. "Bourbon! Sorry. One forgets the extent of American colonialism. Anyway, I thoroughly enjoyed my first attempts at investigation, and I think I left no stone unturned. For instance, did you know that even if you erase something on magnetic tape, you can never quite wipe it electronically clean? No? Well, your conversation with Alice's Recorded Message answering system led me to The Bull at Cowes. And there (forgive me, James) I started recreating the events of that last weekend of yours."

James was spellbound, and did not trust himself to speak.

Freddy went on: "There's a lot I still don't know, and that I want your advice about. Firstly, what's this fellow Moraes like?"

"Moraes? He's a bastard." James found his voice, slightly strangulated.

"He's certainly a clever bastard. And how do you feel about Alice?"

"I love her. I want to marry her."

"Yes, well. Listen, old thing, we must work together about this. Alice is here in Bermuda and she's married to Peter Moraes."

"*Balls.*"

"Sorry, but it's true." A pause.

Then again: "Sorry, James, but it's true."

James had an almost overwhelming desire to abandon this problem for the moment and faint, but the thought that this would be culpably weak in front of his cousin just enabled him to fight off a complete melt-down that was rising up inside him like vomit. Through his mind streamed all sorts of strange and vivid ideas, glissading into each other and confusing him. He could not think straight. He could not think at all. These wild thoughts were invading his mind, and he knew he would be unable to comprehend anything until he had cleared them out of the way. It's not fair, he thought. I'm really not fit. I can't cope with all this. It's not at all fair.

Luckily Freddy was getting some more drinks. He came back from the bar looking serious.

"Scotch this time anyway. Drink up; you look as though you need it. What I think happened was this. Moraes somehow (heaven knows how) managed to remove Alice after that party and persuade her to marry him. They were actually married by special licence under Ecuadorean law – he had to produce the marriage certificate to the immigration office here, and a chap there who turned out to be an old friend of UA said it was undoubtedly authentic, but he couldn't then remember the date. Alice arrived here in November in company with a certain Miss Ishbel Fergus, and I think has been staying here ever since. The routine police check which they make for all missing people with immigration authorities didn't connect Miss Cullerby with Señora Moraes."

James gasped at the name. The swine. *The swine.*

"I was led to all of this by a process of elimination that Sherlock Holmes would have been proud of," Freddy was continuing. "It seemed to me obvious when I'd discovered something about Alice's movements on that Cowes weekend that her disappearance could only be connected with either you or Moraes. Now I know you went to a pretty peculiar school, but even so I didn't think you were capable of running off with a girl and not even telling her parents she was still alive. So I enquired about Moraes, and everyone in Cowes thought him a most unpleasant fellow. Capable of abducting your girl? Easily, it seemed to me. So I thought I'd better catch up with your *Mozart* and tried to get some more money from the firm. At this stage I rang up your mother to find out where you'd got to, and quite by chance she mentioned *en passant* that you'd said Peter Moraes had suddenly abandoned the ship in Bermuda. This was a fairly clear lead, but it took some time to get the necessary funds, with the result that I only got here ten days ago. But I didn't waste my time, and three days ago I discovered where Alice has been living all this time …"

"Spanish Point?"

"So you know about this Swallow chap. Well, I've been keeping that house under observation through a telescope – they certainly give some parties! Practically every evening there seems to be a beach party there, with a barbecue on a little island just off shore."

"Have you seen her?"

"Well, it's usually pretty dark, and I don't know precisely what she looks like. But all those girls look gorgeous to me. Being a peeping tom can be quite entertaining. Anyway, yesterday our friend in

Immigration rang me up and said that a man called Moraes had just flown in from Santa Rosa. Sure enough, a darkish character turned up in my telescope that evening! So I reckoned I was getting warm. I had a splendid plan afoot to penetrate the household in the guise of a lavish playboy when, blow me, that Immigration fellow rang up *again*. A stretcher-case called Huwes had just been cleared for medical attention on arrival from Santa Rosa – was it of any relevance or was I interested? And I decided of course to see you before doing anything else. So ..."

"Have you told her parents you've probably found her?" said James.

"No, I've told nobody yet."

"Do you know what state of mind she's in?"

"Again no. You will think she's being detained against her will. But look, James: there she was, an ordinary girl, come down to spend a weekend with her boyfriend, suddenly leaving you without a word ..."

"There was a note."

"I heard about the note from that landlady person, who, with a little financial encouragement, revealed she had held the envelope up to the light and read it, I'm sorry to say. So it seems Alice left of her own accord, and even Machiavelli Moraes could hardly have married her against her will."

"I wouldn't put it past him."

"Or brought her to Bermuda involuntarily. But what makes me so suspicious of things is that just before she came down to Cowes she was wildly, helplessly in love with you."

James's skin down his spine shivered.

"Jane Thompson told me," said Freddy. "She said Alice had declared her undying devotion the day before in terms which made me green with envy."

James felt transfigured. He could do anything now, and the leadership of the conversation suddenly became his.

"Now listen, Freddy. Firstly, I'm not catching that plane."

"Right."

"Secondly, I must see Alice. As soon as possible. Regardless."

"Mm?"

"And you've got to help me, as I'm not awfully fit."

"I can see that."

"Finally, there's one or two things you ought to know about Moraes and his cronies and their recent activities."

"Fire away, old thing. There's lots I still don't understand."

James gave him a brief résumé of his story, finishing with the underwater battle in the mud of Santa Rosa.

Freddy said: "My dear courageous coz. What a saga! So now we know we're dealing with an unscrupulous murderer. That makes things both easier and more difficult. In fact, I'm beginning to think the whole business is becoming a bit more than I can handle. Perhaps we should get the police."

Some basic instinct in James was protective and cautious.

"I'm not sure, Freddy. I'd like to see Alice first."

"*How*, do you suggest?"

"I'm thinking."

"Well, keep at it." Freddy moved to the door. "I'm going to cancel your flight. Don't move from here. You're quite safe inside the airport barrier. Outside …" Freddy looked out of the door along a dimly lit passage, quite deserted. "… Outside anything might happen."

James was indeed thinking, and thinking with an intensity which people seldom achieve except under pressure of love or death. When Freddy came back he had the outline of a scheme. After a telephone call and half an hour's detailed planning, it was complete.

CHAPTER FOURTEEN

Freddy was rowing. The night was very black and breathlessly quiet. James sat in the stern of the boat, and his heart knocked at his ribs with excitement and fear. He pondered fear, for he was certainly afraid. There was an air of boldness about their plan which verged on desperation, and if they failed the consequences would be grisly. Yet, as he considered it more carefully, it was not so much the physical consequences of failure but the fearful burden of doing the unsuccessful thing – and therefore the wrong thing – that frightened him.

The plan was undeniably a leap in the dark. The odds were perhaps fair, but the stakes were enormous. He was gambling with Alice.

He realised, without finding it surprising, that he must be very sure of his love for her. But what about her love for him?

Freddy rowed effortlessly and superbly straight.

He had said that her friend had said that she had said she loved him wildly. What kind of reassurance could one get from a chain of hearsay as flimsy as that?

And now like one who rows,
Proud of his skill, to reach a chosen point
With an unswerving line ...

His old schoolmaster, Toebang, intruding onto the scene again.

It was a lovely night, clear, velvet-black, reminiscent. The stars were incredibly numerous, and the whole panoply swung gently with the heave of the oars. At school those same stars had swung through the firs outside the dormitory window, and sometimes he had got out of bed to watch them and to see the lights moving on the far hills. Lights would still be flashing across the valley to that very window, and those same beds would contain much the same size and shape of boy. They are safe in their own world, thought James, while I in mine am only full of anxiety. Here, lights are shimmering across the ripple of Grassy Bay from the inordinately expensive houses of rich Bermudians. It's a glorious night, but my heart is knocking at my ribs.

But it always diminishes fear to identify it correctly, and anyway Freddy was still rowing. He had been quite a distinguished oarsman, James remembered. That was reassuring, a little. What a stroke of luck to have Freddy on one's side.

James took stock of the situation. They were heading straight towards grand-piano island, behind which the Swallow house would be entertaining its inmates at one of their beach parties. The boat was a fifteen-foot dinghy, borrowed for the evening by some clever arrangement of Freddy's. Astern, the lights of HMS *Fowey* stood out against the dark bulk of Ireland Island. A red flashing buoy on their port hand marked the edge of the coral reef. Equipment in the boat included a watertight electric torch, a snorkel-mask and some fins. James was carrying all the money he possessed, plus a hundred pounds Freddy had lent him. He thought about that hundred pounds. In effect he had borrowed it from Alice's father.

He looked for the island ahead, and the outline was just starting to take shape, black and reminiscent also. A very bright star was rising over its hut like an omen. It must be Sirius, the dog star, something to do with the dog-days of the ancient Greeks, or was it Egyptians? Was the omen good or bad? Hell, he thought, but this is a dodgy do.

Freddy slowed down his stroke. He was now rowing so quietly that the only sound was the dripping of water off his blade.

He stopped altogether. The boat slowly moved into the black shadow of the island.

"About here, I think," whispered Freddy. "Can you take the oars now? Just stay in this spot – I should keep the top of the hut in line with that bright star. I may be gone some time. We mustn't rush this bit, whatever happens. Will you be okay?"

"Of course."

James watched his cousin take off shirt and trousers. He had swimming trunks on underneath. He slipped into the water and adjusted his face mask and fins, one hand on the gunwale, the boat rocking gently.

"Dark, tallish, and speaks beautifully. Possibly she'll also have a faraway, crossed-in-love look in her eyes. I'll do my best. Don't worry."

"I won't. And Freddy ..."

"Yes, old thing?"

"Thanks, Freddy."

He slipped away. With just the tip of his snorkel tube showing above the water, he disappeared from view almost immediately.

James lay on his oars. Their crazy scheme was on. There was nothing to do now but pass the time.

It passed slowly. He visualised Freddy going round to the other side of the island, observing the beach party; waiting till most of them were in the water; swimming up by stealth and joining them unobserved; identifying Alice; inviting her to swim back to the boat to see James. The trouble was that one could visualise all the events of that simple plan in about ten seconds. It was then impossible not to visualise all the things that could go wrong. Perhaps, for some reason, there was no party tonight. Perhaps they weren't swimming.

Perhaps Freddy would be unable to inveigle himself into the group without being rumbled. Maybe Alice wouldn't come. She was, after all, married to the man.

But James remembered gatecrashing a midnight swim off Tigne Beach, years ago. It had not been too difficult. Unidentifiable heads in the dark were expected to pop up anywhere. And the girls had made the most of the unknown on that occasion, losing all sorts of inhibitions in a way that would have been surprising in broad daylight. Success would depend very largely on the size of the party, but if anyone could manage it, Freddy would. As for whether she would come or not, this at least would settle things. He reflected that the next hour or so would determine his entire future. So ...

He either fears his fate too much
Or his deserts are small
Who dares not put it to the touch
To gain or lose it all.

With a sense of history in the making he watched Sirius, perhaps his lucky star, slowly rise above the hut. No one could feel frightened for long under such a deep and starry sky. If Alice and I ever have a son, he thought, Sirius would not be a bad name.

What a beautiful thought, he suddenly caught himself thinking. And absurd. Ridiculous.

Sirius brightened and became steadier. He kept it over the black hut on the island – easy in a very slight set and no wind. Time to consider the rest of their madcap scheme. With *Fowey* sailing tomorrow morning for Jamestown there would be no second chances. Was it right to involve Mark Hillier? He had been enthusiastic on the telephone with the boyish glee of an undergraduate plotting some outrageous rag. What did he feel now, four hours later?

Five hours later, he corrected himself, looking at Oz's watch. Time did pass, eventually, when there was nothing to do except wait.

He started picking out noises. It was amazing how many sounds were contained in the apparent silence: little wavelets slapping along the crevices of the clinker-built planking; the tiny unavoidable noise of the paddles bearing against the crutches; his own breathing; and – God, why hadn't he noticed it before – people's party-voices from the shore, just perceptible. Perhaps they hadn't been there before.

Perhaps the party was just taking to the water. Better alert all senses and try to keep calm.

And there was, surely, the splash of a swimmer heading towards the hut, none too quietly. He strained his eyes along the water, watching the reflections of stars for any disturbance.

Someone climbed out of the water on to the island, making no attempt to keep quiet. There was a clattering, and then a flickering light was lit the other side of the hut. It blackened the silhouette even further, and made James realise how appallingly close he was. Stealthily, he nosed the boat out to sea.

The person on the island had lit the charcoal burner, and seemed to be preparing for a barbecue. Click! The sound came from the hut. A discordant noise came from the keys of the piano, as someone hit them indiscriminately. Ah, that piano …

Then La Rue announced herself as clearly as if she had shouted her name. She began to play with her signature touch those rolling arpeggios of Liszt, the very piece she had played to James five months before in very different circumstances.

He was too keyed up to feel any sense of embarrassment. This is done for a purpose, he thought. A signal. She must be on my side. What can she be driving at? Has she spoken to Freddy?

She stopped playing, and there were sounds of further preparations for the barbecue. Then more people started climbing out of the water on to the island, and dark figures moved against the flickering edges of light.

James continued to nudge the boat slowly out to sea, until he felt he was at a safe distance. Still nothing to do but wait.

Freddy must have spoken to slim La Rue. Those few bars on the piano were a private signal from her – how else could she have known he was there? But was it a signal to do something specific, some development in the plan? What could it mean? Considering the associations of that piece, it was hardly a tactful choice. He remembered her lovemaking – amused, skilful, then suddenly passionate. They had parted with affection. She was surely on his side. She could not mean him to break his rendezvous with Freddy and Alice. Indeed the idea of them swimming out to sea and finding no boat was unthinkable.

There was now a good deal of noise coming from the island. The piano was going again. There might well be a fairly large party, he thought. Which is all to the good.

And then he saw a thin silvery ripple which told him quite certainly that someone was swimming towards him. Consumed with excitement and apprehension, all he could do was to ship the oars and wait, always wait.

Freddy suddenly surfaced beside the boat, and James was taken unawares.

"She's coming," said Freddy in a whisper. "I'll push the boat further out before we climb in."

Another ripple, slightly bigger, was coming their way.

That ripple is Alice, he told himself almost unbelievingly. It reached them slowly. She was swimming inside a lifebelt. Long black hair framed her face. It really was Alice. She looked young, frightened, as she put a hand on the boat's side.

"Darling," he said, "I love you. Will you marry me, Alice?"

"I love you too," she whispered. "I always have."

"Shut up and be quiet." It was Freddy, who with both hands on the taffrail was noiselessly propelling them out to sea.

James closed his hand over hers, and desire flowed into him like an electric current. Not here, not just now, but soon, please God soon. Gently he removed the lifebelt from her and placed it in the boat.

He bent his head to hers. "How did you get away?"

"La Rue helped me. They won't miss me for an hour or so."

"My love."

"James … you know I'm married."

"Yes. It doesn't matter."

"What are we going to do?"

"Go away. I'll look after you."

"James … you must understand that I've always loved you, ever since I can remember anything I've loved you. So I must tell you …"

Freddy had stopped pushing the boat and was trying to help her into it. She didn't seem to understand. He said: "Jump in now. No one can see us out here."

James took hold of her under the armpits and started pulling her aboard as the dinghy heeled with her weight. In the starlight he could see her beautiful hair fall forward as she bent over the transom. But what was this heavy monster, this hippo climbing out of the water? Was Alice suffering from some gross deformity?

And then in a flash he realised something that made so many things capable of being explained. Alice was pregnant.

"Alice!" he exclaimed, and he couldn't keep the shock out of his voice. "Whose child …?"

"Darling, I don't know," she gasped, half in and half out of the boat. "I simply don't know."

She tumbled on to the bottom-boards, and cried with exhaustion, emotion and fright. James picked her up gently and sat her beside him on the thwart. She was wearing only a nightdress, completely sodden. He put an arm round her cold shoulders. He had found her at last.

"Don't worry, darling," he said. "Don't be anxious. And don't cry. I'll look after you. Don't worry about anything." But she went on crying, close to his side, shivering and speechless.

Freddy began to row.

Hell, thought James, there's a lot more hurdles to jump tonight.

* * * * *

"We made it!" he cried, one hour later. He was tempted to shout, wave his fists, and drum his heels on the deck, but he definitely did not. From now on they must keep quiet.

He had her now, safe. They looked round the brightly lit compartment that was to be their hideaway for the next two days. It was the Baggage Store of HMS *Fowey*, and from top to bottom it was crammed with suitcases, trunks, kitbags and receptacles of all kinds. There was just enough headroom for a person to stand up, and James felt that with some judicious stowing he might be able to make enough space to sleep in. Mark had said there would not be room to swing a kitten; for once the phrase had not been an exaggeration. It was also extremely hot.

Alice sat on a trunk. She looked all in. Mark's naval Burberry was over her wet nightdress.

"Not much of a place for pregnant mums," he said cheerfully, "but we'll make it as comfortable for you as we can. Just sit there, and don't run away."

She smiled weakly. Weak as it was, it was a smile that would tempt a saint.

God, it was a joy to have her. After all these months of wondering and worrying, now she was here. He thought of their lives together, stretching out ahead of them from this moment onwards, Alice and James, inseparable. There was so much to tell her about; so much to hear from her. Two days wouldn't be enough to tell it all.

Just before Mark had locked them into this cell he had given James a key. "That's the key of my tin trunk," he had said. "I've tried to collect together some things that might be of use to you – they're all in my trunk. When you leave, lock in it every single sign of your presence and I'll dispose of it. No one can get in to the store, as I'm keeping both keys, and in the unlikely event of anyone wanting a trunk they can't do anything until one of the keys is found. I'll come and see you sometime between one and three each night if I can, with whatever food I can scrounge. Otherwise you're on your own."

James looked around him, and his eye was caught by a black steel trunk marked "HILLIER, M.H." There it was. Why on earth did they always put the initials after the surname?

He heaved on the heavy trunk and managed to slide it down. He opened it with his key; it contained tins, chocolate, packets of biscuits, two blankets, a few stoppered bottles full of water, and several polythene bags.

"Fine," he said. "Enough here to see us through nicely."

But she was too exhausted even to answer him. Poor girl, she has suffered such a lot, he thought, much more than I yet know. Better get her to sleep as quickly as possible.

He started stowing a pile of suitcases into a corner to make some room, careful and slow. It was hard work; his back began to throb and the sweat to pour down his arms and chest, soaking his shirt. The temperature must be in the nineties.

At last he had cleared a space for her. He laid both blankets on the deck, and rolled up an empty kitbag for a pillow.

"Here you are, my love. I hope you won't find it impossibly hard."

"I could sleep anywhere," she said. It sounded difficult to say through her exhaustion.

"Sleep now; talk tomorrow."

He helped her to her feet, and took the heavy Burberry off. Her nightdress was sticking to her, clammy and transparent, but she was much too tired for any kind of modesty or coquetry. He helped her peel it off and lie down. She was asleep, or nearly so, almost immediately, curling up on one side with her head on her arm. He looked at her, delighted with her round breasts, fuller than before, and the young rosy nipples that somehow made her look so perfect, so endearing. His eyes wandered over her greatly distended belly, firmly curving down to her thighs, dark and fondly remembered silky-soft fur, nice long legs, back suntanned and shapely. Toenails neatly cut, he noted. Fingernails carefully painted. Legs and armpits shaved that morning. No wedding ring, but – wow! – a massive emerald on the right hand. Hair as it always was, long, dark and straight. But his gaze returned to her breasts, and without ordinary desire he adored her with an intensity that astonished him.

I can never love anyone again like this, he thought; perhaps not even her.

He bent down, and chastely kissed her on the cheek. She did not stir.

He thought of all she had been through and all the might-have-beens in both their lives, feeling as he had felt years ago when coming across his dead father's half-worn shoes. A quiet sadness settled on him.

CHAPTER FIFTEEN

Fearful nightmares were chasing him as he swam through heavy glue, and he wasn't sure if he could wake up in time. With a great effort he wrenched himself free of his dream. The light was glaring. He found himself propped up on a packing case soaked in his own sweat. His neck ached, and there was the central portion of a naked girl in view, lying next to him.

He could not quite remember the reason why but he was aware of a heart-warming glow of triumph, like the Cheshire cat whose grin appeared before anything else. Gradually the details faded in. He'd got Alice and he was damned lucky to have her. He began to remember everything about last night, all that extraordinary and fortunate sequence of events. Freddy had rowed across Grassy Bay, going fast for they were later than they had expected. The tidal stream was now against them, and Freddy had to put his strength into it. At last they drew near the breakwater of Ireland Island harbour, and alongside the old dockyard wall was the outline of HMS *Fowey*. The floodlighting had been switched off by that time, and the upper-deck lights cast no illumination on the ship's side. When they reached it they found the Jacob's ladder that Mark on the telephone had promised he would leave out for them. But they were late and Mark was not to be seen – were all their plans to be ruined at the eleventh hour? James remembered slipping on board furtively. There was not a soul about, and he guessed his way to the navigator's cabin. "Lieutenant M.H. Hillier, Royal Navy, United Service Club" said the card in its holder on the door. James knocked softly and walked in. Mark was in mess undress, smoking a pipe and painting a seascape in oils.

"Hello there," Mark said lustily. "I thought you'd never come. Everything's ready for you, although the Baggage Store won't be exactly palatial. It's sufficiently ventilated but it'll be bloody hot. Did you get the girl?"

James said yes, she was still in the boat.

"Splendid! Let's see, it's now twenty-five past – no more rounds for at least half an hour. You couldn't be safer. Bring her aboard and then we can all get turned in."

James saw a Burberry hanging on a hook. "Do you think I could borrow this for her?"

"She won't be cold, you know. That store is right over the diesel room. But take it. And don't ever say I don't help lame dogs over stiles." He grinned.

"Thanks, Mark."

"All part of the senior service. Let's go."

They went back through the deserted ship to where the ladder had been secured and he had climbed over the side. James would have walked straight past the place. There was nothing except a small shackle at the base of a guardrail stanchion that was visible from inboard.

"Well concealed," said Mark. "I don't want to make my first court-martial more likely than it is already."

James climbed down the ladder with the Burberry. He had lost his night vision and stumbled into the boat.

"Put this on," he told Alice. "Can you manage to climb up all right?"

"I'll try." She was ready to drop.

"Goodbye, Freddy. Can I leave you with all the sorting out, here and at home? I'll write and tell you our plans when things have settled down a bit. And thank you – thank you more than I can say."

"Not at all, old thing. Here endeth my first proper case. I've enjoyed it. I'll lay a few false trails to confuse the hunt for Alice. My Immigration chum should be able to help. Goodbye, and look after each other."

She went up slowly, rung by rung. It wasn't easy, because the ladder was flat against the ship's side and she had no shoes on. He followed her as close as he could, trying to take some of her weight. As she came level with the guardrails he saw her face in the light for the first time. It expressed great strain.

On deck, Mark shook hands. He looked surprised, but not abashed. "I'm afraid … I didn't realise …" he said.

Alice was speechless with exhaustion.

"Nor did I," said James.

But Mark was used to taking his own decisions. "When is your baby due?" he said rather firmly.

James didn't know. He had to count on his fingers, and half way through he became muddled and had to start again. Mark did not move till he had finished.

"June," said James.

"That's all right then," said Mark, leading the way through a screen door. "I can't risk any maternity dramas among my passengers."

He took them right forward. James thought what a curious party they would have looked to a bosun's mate doing his rounds or a stoker taking his hourly temperature readings: the Navigator in mess undress, followed by a barefoot pregnant girl wearing a Burberry, followed by a dishevelled character with a two days' beard.

But no one saw them, and they had reached the hatch that was the only entrance to their hideaway without incident. Mark had been very confident about them not being discovered.

"Keep quiet in there. It should be a calm passage. There'd be the most unholy row if anyone found you," was the last thing he had said. "I wouldn't have dreamt of doing it if I didn't know it'd work."

And it seems to be working all right, thought James, looking down at Alice. Amazingly, it does seem to be working. But it's not going to be at all comfortable, particularly when we get to sea. It's so infernally hot, and there's a constant low rumbling noise.

She was now lying on her back, and he noticed a pool of sweat glistening in the hollow between her breasts. It was not particularly attractive. He watched, fascinated, as it gently tipped from side to side.

We're rolling, he thought. We must be at sea already.

Conscious of it now, he could feel a slight lift and dip. He must make sure all the trunks and suitcases were properly secure, or they might tumble down if it got rough.

The slight noise of shifting a trunk made Alice stir slightly. She put a hand in front of her eyes, and began to wake up. He loved her still, but that pool of sweat worried him. He couldn't take his eyes off it.

She opened her eyes with a start and sat up.

"Oh!" she cried, looking around, instinctively trying to hide or cover herself up. The sweat poured off her. "Oh!" she said again, disconcerted. But there was nowhere to hide, nothing to cover up with; it was difficult, in fact, to look anywhere but at each other.

"Oh James!" she said despairingly. "Don't look at me. I feel such a mess."

"You look terrific," he said, sitting down on one end of the blanket. "We've got to get used to each other in these conditions. For one thing, we're here for the next two days, and for another there's nothing about you I don't like. Besides," he put an arm on her shoulder, "you're eloping with me. You not allowed to be shy."

"But I am shy, desperately shy. James, let's make love quickly – I shall be miserable with modesty till we do. Then we can talk."

He smiled. "Extraordinary woman!" he said, taking off his sodden clothes and resolving not to put them on again. "There used to be a rule which said *never under the white ensign.* But I don't think it applies to stowaways."

"James! Your back, James! What's been happening to you?"

"It's fine. Just tweaks me a bit when I bend down. We'll exchange memoirs later."

But she was disconcerted. She would need careful loving.

In the hard, narrow space between the packing cases they started making love, and it required a certain amount of adaptation on both sides. "Let's make it a you-one," she whispered. "All right," he said, determined to do no such thing. They began to enjoy each other intensely, bathed in sweat. Suddenly she tossed her head back and all was abandoned, emptied, drowned in a vast sexual wave. Then they lay breathless and ecstatic, telling each other how clever they were. She nuzzled the hair on his chest, and he felt the world could not contain so much happiness.

He closed his eyes, and Alice's pleasant soprano close to his ear was like the music of the gods.

"I've loved you for ever, James. I loved you before we went for that swim in the woods, before you could even remember my name. I simply don't remember ever not loving you, my darling. When you were away at school I used to scratch little marks in the bedhead, a mark for every day till you came back. And then the term would end and I'd be keyed up with excitement, knowing I'd no right to be, because whenever I saw you I was struck dumb. It was the traditional schoolgirl reaction, but I never grew out of it. And people used to say 'James Huwes – he's a nice chap, don't you think?' and I'd feel like a tongue-tied schoolgirl again and would be so afraid to give myself away I'd say nothing at all. And sometimes you'd take me out, and each time I'd think 'I must talk about things more, I must be a bit livelier,' but it never seemed to happen. I was afraid of myself and this great power of loving that bottled me up so torturously. It always surprised me that you were so very kind to me, always, always."

She was talking quietly and steadily. He kissed her neck through a forest of black hair.

"Then I heard you were going to the West Indies, darling, and I felt miserably certain you would meet some gorgeous girl and marry her. In despair, I thought I would probably not see you again. So I decided to seduce you."

He started. "*You* decided to seduce *me*?"

"For purely selfish reasons. I wanted ... to give you something, and have something to remember you by. But having made that decision I found it was then much easier to be natural. Afterwards, although I was more helplessly in love than ever before, I was happier because I felt you'd caught a glimpse of the real me for the first time."

"I liked that glimpse," he said contentedly. "I still do as a matter of fact."

"You're a marvellous lover."

Jackpot, he thought. That's all there is to lovemaking. You make her enjoy it, and she tells you so. Easy. Can't think why people make so many difficulties about it.

"Then you left that Recorded Message," she went on, "and I could hardly think for excitement. I made careful arrangements so that no one would know where I was going, and for four days I felt like a bride. Then, the day before I was due to come down to Cowes, I had the most ghastly apprehension. I thought I might be pregnant. Could it be possible, after the precautions we'd taken – or thought we'd taken? I went over the details in my mind, again and again, and common sense told me, that second time we made love, it might be just possible. I was more anxious and upset than you can imagine, and meanwhile for several days I would not know for certain. I thought of rushing down to see you, or answering one of those pregnancy test advertisements, or jumping under a bus, but eventually I decided to leave everything till I knew definitely one way or another.

"The following day I had to make more deceptions, and I began to feel worried and guilty and devious. I thought people were looking suspiciously at me, all the time realising that was madness. And just before the party – do you remember? – you talked about 'your intentions', and I was so confused my brain didn't function properly. I couldn't make sense of the words you were using. And then I thought you must be stringing me along and I was suddenly miserable. I'd have given the world to be your wife, or even your mistress for as long as you wanted me, but just to be a plaything to be bemused by your words, made pregnant, and left behind – that made me feel utterly wretched. I'm sorry, darling, I should have told you straight away, but I was emotionally stupefied. I knew I had come to a crisis in my life, and I felt incapable of facing it.

"Then at the dance Peter started making up to me and it all became part of the way things were going dreadfully wrong. But he seemed to know, or he pretended to know, just how it stood with us, and I was in such an emotional turmoil that I suppose I told him some more, or he was able to deduce it. Anyway, he asked me if I'd like to see the photo-luminescent panels. You were dancing with someone else so I went along. Then, 'Come and see my cabin,' he said. 'I think it is rather a work of art.' You had shown me yours so I didn't see why not. But once we were in his cabin he locked the door and I was electrified with horror. He told me not to be alarmed, kissed me in the subtlest kind of way, and ... sort of raped me."

James sat bolt upright. "Sort of?"

"I must try to be honest," she said, "and you, my darling, must try to understand things that are often misunderstood. Remember, I had not properly slept with anyone before that first night with you, and I was terribly anxious not to be a failure. My love had been pent up for ten years, you know. I can see now that because I'd made that decision to seduce you I had never been hunted, wooed, captured – I felt it hadn't gone quite right, there was something missing. After that ridiculous slight misunderstanding between us before the party, the bottom seemed to be falling out of my world and I was in a high state of distress. So I can't pretend that Peter didn't fulfil something that lay too deep for ordinary revulsion or self-protection. I hated it, but it was there, and powerful enough. He forced me, yes, but eventually I acquiesced, and I think he knew I would ... I can't explain it better."

There was a pause. James was stunned, and all sorts of ideas were tottering.

"Did he ... um ... was he a very capable lover?"

"Yes."

God, he thought, how little I understood! How absurdly, humiliatingly little! Better start all over again. It's not just a question of orgasms.

"I didn't understand," he said shakily. "I simply didn't begin to realise how you felt."

"I couldn't expect you to, my love. I had concealed my feelings for so long that they never appeared on the surface at all. But imagine how I felt now, in Peter's cabin, with the party going on next door. I was mentally numbed by a confused tangle of sex, fright and shame. Peter suddenly said: 'Marry me, Alice.' I was astonished, and I said I wanted to get back to the party and back to you. He said that if I did that he would have to – 'in all honesty' ..."

"Ha!"

"… in all honesty he would have to tell you, his old school-friend and now his colleague, about what had happened between him and me, and how I had led him on in his cabin. But you have to believe me …" – she burst into tears – "… I absolutely hadn't led him on, hadn't at all."

"Of course I believe you. It doesn't need saying."

"Peter said again, 'Marry me, Alice.' I had a somewhat more coherent moment and asked why. 'Because you toss your head back like wild horses when you make love,' he said. 'You're beautiful. I must have you, and you must marry me.' Sitting there while he stared at me, hating myself, trying to repair my bra, not knowing if I might even be pregnant, and you outside certainly wondering where on earth I'd got to, it seemed the only possible way out of the whole dreadful, miserable, shameful nightmare. I never actually said yes. I think I said: 'What do we do now?' He said: 'Wait here a moment,' and went out.

"He was gone about five minutes, and I thought, shall I go and find James, who must be looking for me – but what if I can't get away from Peter? Even if I can, Peter will tell James his clever lies and then no one will help me. Peter will get at me somehow, and James is sailing away on Monday morning. I felt panic-stricken. Then escape, I thought, at all costs escape, anywhere, but – the door was locked. No escape. I sat on the bed and wept. I would have to go through with it now.

"Peter came back and said the coast was clear. He hustled me through the deserted ship and into his car. We drove through the yard and out of a back entrance. I asked where you were. 'Don't worry about James,' he said with smug satisfaction. 'I spat in his distributor so he won't get very far tonight. I'll put you on one of the early ferries. Meanwhile, you must get some sleep. You look totally shattered.'

"He took me back to his hotel and we went up to his room. He switched on the light and there sleeping in one twin bed was a woman with blonde hair. 'That's my nanny,' he said. 'We sleep together but not *together*. You'll like each other. Wake up, Ishbel! Meet my fiancée!'

"Then he sat me down and told me what sort of note to write to you, and I wrote it. Ishbel went off with it to The Bull; she was going to say I'd had an accident and she needed to collect my things, but I remembered no one had actually seen me there. 'Fine,' Peter told Ishbel, 'just go to the hotel, say you are Miss Cullerby, and you've decided to leave early because you've heard your sister's ill. Make sure the door is locked and collect Alice's things. Leave the note where James will get it in the morning.' Then he gave me something to make me sleep and I got into Ishbel's warm bed. I don't remember anything until the next day.

"When I woke up Peter was there busily writing letters. He explained his plans. As soon as the ship got to Bermuda he would arrange for me to come out and stay there with a friend of his. Meanwhile, I would stay at his house near Malbury and we could get married by proxy. Apparently his lawyer and someone he knew in the Ecuadorean embassy would fix it. Ishbel would take me to his house that morning and he would join me in the evening. He made it all so simple. There seemed to be nothing I could do except rely on him.

"I asked what I should tell my parents. 'Oh no – not at the moment – it has to be a secret,' he said. 'You see, I have to live on board with James, and I don't want him to know just yet. Keep it a dead secret for the present, understood?'

"So you sailed away, and I stayed at Malbury with Ishbel. I signed something in Spanish, and ten days later I was legally married to him. And then also I knew that if I hadn't been pregnant before then I certainly was now. Ishbel and I flew out to Bermuda and stayed at

Angus Swallow's house – Peter and I had the top flat. But it was an impossible marriage – I knew it was wrong from the start."

"Did you, darling?" Her head was on his chest now. Incredibly, wedged in by trunks, they were both quite comfortable. "Tell me why."

"Hundreds of reasons. First, I still loved you! But I'd lost you forever through a misunderstanding – it seemed then a trivial misunderstanding – and perhaps because I was over-sexed, or under-sexed, or something. Also I didn't like giving my parents all that worry about where I was – unnecessarily, I thought. I hope they'll forgive me for it one day. And I discovered soon enough that Peter, who is a very reassuring person when other people are within earshot, has a core of ruthlessness and cruelty when on his own which used to frighten me out of my wits sometimes. Then, as soon as I started getting a tiny bulge he wouldn't sleep with me anymore – just when I needed some support most. He had another girl from the selection Angus always has around and scarcely bothered to conceal it. I had got quite used to sleeping with him – although he dribbles in his sleep – but I was of course dreadfully affronted and humiliated at losing my husband's interest after only three months. Not that I blame him, I've ceased judging people in these matters; he probably couldn't help it. But I had managed to kindle in myself a glimmering of resigned affection for him, and it began to be overlaid with hate.

"And I couldn't help that, either. I had married under false pretences the wrong man for the wrong reasons, and I had only myself to blame. I decided that as soon as I'd had my baby I must certainly try to leave him. I knew he wouldn't let me go easily, so I might have had to run for it. But I didn't relish the idea. He's an incredibly powerful man when he wants to have things his own way."

"What happened last night?"

"I went to bed early. I could hear the usual party noises coming up from the beach, and I think I dozed off. Then suddenly La Rue came in ..."

"La Rue?"

"My greatest friend and ally."

"I see."

"Darling, La Rue and I now have absolutely nothing we have concealed from each other. I had told her all my feelings about Peter and found she was in much the same position with Angus, although not married to him, a sort of emotional prisoner. Anyway, she suddenly burst in and woke me up. 'James has arrived to take you away in a boat,' she said, 'get up immediately – he still loves you.' I was dumbfounded. Apparently Freddy had mistaken her for me on the beach, and when he discovered the mistake she offered to help me get away. I must say I hesitated, but she persuaded me. She said it was my last chance for freedom. I thought it might be my last chance of seeing you. So I left a note for Peter ..."

"Unwise. What did it say?"

"Much the same as the one I left you. Then La Rue took me to where Freddy was hiding in the garden, and went off to start up the barbecue on the island. I waited till they had all gone out there, then took the lifebelt from the swimming pool and paddled out to meet you. It was a long way round, but Freddy towed me most of the way. He was awfully good to me. I knew I was doing the right thing for once – but I get tired so easily."

"I must say, Alice my love, it's good to see you taking things so calmly."

"You'll find I do now. I think having babies makes one docile and purged of all other functions. It's quite a change, I know. I feel cow-like and broody and you'll have to do all the thinking – I'm too busy reproducing the species."

"That suits me. What about the ring?"

She extended the fingers of her right hand like a Thai dancer.

"Not bad, is it? Peter gave it to me a while ago. He's very generous – sometimes. I thought I might as well bring it along."

James thought, three thousand, four thousand pounds? Not bad at all. Nice to save something from the wreck.

CHAPTER SIXTEEN

"Next problem," said Alice. "How do I go to the loo?"

"Oh no! Not again."

"What do you mean, not again? I haven't …"

"Sorry, darling. I meant it wasn't the first time I'd had to face this problem. But this time, I think I have the answer."

The thick plastic bags, provided for the collection of naval refuse, were entirely watertight and served the purpose. He tied the neck with a shoelace and put it out of sight.

"Darling."

"Yes, darling?"

"I just love calling you darling," he said, "but it's occurred to me, this isn't really the ideal place for a honeymoon. We are going to learn more about each other's personal habits in two days than most couples learn in a lifetime. We're going to be completely familiar with all each other's privacies, intimate details, smells, everything, warts and all."

"Good."

"It may be so. But we must be careful not to find each other repellent, don't you think? We haven't even got anything to wash in."

"I love you, silly," she said. "Nothing about you could ever repel me. But I'm afraid you'll have to put up with the raw and unvarnished me for two days. At least it's one way of getting to know each other."

"As *The News of the World* would say: 'Intimacy took place.' Which reminds me …"

"Oh no! Certainly not. Don't even think about it. You must tell me your story now."

"Let me just check that you don't repel me."

"Another us-one?"

"I'll consider it …"

* * * * *

James began his story. It was surely a strange one for a man to be telling a girl. "Your husband is a brute, a murderer of the most despicable kind," – in effect he was saying that. But the words he used did not sound strange to her; rather they brought out into the open something that had already lurked in subconscious corridors of her imagination. She was shocked and horrified, but she felt like someone returning to a rebuilt town after twenty years' absence: it was incredible, but it all fitted in.

He left out little of his adventures. He wanted her to know everything that had happened to him, and he realised that anything he concealed then might become more important as time went on. So he told her all about his encounter with La Rue, the cruise which finished at Santa Rosa, the riot and his imprisonment, the sinking of *Mozart* and his underwater battle, his flight to Bermuda and meeting Freddy, his long and lonely wait in the boat while Sirius rose over the black silhouette of the hut. Told like that, it seemed an astounding tale of high drama. Why had it not seemed so at the time?

She was suitably astounded, and her loving appreciation made him feel like an emperor. After all, he thought, this is why men climb mountains, swim oceans, pit their strength against lions and tigers. We come home and tell our womenfolk and they love us for it. That's what life is all about.

It took him an hour. Then they had a drink of water and made love again.

How young she looks, he thought. How gentle and sweet and … virginal. She is the best possible lover and companion; why did it take me so long to discover that? She is at present entirely dependent on me, prepared to leave all the decisions for me to make, trusting me completely. Long black hair; dark eyes; skin like smooth golden honey. Other men will admire her and envy me. What luck!

They were utterly bound up with each other's company, and enjoyed making light of difficulties. James managed to clear a little more space for them, and found a pile of kitbags, which made a reasonably comfortable mattress when carefully arranged. There were several packets of paper tissues in the trunk, and being often bathed in perspiration, they were able to wipe each other down quite successfully. The tinned and packeted food seemed to allay hunger. He was right in that they got to know each other's intimate privacies – the scatological details which people really do prefer to keep to themselves. But, amazingly, he discovered she was not the least dismayed by any of these things. It was a most flattering declaration of her complete love, and he shared it reciprocally. So they made a virtue out of the situation's necessities, and time passed easily. The only thing they actively disliked was having furry teeth, and there was nothing much they could do about that.

There was a continual hum of machinery in their cell, the lights were bright and inextinguishable, and the temperature remained at about ninety degrees. They talked a good deal.

"Where are we going, by the way?" she asked.

"A place called Jamestown – it's one of the Grenadines."

"What do we do there?"

"Well, firstly we go to a hotel and get ourselves tidied up a bit. I'll buy some clothes for both of us, a toothbrush and things, and a razor. Then after you've been properly rested and fed and spent a few days recovering from this extraordinary escapade, I thought I would try to get a passage for us to Adventa."

"La Rue's home?"

"That's it. She said I could always go there if ever I wanted to. Also I seem to remember her saying that her aunt was the island's doctor, which will come in handy when you have your baby. I think we should be able to lie up there till about August, and then go home – all three of us! Then we can set about getting you a divorce, which shouldn't be impossible, and perhaps bring Black Pedro to justice too."

"How do we do that?"

"Well, I'm not sure about bringing him to justice – proof won't be easy so far away in time and distance. I wonder what Freddy will do about it. I should have discussed it with him. But getting a divorce should be easy enough in these strange circumstances, especially as he was involved with this other girl. We can put Freddy on to that too."

"What about me with you?"

"I don't think that counts, not after you've discovered about him."

"Do you think we'll be safe in Adventa?"

"Don't worry, Alice my darling. I'll look after you, just you wait and see."

"You've certainly done all right so far. It was a stroke of genius to stow away in this ship – he can't possibly find us or follow us, or even know where we've gone."

"It was lucky. We can also rely on Freddy to muddle the search for you. What a splendid fellow he is. We owe him so much."

"Let's ask him to be a godfather."

"Let's call it Freddy."

"Or Frederica."

"And don't forget Mark."

"Frederick Mark Sirius Huwes."

"Or La Rue to be godmother."

"Frederica Marcia Siria La Rue Huwes."

"Known as Freda to her friends."

The ship took on a slow gentle heel. They must be turning, but he was disorientated and did not know which way they were going. A silence dropped between them. They were both thinking the same thing, but from different sides.

"Do you think it is mine?" he asked eventually.

"Darling … I really don't know. Please don't disconcert me."

"Disconcert you!" He flared up, almost for the first time in his life. "*Disconcert* you! How d'you think I feel? What d'you think it's like for me, wondering whose it is, not knowing whether that thing inside you belongs to me – or to a violent criminal?" Damn, he'd made her cry, but he was carried along by his own emotional momentum. "Listen, my Alice. I can hardly bear to think of all you've suffered. But I am human too, and I can't help feeling wretched when I think of him having you so successfully in his cabin during that party and all the months afterwards. And now, not knowing whether it's my child or his – it's almost too much to bear. I thought women were always supposed to know who the father was, anyway."

"I don't know how," she said between sobs. She was crying profusely now.

Well, it had to happen, he thought. I've said it, brutally, and I wish I hadn't. Now I must build everything up again.

"My darling, it's you I love, and I love the child too because it's part of you. It's only because I care for you so much that I feel so helplessly involved in everything that happens to you. All that matters is your peace of mind, more so than my confused feelings or even your love for me. My love for you is quite unshakable, and has been since that night I spent in prison. Let's put all other problems aside till you've had the baby, and then think again. I can do that now. This is something we don't need to face till it happens. We must count our blessings and remember the great piece of good luck that put us here, together. It's not quite how I dreamed it would happen, but as soon as we get to Adventa it will be. I promise. Trust me."

"Oh but I do!"

He put his hand round the back of her neck. She was all compliance, and he was devotion and strength. It was a touching scene, he told himself. She would never nag or try to dominate. She was just right. Not surprising that Moraes had carried her off and married her. He suddenly found himself wishing everyone well – the whole world. After all, under his mixed-up emotion, cynicism and self-analysis, he did love her very much indeed. It made everything else he could think of seem like a colour slide: vivid, attractively unreal. But his love was real. Here at last was something he could devote his life to.

They had little sense of the passing of time, so it came as a shock when Mark suddenly opened the hatch and stepped in, closing it quickly behind him. Alice covered herself with the Burberry; James did not bother. Mark was wearing a white shirt and shorts, and his two gold stripes gleamed on his shoulders. He was carrying some more provisions.

"How are you two doing?" Mark, as usual, talked quickly and decisively. "Sorry this place is so constricting, but stowing-away's a jolly good method of leaving somewhere without trace. Free, too! I must say you both look as though you're thriving on it. There was a fellow I brought back from Poland who almost withered away in this very compartment. I hope you've had enough to eat and drink –

here's some more anyway."

"We're doing fine. What's the time?"

"About two-fifteen. Anything else you need for the next time I come?"

"Would a toothbrush and some toothpaste be possible? And another packet or two of Kleenex?"

"Certainly. We're lucky to have such a calm sea. It can really lurch around down here when we start pitching. Perhaps that's what upset my Polish friend. Look, when we get to Jamestown I will book you into the Palm Beach Hotel, okay? And at some suitable time in the small hours I'll get a taxi alongside and come and collect you. If I'm cunning I can get you off unobserved. After that, you're on your own. The only thing is, could I have my Burberry back some time?"

"Mark, you shall have a thousand Burberries if you want them, all trimmed with mink."

"Just one. Good. Well, I'll be off now, and I'll take the gash and drop it over the side. No trouble. See you about this time tomorrow."

"Thanks, Mark, more than I can say."

"Not at all. I always welcome desperate calls for help. They give one an excuse for doing crazy things. And I haven't done a crazy thing for much too long."

"Mark," said Alice, "we're going to call the baby after you."

He emitted a subdued peal of laughter, very pleased, very amused. Chuckling, he opened the hatch and let himself out.

They found they were smiling to themselves and each other. Having babies is a rather entertaining business, thought James. And then, with a twinge of anguish: O God, I hope it's mine.

CHAPTER SEVENTEEN

The morning sun was streaming through the open French windows past a ridiculously gaudy hibiscus. He was shaving. She caught him smiling to himself in the mirror.

"What are you smiling at, my love?" She put her arms round his waist from behind.

"I've just discovered life's greatest secret."

"Clever chap. Tell."

"You guess."

She pondered, swaying him a little from side to side. "Sex?"

"Too limited a secret, even for women."

"Success?"

"Too broad a definition, even for men."

"Full of epigrams this morning. How about happiness?"

"Getting warm."

"The pursuit of happiness?"

"Fatal."

"Give it up."

"Recognizing happiness when it actually happens."

"Which is now."

He felt her lay her head between his shoulder blades, and he went on shaving. Firm, deft strokes with a sharp blade, stripping off the soap and the bristles; clean, cool, brown face – this was how men were meant to shave.

She said: "Can you describe your happiness, darling?"

He tried, thought by thought. "The sun. An unhurried shave. Being idle. My delicious woman. Hungry for breakfast. Nakedness. The beach, palm trees, shade, cool salt water ..."

But his mind was wandering. He was thinking over the events of the last two weeks. Common sense told him they had been incredibly lucky. Everything had worked out as though a guardian angel had planned and executed it. Off the ship undetected, a week recuperating in a hotel, the passage to Adventa in the mail boat, and the arrival in the same mail boat of a letter from La Rue to her aunt which ensured that they were welcomed and quickly installed at the house at Brave Dolphin Bay – it all seemed very much too good to be true. Since then the idyll had proceeded unspoilt for a week, so perfect a dream that one half of James's mind kept asking, where's the catch? – this has never happened before, it can't last; while the other half now calmed him: relax, recognize a great happiness when it comes your way.

James looked at his face in the glass. Shaving was the one occasion when a man could legitimately indulge any lingering narcissistic tendencies. He had a lean smooth chin. No spots nowadays, he thought. Haven't had any spots for a year or so, thank the Lord. Must be getting old. And that hairline, wasn't there just a trace of thinness either side of that bit in front? You'll be going grey soon, laddie. Father's hair was completely silver and he always said he was half-grey at thirty. Eyes quite blue. Nose a bit red and pudgy. But mouth good and cheerful. And not a bad chin. Perhaps the chin's the best feature.

"Your cut has healed beautifully, James," she said. "The scar will hardly show at all. Doctor Meg took the stitches out very neatly." She ran her finger gently across his back.

"Blast!" She had touched a sensitive spot, and he started and nicked his upper lip.

"Oh darling, I'm so sorry." But it was only a tiny little cut.

"It's nothing. A scratch."

"Oh, but I'm so sorry." She was inconsolable. "I'll get you some Dettol. My poor love."

She hurried off to the medicine chest, unhappy but somehow carrying her great load proudly.

Christ! he thought. What on earth does she see in me? She must have been born with that generous talent for loving and sympathy, but why for me? Perhaps it's something biological to do with having babies.

She was back, dabbing the almost invisible cut. "What shall we do today?" he said.

"I don't mind, darling. Anything you want to do. Nothing."

He couldn't help smiling. "All I want is to make love to you, too. But let's go for that walk up Mount Shakespeare this morning, before it gets too hot, do you think you could manage that?"

"Easily."

"And then it might be rather fun to go for a swim with the snorkel masks this afternoon."

"*Great* fun. I'll get a picnic lunch ready and we can have it up by the fort."

"Just making everyday plans together is extraordinarily pleasurable."

"*Ogni piacer più grato mi fia con te diviso.*"

"What does that mean?"

"Every wonderful pleasure I will share with you."

"Will you teach me Italian?"

"Oh, I only know operatic Italian. I've found it doesn't much help when trying to buy an ice-cream. But it seems to say everything that can be said about love."

"That's all I shall need."

She was enthusiastic, pretty and good company. Life with Alice would never be dull. How could he ever have thought her dull?

After breakfast he strolled into the garden, quietly relishing both his happiness and having nothing he felt obliged to do. Brave Dolphin House was about fifty yards from the beach, and a flat swathe little more than the width of the building had been cleared through the secondary vegetation between house and sea. The garden so formed was a haphazard combination of cultured flowers run wild and wild things imperfectly controlled, and there were many over-flowering bushes, which were difficult to place definitely in either category. At the water's edge the white sand was fringed with palm trees, and through them the sea twinkled with occasional flashes of reflected light. On the left was a small stream with a wooden bridge over it, and where it ran into the sea there stood a boat shelter. There was no knowing how far the property extended in either direction, as no one had marked it or fenced it. It was completely secluded.

Indeed, when the house had been built, about a hundred and fifty years before, La Rue's whiskery ancestors had probably owned most of Adventa that was worth owning. Their sugar-cane plantations were still all over the island, but now had chiefly been bought by the big West Indian combines, as generations of male Fafoux, born in Adventa but feeling the tug of the outside world, had sold up and left. The last of the family, which had started as Franco-Dutch but had been British for at least a hundred years, were now La Rue and her Aunt Meg. And the old home seemed somehow to be aware that the family was dispersing; it might last a little longer, but one day soon it would crumble away into its own jungle.

It was a fine building, designed in a gracious manner with no fuss. It had a long, wide roof with a high gable at one end. The house was supported by stone pillars on three sides, made out of coral blocks. The space between these pillars and the walls formed a wide veranda, which made the house look much bigger than it was. The windows were large and plentiful and framed by green shutters. Someone with a splendid lack of propriety had added a stoep, a covered alcove of wood and palm thatch that adjoined the house over the French windows, making a kind of indoor-outdoor shed or shelter. Otherwise there was nothing between the square tiles of the veranda and the rough grass of the garden. The house appeared to be growing where it stood.

Inside was a quaint mixture of the luxurious and the ramshackle. The drawing-room was well furnished, with a grand piano painted white. The main bedroom had little furniture except an enormous bed. Surprisingly, it seemed to be the only bed in the house. But there were two bathrooms, and two kitchens. At some stage the house must have been divided.

Alice came out into the garden with a basket.

"Picnic's ready."

"Let's go. We'll walk slowly, and you let me know *before* you get tired."

"Oh, I shan't tire. I'm really very energetic."

"You were very quick with the picnic."

"There wasn't much to do. And the maid helped me."

"What's her name?"

"Spottiswoode."

"Hadn't we better call her by her Christian name?"

"Darling, that is her Christian name. And she calls me Alice. She's a gem. She keeps quoting Shakespeare."

"Really?"

"Seems to know it all off by heart. She says she lives in the shadow of Mount Shakespeare, and she and her children read a page or two every evening."

"Why is she called Spottiswoode?

"Her elder brother was Eyre."

"So?"

"They were the first two names in the family bible."

They crossed the wooden bridge and walked slowly along the path through the trees. Were they pines? Or firs? Or casuarinas? It would be nice to know something about trees.

Mount Shakespeare was a small hill, so perfectly conical that it must have been volcanic in origin, and Meg had recommended the view from the ruined fort at the top.

"When we're married, darling …" She spoke well. Her voice was high and clear.

"Mm?" He wanted to hear her say it again.

"When we're married, don't expect much of a dowry. As far as I can see I won't have anything much till everyone dies."

"We'll manage."

He was thinking what a pity it was that they had had to sell that emerald for $950. It was surely worth a lot more, but no one in Jamestown could have paid more. Still, it was all profit. $950 would see them through for a good while.

"What do you think of Doctor Meg?" she said.

"I like her. She's a bit severe, perhaps a little self-centred – not selfish, more introspective – but when it occurs to her she's remarkably kind and thoughtful, I think."

"She unnerves me a little, with her very pale complexion, and her way of darting her eyebrows up and down. An unusual face."

"I think she's a damn good doctor."

How did one know? But it was important for Alice to think so. She had certainly removed those stitches very competently.

They were climbing steadily now, and the view was appearing over the tops of the trees. Brave Dolphin Bay was approximately semicircular, and just to seaward of it was the dark blue line where the reef began. They would take a boat and explore that reef one day; the coral and fish life were reputed to be superb. Meg had told them about the old legend of the boat that was wrecked on the reef, and the dolphin that fought off the sharks while the crew were struggling ashore; but no one had ever seen a shark inside the reef within living memory.

Behind them the Green Mountains, the island's backbone, cut jerkily into the sky; ahead of them the sea fell away towards the horizon in a hazy sweep of wrinkled blue. It would have gladdened anyone's heart. James walked easily, and sometimes the metal tips on the heels of his brown leather shoes clinked on a stone. There was a great reserve of energy inside him, and he had to restrain an inclination to cavort through the trees doing cartwheels, or leap into the air and soar down the hill like a sea-hawk. He felt elated, virile, loving, and lively. There was nothing he could not do.

They came to an intermittent stone wall, and then the fort itself. A broken-down memorial to Nelson's mastery of the Caribbean, it was now scarcely more than a pile of stones. He put down their basket on a long, flat rock that might have marked the gateway.

"Let's picnic here."

The view was amazing. The whole of the south and west coasts of Adventa were spread out neatly and brightly in the sun. There was a ship far out, the weekly mail boat, coming towards them slowly.

"It's absolutely breath-taking," he said. "It's terrific. Majestic." Palm tree and sugar cane, rock and sand had confused his sense of description. How could one communicate except in clichés? But one had to keep trying.

"Fantastic," he went on. "Millionaires would pay the earth for this view. I love the way the palms fringe the shore. And do you hear that low rustle, the sugar cane? This is the West Indies just showing off. It's just about as perfect as you could wish for. 'If there be a heaven on earth' etcetera. And we have each other, almost alone on a desert island ..."

"I love this place," she said beside him. "We're so lucky."

Something in the slope of her back or the soft hair at the nape of her neck was particularly rousing. He stirred towards her, and gripped her warm brown shoulders.

"Darling ..."

"No, my love," she said gently. "Not here, not just now. Really I'd rather not, unless you're quite desperate."

"Oh no." She must know it wasn't like that.

He subsided slowly. Of course she was right. It would be awkward, absurd and uncomfortable. Mature people did not behave like that. It displayed a frantic, adolescent desire that was probably most unflattering to Alice. Think about something else. Love should be more than just sex.

He sat on the rock and ate a banana, and the sea sparkled for miles and miles. They were indeed so lucky. But he felt an irritating grain of sadness. It would have been nice to make love on the top of Mount Shakespeare.

"James!"

She sat down beside him and leaned up against his side. "I'm sorry James. It's the child-bearing me, not the real me."

She was always extremely *simpatica*. Sometimes verging on the too-much so.

"You don't mind?" she said. "I know it's important to you."

"It's all right," he said.

I suppose it's all right, he thought.

* * * * *

After their picnic they explored the ruins for a while, and then came down the hill slowly. The sun was very hot now, and they were both perspiring. The mail boat was quite close, making round the headland for Adventa harbour.

When they reached the house he changed immediately into swimming trunks and collected the face mask and fins.

"Coming for a swim, Alice?"

"No, I've probably done enough for one day, darling. I'll just lie down for an hour. Might join you later."

He padded across the grass and slipped into the cool, sensuous water. Fins on; wet the mask, fit it on. And all at once the seabed leapt into view, a gaudy new dimension of sand and coral and small stripy fish. It was enchanting. The buoyancy of his fins and mask kept him afloat with just a slow swish of his feet. He floated out, and the underwater landscape became more and more fantastic, with sea eggs, anemones, fists and fans of coral, wonderful shells, and bigger fish coloured as though by some child with a new paint box. He drifted for an hour, absorbed in this impossibly bright world. His movements became slow and deliberate; fish peered and darted and then ignored him.

He was suddenly conscious of the feeling of having been this way before. It might be the familiar colouring of a fish, he thought, or the shape of a piece of coral. But no – it was a slight noise; the noise, he remembered, of a swimmer coming through the water towards you. He searched around. Someone was about fifty yards away, low in the water and head down, doing an expert effortless crawl towards him. At twenty yards the swimmer stopped and looked up, long blonde hair streaming with water, and then submerged.

La Rue. For heaven's sake. How did she get here?

She came towards him under water, slim and fair with hair sleeked back, and he saw she was not wearing any bathing dress.

Holy Jesus, he thought, doesn't she know my obsession about nakedness? Because this is no time to start teasing me.

She swam underneath him, and he had a glimpse of small breasts and brown thighs, and the darker triangle of her groin that blazed at him like a flame-thrower.

For God's sake, he thought. For God's sake.

She surfaced about five yards away. He pushed the mask on to his forehead.

Real La Rue. Nude La Rue.

"Well, well, well," she said, gasping. "Fan-cy seeing you."

She was breathless, but she still drawled.

"Indeed, fancy."

"Aren't you pleased to see me?"

"Of course I am. How did you get here?"

"In the mail boat, of course. There's no other way. Angus more or less let me go."

"More or less?"

"Or perhaps not. He will be mad at me, but he has other interests now. I think he knows I hate him."

"Have you seen Alice yet?"

"Of course I have, James. We had a long talk."

"Does she know that you ... that we ..."

"Alice and I have no secrets. She knows I never wear any ba-thing things in my bay. I never have done. Does it worry you?"

"Worry, no."

"In fact I've always thought wearing clothing for swimming slightly ridiculous."

"Well, I suppose so."

"Come on in now. I want to hear all your news. Race you to the beach!"

"You know you'll win."

But it would be as well to do something energetic. He was all steamed up, and this she knew.

She beat him to the shore by a good margin, and he saw her like the birth of Venus rise from the waves, water cascading down her brown body, her beautiful breasts defying the laws of gravity. Then she scampered up the sand to the protection of a large towel that was soon wrapped round her like a shroud. She waited for him, and they walked towards the house together. What was she playing at?

"How do you like it here?" she asked.

"I love it. We both love it hugely. Thank you so much for letting us be here."

"It's exhilarating being back. I feel quite absur-dly happy."

"La Rue, we've been happy too …"

"It's all *right*, James. I know what I'm doing."

"Yeah."

They were at the French windows, and she went off to get changed.

I'd better get changed too, he thought. And talk to Alice. Where's La Rue going to sleep?

But while he was brushing his hair La Rue came in, wearing a young flowery dress.

"Well," she said, and sat on the bed.

"Well."

She was brushing her hair too. He couldn't go on brushing his for much longer.

He could just hear Alice singing in the kitchen. The pause lengthened into something significant.

"La Rue, I've been thinking. We only managed to find one bed in the house, that's this one. Would you mind if just for tonight you and Alice shared it? I can sleep on the sofa, but she deserves a comfortable night."

"There is in fact another bed stowed in the garret somewhere ... but why don't we all sleep together?"

"Impossible."

"Don't you think it might be rather amu-sing?"

"It would be fascinating, but still impossible. And embarrassing for Alice. Undignified. And not exactly the right thing to do."

"Not the right thing? It's all a question of attitudes," she said. "Preconceived attitudes."

"Precisely. I might get fonder of you than I am of her."

"What non-sense."

"She wouldn't do it, anyway."

"Why not ask?"

"Have you discussed this with her?"

"Not exactly."

Abruptly he left her sitting on the bed, and went outside into the soft twilight.

Well I'll be damned, he thought. I'll be damned.

CHAPTER EIGHTEEN

But out there in the half-light, amongst the grasshopper and saw-bird noises, the idea was busy making excuses for itself, and it quickly became more possible and less embarrassing. It was after all, he told himself, the Swinging Sixties. Then it didn't seem too difficult to make up his mind.

He went round to the kitchen. Alice was putting things on a tray.

"Alice, La Rue and I thought, as there's only one bed, if you didn't mind, if she was to sleep with us ... that is, if I sleep with her too ..."

"Of course." She was as bland as butter.

"You don't mind?"

"No," she said lightly. "Supper's nearly ready. I thought we'd have a sort of buffet as I'm a bit tired."

"Well, you bloody well ought to mind."

He was nonplussed as well as curiously angry. He would go next door and have La Rue now, if she wasn't careful. And supper would have to wait.

"Calm down, darling. Let's be civilised."

"Well, really. I should have thought you would have been a bit less casual about it. I would almost say you had a wifely obligation to raise some slight objections."

"So far as I have any wifely obligation it might be to entertain you. And we both ought to be honest. Don't pretend you wouldn't find it interesting, sleeping with two girls at once. And it's just possible you might not be the only one to enjoy it."

Her brazenness staggered him. He felt half proud of her, but not proud of being proud.

"I think it would be a great joke," she said, "sharing you with La Rue."

There was a slight pause, and then she went on: "I always knew life with you would never be ordinary."

"You're not jealous?"

"Darling, it's only because I feel so certain of your love that this could possibly be fun and not a disaster. Isn't that obvious?"

"I suppose so …"

He suddenly felt dispirited and weary. Some kind of collusion seemed certain, but he couldn't face thinking it all out, not tonight. He wished he was in bed, just dropping off to sleep, having made love briefly to one or other of them. God, he thought, these women run rings round me. I really can't cope with both of them.

There was a knock on the front door.

"I'll go." Answering the door, that was something he could do.

Standing in the porch was a small black postman, grasping a letter.

"Just sorted dat mail. Letter for Miss La Rue. Nice to have Miss La Rue back here again. Night." His voice hadn't even broken, but he had the self-assurance of a Moraes.

James brought the letter to La Rue, who was piling mangoes on to a plate.

"It's for you. It came in the mail-boat. They've just sorted it."

"It's from Freddy," said La Rue, and started to blush, her ears and cheeks glowing a beautiful pink. "Ex-cuse me." And she left the room.

He felt better. Dear, sophisticated, playgirl La Rue, blushing like a schoolgirl.

She returned when they had almost finished their dinner, freshly powdered and suave again.

"Freddy sends his very best wishes to you both," she said. "He has passed up Universal Agents and he's coming here next week ... I'm so pleased."

She sat down gracefully. "I'm really so pleased," she said again.

Alice and La Rue looked at each other. James looked at both of them, and then at his plate. Human relationships on this level were bewildering, and he felt drained of emotional energy. Mangoes require a certain amount of expertise and he concentrated on his, determined that no indignities should be allowed to enter the mango sphere. Outside it, anything might be about to happen now.

"James," said La Rue, "I'm sorry. I've been behaving abom-inably. I'm a little confused ..."

"Ha?"

"And I know you'll understand ... it must be the intox-icating effect of coming home after all the tensions and excitements of the past year. Would you mind aw-fully helping me get that bed down from the garret? ... I won't be able to manage it on my own."

"Yes."

"Bless you."

"I mean yes, I would mind. I'm absolutely whacked. You and Alice can sleep in the double bed, and I'll sleep here on the sofa. As I suggested in the first place. I'll get the other bed down in the morning, if you don't mind."

He left them and went out into the garden, thinking, why do I always get up and go when things become sticky; it's a sign of weakness. I've been hideously weak all along in this business; no wonder they scheme about me. I should have taken charge from the beginning. And now I will have to sleep alone tonight. I've mismanaged everything. Oh, the pity of it all!

He sat on a log and began to fill his pipe, slowly and carefully, taking pride in doing it unnecessarily well. Roll the little curls out, not too smoothly; tamp them down evenly but not in layers; and let the tobacco work its familiar magic. He drew the flame steadily across the bowl. Smoking a pipe was good.

The night sounds were mysterious and plentiful, and he allowed them to distract his mind from more important things. Rustlings and chirpings and possibly nightjar noises. He was tired. It had somehow been an exhausting day. Forget about women for tonight, he told himself; things are too complicated, and I'll sort everything out in the morning.

When he came indoors they had made up his bedding on the sofa and were preparing for bed themselves. They talked easily to each other, with the long pauses allowed only in the conversation of close friends. He kissed them both goodnight, about equally, and turned in on the sofa.

But he couldn't get to sleep at all. The day's events paraded feverishly in front of him, revolving and merging like garish horses on a merry-go-round. Coral, forts, postmen; feeling happy, feeling frustrated, feeling silly; Alice laying her head between his shoulder-blades, and La Rue swimming towards him under water.

He sat up suddenly. Sex reared its head, stopped the merry-go-round, woke him up irrevocably, and leered at him. Ach! He was aroused and very angry.

I'll bloody well go in there and take the first one I come to, he thought. And then the other one. I'll show them who's running this festering household. If they think they can just plot things cleverly with each other, I'll teach them a thing or two.

"I bloody well will." He found he had said it aloud, going noisily along the passage to the bedroom.

Alice was first, La Rue gently contributing. La Rue next, so soft, so different, with Alice's arms around them both. Then he curled up between them, and sleep enveloped them all most gratifyingly.

* * * * *

The morning sun, streaming through the wide-open windows, solved everything. Together they all got up late, and there was lightness in the air as they jockeyed for position under the shower. Alice and La Rue competed with each other in playfulness and high good humour. James felt overjoyed with his harem as he watched them dress, the two people in the world he loved most, one warm-heartedly, the other utterly. He delighted in their differences – their different shapes, different textures of skin and hair, different kinds of love and the lovemaking that expressed it. All was right with the world.

It certainly seems possible, he thought, for a man to live honestly with two women, and the three of them to love each other without meanness or jealousy. Western religions and literature and ethical traditions are all dead wrong. That's a remarkable discovery. And at last we can touch one another and talk easily; as a civilisation we are uncurling and growing up. Silly ghosts are being exorcised.

La Rue kissed him cheerfully on the forehead, and Alice kissed him properly. Exactly right.

He spent an agreeable morning with both of them. La Rue's personality charmed him once again. She was understanding and funny. As she helped him bring the bed down from the garret she explained to him her feelings for Freddy, and her straightforward intention to become devoted to him. They had seen a good deal of each other in Bermuda after James and Alice had left, but they had had a quarrel just before La Rue decided to break with Angus Swallow. Until yesterday's letter she thought she had lost him. But the letter had changed all that.

Alice was happy and particularly loving. "I'm sorry I was such a minx yesterday," she said. "I can't think what possessed me to be so unfeeling, and not a bit more understanding of how things were from your point of view. It must be this cow-like having-babies quality."

"That's all right, my own darling. I was unfeeling, too, and ridiculously proud and selfish. It won't happen again."

"No, it won't. I know you better now, and love you even more than ever. You have just the right veneer of civilisation over a hard core of primitive lustfulness."

"Thanks very much!"

He was pleased. Last night could so easily have snarled up everything, but it was turning out to be something of a triumph. Life, he thought, is an unpredictable business.

So they had a pleasant week, waiting for Freddy. La Rue slept in the big bedroom at the other end of the house, and spent the day playing the piano and painting in oils in the garret. Her paintings were weird neat little structures in seas of white or blue, and she described them mock-knowingly as neo-definitist. She had certainly found a light happy touch with painting, as with living. Alice sailed round the house and garden like a queen, sometimes singing *bel canto* arias that drifted out among the palms. She said she had never felt so secure and so fertile. James, reckoning he was responsible for both feelings, for the time was too busy with pleasant domestic activities to harbour any doubts. There were the speed-boat and the Sunfish to collect from the yacht club and bring round to the boathouse. A tile on the roof needed fixing. Meg was to be visited and asked back to dinner. They spent a lot of time lying on the beach, or half immersed in their private piece of sea.

Over everything the West Indian sun shone hot and steady all day. And the moon (said La Rue) shone clear and hopeful all night long.

She often used to watch the moon. And those extraordinary dreams she would describe at breakfast time, they were almost always about the moon.

CHAPTER NINETEEN

James lay stretched out on the sand and watched the palm fronds sway above him. It was his favourite spot, a gentle slope of beach and a wide enough patch of shade not to have to keep moving. In fact the sun was almost directly overhead. Tiny chinks of brilliant light blinked through the leaves at him. Odd, he thought, how the chinks are perfectly round and slightly grainy towards the centre, like the blur of a spoked wheel on the move. Odd, too, how they look white with a bluish tinge, slightly different from the colour of sun in the open. But steady, he thought, isn't sunlight pure white? So how can filtered sunlight look whiter? There may be an explanation. But who cares.

He lay quite still with his arms stretched out, soaking up warmth, and coolness, and the scarcely perceptible sounds of the sea. The rush mat he was lying on transmitted the shape of his back to the conforming sand. Glorious sand, he thought, letting it run through his fingers; it's strange how we always let sand run through our fingers. It seems to approach some deep-seated, subconscious idea – time's ruin; smoothness and grittiness; salty, dry; and we grasp with emptying fists. And we can make all that strangely symbolic, basking in warmth and dryness as the hourglass drains away.

He singled out one grain, and rolled it between finger and thumb. Here, now, for him that particle of sand marked the present. He raised himself on to one elbow to examine it. It was a minute world in itself, with its own shape, weight and identity. He let it roll off his finger, to be lost instantly amongst its competitors. His mind was distracted by the vast, but finite, comprehension of each and every grain; but the concept of nowness remained.

He had been aware of a growing sense of the present lately. Alice's baby was due in ten days' time, and her calm mind was uncluttered by any thoughts except having it properly. But James's had been racing ahead. What would it be? *Whose* would it be? If it had black hair and brown eyes and a swarthy skin, how would he feel about it? And what would he do about it? The prospect of raising a Moraes was not particularly appealing. Where would they all go from here? He avoided answering these questions as much as he could. There were still too many imponderables, and the factor he could predict least was his own reaction. In ten days' time things would be irrevocably and absolutely changed, and no power on earth could alter that fact. A new personality would intrude upon the scene, with arms and legs and its own special being, and he might feel fatherly or live forever after in a state of chronic pique. These considerations drove him away from an uncertain future back into the vivid present of sunshine and happiness. Give the hourglass a run for its money, he told himself. Wait and see.

And indeed Alice could not have been more beautiful or loving. He looked over his shoulder towards the house. She was wearing a big stripy dress, and gathering some tall gladioli. He loved the arch of her neck as she stooped forward, and the grace and pride of bearing that made her careful movements attractive and exciting. She would turn round and smile at him in a moment. The future might possibly exist, but it didn't matter now.

She turned round and smiled at him. He was enslaved, and observed it in himself with mild astonishment at the concentration of time and effort lavished on one person. He loved everything about her, but particularly he loved her when she smiled.

> *What though the tide*
> *Advances slowly*
> *When my fair Alice*
> *Picks gladioli?*

Stop, fool!

> *And the future stays*
> *Uncertain wholly –*
> *My own love, Alice,*
> *Picks gladioli.*

Here, now, he loved her without qualification, every inch, every pore, every hair. Whatever happens from now on, he thought, this will have been real.

La Rue and Freddy had gone off in the little speedboat, equipped with water-skis, harpoons and a picnic lunch. They would not be seen till late afternoon when they would return, sunburnt and salty, carrying their fish proudly like the spoils of war. The reef that almost surrounded the island of Adventa was famous for its marine life. They ate fish almost daily, and the house was full of coral and shells, trophies that they never tired of bringing home. Then in the evening as the sun moved to the right and slid down towards the palms they would all come out on to the stoep, freshly showered and groomed, for the sundowner, a special planters' punch whose ingredients Freddy never precisely revealed. Two or three punches, dinner by candlelight with a bottle of wine, whisky with conversation, and a pipe under the stars – that was the pattern of a normal evening, before they all went to bed in their respective ends of the house. Could the jealous fates ever offer more?

A great glow of satisfaction stole through James, tightening his stomach muscles and his throat most pleasurably. This is the life! Talk about having one's cake and eating it! As usual, he found himself thinking in clichés, but they were not less real for being second-hand.

As for Freddy and La Rue, what would happen there? No one could doubt that she had him under a powerful spell, and that he was delighted for the moment to be so detained. Freddy would certainly stay here for some time. But it was difficult to tell how deep their relationship went, and although Alice believed that La Rue was firmly in love with Freddy, James found it impossible to tell what Freddy thought himself. Indeed James had asked him the previous night after dinner, lighting his pipe in the garden while slim La Rue ad-libbed some absurd faux-Handeliana from the drawing-room.

"She plays well, Freddy."

"She does."

"Nice girl, Freddy."

"I like her too."

"Have you any thoughts about moving the situation forward?"

But Freddy had only laughed, and then, more significantly, smiled.

James knew his cousin well enough not to have to go on talking, and they had sat in silence, smoking at the stars. It wasn't easy to discover what Freddy would do. But they were both abundantly happy, those two. And I'm happy, he thought. Alice's happy, although naturally a bit apprehensive about having her baby. So we're all happy. No need to probe any more.

Footsteps sounded on the grass behind him, too quick to be Alice's. It was Spottiswoode, looking large and shiny, carrying a mountain of things, mostly edibles.

"Hi James!" she said, as though they hadn't met for weeks. Spottiswoode had never been known to call people by anything other than their Christian name.

"Hello, Spotto. Is that our lunch you're bringing?"

"Yes, man. Alice says, you like it right out here in the shade of the big palm, all's right? Won't that be nice? She just-arranging some flowers she's been a-picking. She say, you take out these things, Spotto, you just-put them under that big palm tree, and Ah'll be out there toreckly."

"Many thanks, Spotto. How's the family?"

"Wild, James, just wild-wild. That young Marcus, he more trouble than all the rest. Always a-running round like a mad thing, always running, mad as a tabby. Till he goes to school I very vex with him. But Ramjohn, he the eldest, he's a fine big punksey boy now. And little Elizabeth, she seeing Doctor Meg about her funny-up feet, but she quite spractious already."

"How do you like the thought of another baby in Brave Dolphin?"

"There, Alice making small bones for you, Jim-boy." Spottiswoode managed to look both motherly and coy, and her white eyeballs flashed. "There, a baby for Alice and James. There's a fine thing, and no mistake."

"You'll help us, won't you, Spotto?"

"You send me word, you just-send word to me, and Ah'll be vyee down de broadroad on my bike, all's right."

"I know you will, Spotto."

"My! The clock upbraids me with a waste of time. Ah must be gone, feed my own babies. Bye, James. You just-send me word."

Spottiswoode handed him a long drink and departed, having unloaded the lunch. It was mostly fruit. He reflected that, apart from fish, they were all practically vegetarians now, not for any doctrinaire reasons but because fruit and vegetables were good and cheap, and required less time to buy, prepare, and clear up after. And somehow one wanted meat less in a hot climate.

He sipped his drink, cherishing a pleasant thought without quite knowing what the thought was. They were lucky to have Spottiswoode. She came in every morning except Sunday, bustled round, swept, tidied, got the lunch, and left to go back to her own family. She had a happy fluid voice and a gift for wearing exotic colourful clothes. Everybody liked Spottiswoode.

The pleasant thought recurred at the back of his mind, and this time he took the trouble to unearth it and find out what it was. Of course – Alice was coming in a moment to join him. It was doubly pleasant to identify the thought, and then return it securely to the subconscious knowing that it was still valid. The prospect of her company gave him a particular sensation which he eventually decided to call joyousness. She was so young, so splendidly pregnant. But where was she?

A distant cry brought him to his feet.

"James," he heard faintly from the direction of the house. "*James!*"

It was probably eight seconds before he reached the house, time enough for his imagination to go through some gruesome antics. God, he couldn't find her, although she was still calling. Panic! Through the stoep, drawing-room, bedroom, kitchen, bathroom, back through the bedroom – and there she was in the hall, head bowed, sobbing wildly as though her life depended on it.

She could not tell him what had happened and he had no way of knowing. She seemed physically unhurt and clung to him desperately. He had the feeling that somehow she had been threatened. Sick with worry, he helped her into the bedroom. She sat on the bed with her head in her hands, shoulders shaking. He could only put a firm arm round her and wait.

Eventually she was able to talk.

"I went to the door, and there was this horrible man with white eyes, standing there ..."

"What sort of man?"

"Very large, and very black, and he had long hair that stuck out in all directions, and a long dirty beard ... and sort of pinkish-white eyes."

"What did he do to you?"

"He held out his hand and started gabbling something I couldn't understand. I thought he was asking for money, and I'd have given him some just to make him go away if I'd had any and he hadn't looked so horrible. He was wearing a reddish cloak-thing covered with crosses crudely splashed on with paint, and there were all sorts of things hanging from his clothes ..."

"What things, Alice?"

"Dead birds, and knives, and a snake skin, and clay objects, and he looked just *horrible*, and I tried to shut the door but he pushed it back and Spottiswoode had gone and you were out of earshot, and I didn't know what to do. He moved so quickly and talked so fast and eerily I thought he must be some kind of witchdoctor. He had a fragment of mirror he kept flashing at me, and everywhere I looked I saw my reflection in this broken bit of glass. It was so weird, so sinister. And then he grabbed me ..."

"*Where?*"

"My wrist. He chanted something and then scratched the back of my hand, and then ... cursed."

"How do you mean, cursed?"

She was shivering now. He thought, how desperately vulnerable she is. How could I have left her alone, unprotected? God, how could I?

"He cursed my baby," she sobbed. "He was evil, and he cursed my baby."

James glimpsed the powerful spectre of superstition that sometimes haunts pregnant women. Some villainous savage had scared the wits out of her.

He stood up, white with temper and suppressed violence.

"Oh, don't go! Please don't leave me."

He hesitated, but furious instincts got the better of him. He went to the door and opened it. Not a soul in sight. He stood in the doorway listening to the sounds of West Indian fauna and flora, the rustle of palm trees, the whirr of nameless unseen birds, the crickets; the faraway noise of humanity and radios that came from the village; and was that the sound of manic laughter, coming faintly from the sugar plantation?

He remembered striding out into the black confusion of the Cowes dockyard; years ago, was it? It seemed an age ago. No good doing that again. His place was by her side.

He went back to the bedroom and sat down. She needed him here in this hideous business. She was quite broken up. His wild feelings gave place to a vast affection and sadness. Ah, what a tragedy it all had to happen just now!

"My love, let's walk in the garden. Come out in the sun while it's still shining and try to think of happier things. In a moment I'm going to ring up the police, and they will soon sort this fellow out. He's probably a well-known troublemaker and I expect they'll have no difficulty catching up with him. And you mustn't feel superstitious about whatever he said to you – did you understand a single word?"

She shook her head.

"There you are, then. He may have been wishing you well."

It was a foolish suggestion, and she shook her head again.

"Anyway, darling, you simply must not worry or be frightened any more. I shan't let you out of my sight," he took her by the hand, "and we'll go and have lunch under the big palm. Don't worry, my darling, please. Forget it if you possibly can."

But across the back of her hand, scratched with a sharp point and not quite breaking the skin, was a small upside-down cross. A sense of violation almost overcame him. Of course she wouldn't forget her horrible experience. Nor would he.

They went out into the garden. There was a curious heavy stillness in the air, like an examination room. She walked slowly, recovering. She was much better now, but an occasional shudder revealed her nervousness and state of shock. It was not surprising.

They sat under the big palm, and the world seemed different from that other world of ten minutes before, when he had stretched out on the same spot. Sometimes, he thought, we have been so fortunate in our affairs that we have had to invoke a guardian angel. At other times we have just been incomprehensibly unlucky. Is life always like that, or are we rather special?

"Was he a witchdoctor, do you think?" said Alice.

"Darling, I don't know."

"What did he mean by flashing that piece of mirror at me?"

"Alice ... I don't know ... nothing."

"Do you think witchcraft can have any effect on you if you don't believe in it?"

"Of course not. And you don't believe in it, do you?"

"No ... of course not. But if he laid a curse?"

"He didn't lay a curse, my darling," but he was not able to keep a note of pleading out of his voice.

They each ate an apple, thoughtfully.

"Do you mind if I go and ring up the police now?" he said.

"I'll come with you."

They walked back to the house again. He went to the telephone and lifted the receiver off its bracket on the wall. He listened. There was a vaguely echoing sound, but no one answered.

"Can't get the exchange."

"Is it making one of its end-of-a-long-corridor noises?"

"Sort of." He flicked the ancient iron telephone fitting that in England would only have been found in an antique shop.

"The barometer went wrong this morning," she said, "and now the telephone."

"The telephone's always going wrong."

"What do we do now?"

"We go back and finish our lunch. Then when Freddy gets back one of us can go off and tell the police station."

"There won't be anyone there then."

"Spottiswoode will know what to do, whom to tell."

Once more they walked out into the garden. The atmosphere was unusually stifling. Back under the big palm they ate their fruit silently, both of them unable for the moment to communicate their thoughts. The only reassurance he was able to give her was a gentle squeeze of her hand. He felt inadequate to the situation.

Lying back, he found himself again grasping a handful of sand. Extraordinary how that creature had come to the door. Why had he chosen to do so just now? What was he after? Extorting money? Spreading uneasiness? Repulsive, the way he had scratched the back of her hand. That was in legal terms an assault, and assaulting a pregnant woman was a disgusting thing to do. As for cursing the baby – it was an utterly unspeakable business. The man was obviously mad and should be locked up. Only a lunatic could have uttered that crazy laughter – if it had in fact existed. It was of course easy to imagine things when one strained one's ears.

He was straining his ears now. It was remarkably quiet. The palm leaves had stopped rustling, and he couldn't hear any crickets. But a frigate-bird flew along the beach with a distinctive pulsing of wings. He had never seen one so close to the shore. He could hear Alice stirring slightly on the dry sand beside him, and also the gentle plash of waves crawling backwards and forwards at the edge of the sea. And above these slight noises, clearly now, the distant thump of a heavy wave on the reef that shielded Brave Dolphin Bay from the Atlantic Ocean.

He sat up suddenly; that had never happened before. During the weeks they had stayed in Adventa, he felt sure that the sea had never broken over the reef. Yet there it was, undeniably, an enormous wave breaking all along the reef except for a small section in the middle where the channel led through the coral heads. Why should this be? It was an extraordinary phenomenon and he watched in bewilderment as the cascading ridge of white foam advanced like a battalion in line abreast. Was the whole world going mad, or was there a simple explanation? Was it a dream? Or was he mad himself?

"James," said Alice, "there's something not quite right." And something in the back of his mind comprehended.

"Get up," he said. If she was better at sixth senses he was better at decisions. "*Get up*," he said more sharply, "quickly please."

She obeyed him without a word. The wave was gathering itself again, pushing a great volume of churned up water ahead, and building up ready to break. Somehow, inconceivably, a deep-sea wave had invaded their bay and was about to thunder up the beach.

"Back from the shore!" He took her hand and made her hurry on to the grass, just as the wave crashed over all its length and reinforced the white torrent of foam that was violently roaring forward. It seethed up the beach, swallowing their lunch at one gulp, and boiled round the roots of the palms. The noise was astonishing.

They watched it, fascinated. They had only just got clear in time. The foam subsided, and began to drain back into the sea.

"Was that a tidal wave?" she said.

"Something of the kind."

"What does it mean?"

"I'll just have a look at the barometer."

"I don't think it's working properly. This morning I found the pointer right over to one side."

He walked quickly into the house and straight up to the barometer. It was reading 970. The signs were now unmistakable.

"Hurricane," he said. "But *June*? – it should be too early for hurricanes." He tapped the glass lightly with a fingernail. The needle jumped down to 968.

"Hurricane," he said again.

"Is there a hurricane coming our way?"

"Yes. Help me close all the windows as firmly as possible. We may not have much time."

And already, as he looked out of the window, the palms were beginning to wave jerkily, and another gigantic wave was pounding over the reef. A great bank of cumulo-nimbus had risen out of the trees on the right, and was about to obscure the sun.

CHAPTER TWENTY

The house had wooden shutters, installed no doubt for just this kind of emergency because they were never shut in the normal course of events. While Alice closed all the windows from inside, James went round the outside dealing with the shutters. But he found them difficult to move. Some lazy and unsupervised painter, ages ago, had decided not to bother to paint the inside, and as they were seldom moved and generations of lazy and unsupervised painters had followed suit, the hinges were practically solid under layers of ancient paint. Those that could be moved revealed an inside rotten with fifty years of neglect.

He tugged at the creaking woodwork, and the wind tugged at his shirt. What a hell of a thing to happen, with Alice in a state and Freddy and La Rue out in the boat. The wind had a viciousness in the gusts which he found alarming. The storm was coming on so quickly.

He managed to close about half the shutters and secure them with their wooden drop-latches. He caught sight of Alice inside the house, moving about checking the windows with a look of concentration. He stood for a moment with his legs braced and the wind buffeting his hair, and watched as she knelt on the window-ledge and stretched up to fasten the top catch, appealingly kangaroo-shaped, head thrown back, breasts and belly flattened against the glass. She would know he was watching, thinking that she shouldn't be stretching up like that.

Without taking her eyes from what she was doing her features softened as she thought of him watching her. Oh, keep her safe, he thought. God keep her safe from harm. I'll do anything …

He started clearing the stoep of its deckchairs and lilos, putting them just inside the door in a heap, and the door was a dead weight against the wind as he closed it. A rubber beach ball was careering round the inside of the stoep as though possessed by erratic and freakish devils. He captured it and thrust it through the door where it bounded dramatically along the corridor. Anything else he ought to do?

He suddenly remembered the Sunfish. Hallelujah! He should have thought of that before. He hurried down to the boathouse, breasting himself forward carefully against the unpredictable forces of the wind. The heavy swell was now breaking continuously over the reef, and a high steep sea was being whipped up. Long rollers were thundering in to the shore, and spindrift was being lifted off the tops and blown in great streaky patches across the bay. It now began to rain copiously. He became quite drenched in rain and spray. An hour ago, he thought, I was lying under that palm with the sun glinting through it. Now – he gasped as the spray hit him – I'm fighting the elements, and it feels cold.

He made for the boat shelter, dodging the bigger waves that were coming well up over the grass. The entrance was to seaward, and he had to pick his way through flotsam that was being strewn all over the garden. Thigh-deep in spume he looked inside. The boat was not there. His first reaction was that it had drifted away, but then he saw the painter still made fast to its ring and thrashing around in the wind. The boat was smashed. Bits of wood surged in and out of the shelter with the surf; they were all that was left.

Tragedy number one, he thought. La Rue's poor Sunfish. A leaden sense of responsibility in the pit of his stomach told him that there would be plenty more to come.

He braced himself against another big wave. It was getting darker.

The storm was only just beginning.

He went back to the house. Alice must have been watching him, because she opened the door for him and was nearly bowled over by the wind. Inside, he pushed the door shut with both hands, and the incredible shelter of the house enveloped him. It was like entering a calm harbour in a small boat when a big sea is running outside. He gasped with relief and stood there dripping.

"Well done, darling," she said. "All well outside?"

"No. The Sunfish is smashed to pieces."

"God, how awful! Ruined?"

"Completely. And there's more to come. Anything on the radio?"

"They keep saying 'Stand by for an important announcement', but so far no announcement."

They were in the drawing-room. A crackle of static was coming from the radio, punctuated by snatches of an advertisement for some of the newest American cars. He thought, irrelevantly, it was most improbable that any of the models being described would ever reach the narrow asphalt lanes of Adventa. The drawing-room windows rattled furiously and they were misty with spray.

"The wireless is impossible," she said. "It's never been so bad before. Just when we need it most."

"Come in to the bedroom," he said, piloting her there. "I don't like you being behind unshuttered windows. If they blow in in this gale it won't be any fun at all."

He sat her on the bed and put the radio beside her.

"You must listen carefully for any announcement about the weather." She turned to him in dismay. "Yes, I've got to go – to see what's happened to La Rue and Freddy – I won't be long."

An announcement interrupted him. Through the static came an unfamiliar voice, speaking slowly: "This is a hurricane warning.

Hurricane Anthea is believed to be centred forty miles, that is four-zero miles, east of Adventa, moving west at twelve knots, that is one-two knots. Very high winds and mountainous seas are being experienced throughout the area at this time. You are advised to close all windows and shutters, and remain indoors. I will repeat that ..."

Well, well, he thought. Fate loves to pile on the agony. On one hand a frightened pregnant wife – near-wife – in a rickety house, right in the path of a full-scale hurricane, and on the other a cousin I owe everything to and his beautiful girl perilously at sea. I have to choose between them. Can't have both.

Automatically he referred the matter back to his vague sense of heroic precedent. The decision was obvious really. While Alice was not actually in danger, his clear duty was to see if the others were safe, no matter how much she hated to be left. If La Rue and Freddy were to drown for lack of assistance while he stayed indoors comforting his almost-wife – it was unthinkable.

"Are you still going?" she asked.

"I could not love thee, dear, so much ..."

"That means yes?"

"Yes."

"Don't be long, darling. Keep safe."

He abandoned her. With a sickening realisation that he had never left her in time of stress without some disaster occurring, he battled his way out through the front door.

It was certainly getting worse. Wind and vicious rain (or was it spray?) lashed at him from several directions, and a hysterical frou-frou from sugarcane and thrashing palm trees drowned all other noises. He knew what he had to do and set off for Mount Shakespeare, a distance of about half a mile. But the forces of the gale against his body were strong and capricious. At one moment he was stooping down against a powerful headwind, and the next he was stumbling forward as though he had been hit in the back. The result of these random uncertainties was to make him feel like a man walking barefoot and blindfold over rocky country: it required a good deal of energy just to keep going, and he took a lot of knocks. Pieces of sugarcane and palm leaves were flying through the air, and the path was strewn with broken branches.

A long, reed-like leaf with sharp spikes, tough as a whip, slapped him hard across the mouth. The blood that ran down his chin and spattered over his shirt increased his determination. He was grimly resolved to make the top of Mount Shakespeare, because from it you could see the whole of the south-west coast. If La Rue and Freddy were still at sea (and God forbid) they should be visible from there.

As he climbed higher he became more exposed, and he began to fear that he might be simply lifted off his feet and swept away. But although stronger the wind was steadier, and there were less objects flying around. The path led slightly to landward of the summit, and he was grateful for what protection it afforded.

Near the top he stopped by a large thrashing casuarina tree to regain his breath. With one hand on the trunk to steady himself, he watched the effect of a hurricane on the green landscape of a small West Indian island. It was awesome. Great gusts of ferocious strength were ravaging across plantations and pines and palms, and a loud noise of panic-stricken vegetation competed with the shrieking of the wind. The village, half hidden on his left, seemed to be closed down. It was impossible to tell how much damage would be done. This wind, he thought, is invincible. It will tear us all to pieces if it cares to.

Just above him on the top of the hill was the ruined fort. He went towards it painfully on hands and knees, holding on, the wind tugging at his clothes but not yet prepared to dislodge him. A gap in the stone wall would give him the view he wanted. He crawled up to it, and looked over.

The blast of air howled in his ears and shook him menacingly. Not being able either to see or breathe, he had to duck down again behind the protection of the wall. His hearing was numbed, and his eyelids blown about. Take it slowly, he told himself. People can see through stronger winds than this.

He inched his head up into the slipstream, and found he could just keep his eyes within the sheltered airflow where the wall deflected the blast and the rain like a baffle. And there in front of him was the terrifying sea.

He had never seen such an ugly and ferocious sea. The long swell which had broken over the reef and given him his first inkling of the hurricane was gone, submerged in quick steep waves of astounding size which raced and crashed towards the shore, lurching confusedly, stampeding, piling up into super waves which the wind attacked and scattered in great foamy convulsions over hundreds of yards. The air was filled with spray, and he could only see a mile or so out to sea. No small boat could possibly survive in that turmoil; not the remotest slightest chance. The sudden prospect that La Rue and Freddy must be actually dead struck him sickeningly and for the first time. But they might have got ashore somewhere, he told himself; they might be safe; Freddy would have had warning, would have seen the storm coming.

And he answered himself, how much warning did I get? The hurricane came at us out of a clear blue sky. We were nearly drowned just lying on the beach. There's no hope. They've had it.

He put his head down again, inside the shelter of the wall, and his eyelids dropped themselves shut with relief from the blast. In the comparative stillness misery struck him like a clout to the head. Freddy doesn't exist anymore. La Rue gone, drowned. Capsized in a hurricane, spluttering against the waves, grasping each other for a second or two, then – overwhelmed in an uproar of white-black turbulence, thrown about, sucked under, choking, and cold salty liquid seeking out the frantic lungs, water-logging the brain. With his eyes closed he saw them vividly, several fathoms down, splayed out among the coral-heads, hair a-stream, suntanned limbs dangling; and the light shifted and slanted with the heave of the sea above them. He felt as though he was about to throw up. I'm no hero, he thought. This kind of life isn't for me. What a foul death for poor slim La Rue and faithful Freddy.

He vomited copiously through his mouth and nose. It was unlike being sick for a physical upset, and brought no relief. He felt hideously worse. The vision of drowning had mentally drained him, for it was now as certain as his vision of Alice in the prison cell.

But his upbringing told him he should pretend to be a man of action and not give up, even when friends get killed. He looked over the wall again and saw – Christ! – a boat perched precariously on the top of a wave. He ignored the acrid taste that the wind was driving back down his nostrils, but by the time he had blinked the boat was no longer to be seen. Another vision? No, quite different from a vision, and not La Rue's boat anyway. There it was again, miraculously alive where no boat had a claim to live. It was a cabin cruiser, low and heavy in the water, and it was taking such a pounding from the waves that it was only visible on the crests, even from a height. James watched and was appalled at the task facing the human being who must be at the helm. He was doing the only thing possible – running before the wind towards the shore. It would have been suicide for him to attempt to turn away, as one wave broadside on would swamp the boat in a trice. His only chance would be to keep on with as much steerageway as possible and attempt to make the beach. It was a forlorn hope, and the boat was certainly doomed in any case, but it was all that could be done.

James watched the boat leaping in and out of sight like a dolphin. As long as the waves did not break, the helmsman could steer. But then a large wave combined with another, the resultant monster toppled in a cataract of foam, and the little boat was swept forward and hurled under like a toy.

He was up and through the gap in the wall into the wind's teeth. Let the dead bury their dead, must be his attitude. There's someone out there in life-and-death trouble.

He staggered down the hill against the full force of the wind, with torrents of rainwater sluicing around his feet. Flying debris was plentiful now, and he tried to keep one hand in front of his face for protection. About a third of all the trees had been uprooted, and none seemed to be undamaged. His hearing was deadened by the frenzied screeching of the wind. So this is a hurricane, he thought, as he tried to avoid a branch that hit him in the stomach and winded him. A hurricane in June, he thought, doubled up and not being able to breathe or even gasp. But the hurricane season is not supposed to start till July. He got his breath back and tried to straighten up. Well, fight on!

The wind was not slackening. If anything it seemed to be getting stronger, and veering a bit towards the east.

Of course the person in that boat hasn't a hope, he thought. Even wearing a lifejacket he couldn't have lasted more than a moment in that sea. The boat will certainly be driven ashore through that fantastic surf and crumpled up on the beach. But I must get there – do what I can. God, this wind.

As he neared sea level and approached the sea, he began to be hit by salt spray again. It stung his face and arms. He pressed on, carefully placing his feet, head down. He could feel the ground shudder as the waves crashed on to the beach, but the noise itself only reached him faintly, filtered through a merciful near-deafness. Looking up between gusts he could see enormous waves over the top of a low sandy bank. He watched fascinated; all along the bank and above the level of his head waves were forming and reforming. It was as though two identical slides were being flashed alternately on a screen: a long, cavernous, impossibly high wave, which then suddenly collapsed and disappeared, to be replaced by another exactly the same; and all the while a constant flurry of spray and spume billowed over the bank towards him. Shielding his eyes with both hands he thought, it's uncanny; magnificent; awesome; almost inspiring; and then he saw the boat.

At first he did not recognise it as the cabin cruiser, it being so shattered and split. It was wrapped round a palm tree growing just on the landward side of the bank, and must have rolled over and over up the beach with the force of wind and sea. He went towards it gingerly. What an unutterable shambles; dreadful. Worse than the worst motor-smash photograph a newspaper would ever dare print. A sheep's carcase of planks jutted stark in the air, and the hurricane thundered through them.

As he reached the wreckage three things happened very quickly. First, he saw the name on a broken plank, *Peccavi*. Secondly, before he had grasped the implications of that, he saw a battered corpse sprawled half out of the cockpit. It was Angus Swallow, horrifyingly dead. And then he found himself staring into the albino eyes of a great bearded black man who was picking over the body.

CHAPTER TWENTY-ONE

Before the full shock of this grisly tableau had time to have any effect, the witchdoctor with albino eyes leapt out of the boat with a loud shriek. He leapt so easily and effortlessly that James would have been tempted to believe he was in the presence of all sorts of supernatural powers, had the man not caught his foot on one of the splintered planks as he sailed through the air. He landed on the sand and emitted a swear word so crude, so English, so un-witchdoctor-like, that James who clearly heard it above the wind lost all fear of the situation. The man scrabbled in the sand wildly throwing up a sandstorm, and eventually found his feet and bolted with signs of the utmost panic. His yells merged with the wind.

James picked up a piece of glass that the creature had dropped in flight. It was a wedge-shaped splinter of ordinary mirror. He caught sight of himself in it, and for a second was appalled and incredulous. No wonder the fellow had taken fright. James saw his face matted with blood and vomit, his shirt flapping in rags, his hair thrashing wildly. Quite an apparition to put its head suddenly over what was left of the gunwale! Well, that just about levelled the score.

He turned back to the shattered boat. So this was the end of the Red Terror, Angus Swallow, the end of *Peccavi* and the Swallowtails, the end of that wild set-up in Bermuda. He peered into the boat guardedly. Everything movable was being torn out by the gale. But the dead Angus was immovable; he had lashed himself to the bulkhead with a length of two-inch manila, so that he would not be swept off the wheel. James looked at the gaping fat body. It was dreadfully broken, bleeding and crushed. He hoped the man had been quickly drowned. Otherwise, with the wreck cartwheeling up and over the beach and Angus tied with his own rope – it did not bear thinking about. But what was he doing, coming to Adventa in a cabin cruiser? He put the question aside as matter for further thought when there was more time. And Angus couldn't have been alone – he must have had some supporters, if only to crew the boat for him. But there was certainly no one else in the jumble of spillikin wood that was now *Peccavi*.

The wind was assaulting the wreck as though revengeful of anything that could survive its masterpiece of a sea. James grasped the inshore side of the boat, and a jagged piece of wood from the deckhouse sliced past him in the air. Best to abandon her before she claimed another life. Must get back to Alice.

He staggered away, bracing himself against the full force of the wind. It was certainly not weakening; in fact, although he was becoming more used to moving and breathing in it, he felt it was stronger. And stronger too were the almost solid sheets of rain – but do you call it rain when it is mixed with spray and coming at you horizontally? He tried to gauge the wind speed by imagining a car moving at the same speed as some of the airborne planks: a hundred miles an hour, ninety knots or so. Not surprising the sea was in such a fantastic state of riot.

He was by now quite skilful at walking, but he was not prepared for a great gust of exceptional strength. It bowled him over and he lay prostrate on the ground, and high-velocity sand abraded all exposed parts of his skin like emery cloth. His hearing, although deadened to the howl and screech of the wind, picked out the sharp tearing sound of some vast upheaval. As the gust subsided and he extricated himself from a little grave of sand, he could see that the palm tree he had just left had been uprooted, and the debris was being broadcast inland. As for the wreck of the *Peccavi*, it simply did not exist anymore. It was dispersed, scattered like chaff over several acres.

He found himself thinking that if you had managed to film that scene it would be interesting to run it backwards.

Well, home! Alice has been on her own quite long enough. Couldn't say quite how long but it's getting darker. Back to Brave Dolphin. Done my stuff anyway. No one can say I haven't tried. And for most of the way home I've got the shelter of Mount Shakespeare – for what it's worth.

It was worth a little, and with the hurricane blowing with renewed fury out of a darkening sky he was grateful for any help. There were more trees down across his path. He noticed that the ones that seemed to have fallen most recently were lying at a slightly different angle. Perhaps the wind was indeed veering now. If so – what was that confounded rule?

Face the wind in northern seas:
Abaft the beam twice ten degrees
The storm to starboard may be sought.
(If south it's just the same but port.)

So maybe the eye of the hurricane was passing to the south. That was surely something to be grateful for.

As he stumbled back along the path he experienced a certain tired elation, as if he was returning to the club-house after a successful round of golf. The colossal wind had blown its worst, but a small human equipped only with determination had defied it, and was coming home.

And then he remembered La Rue and Freddy, undoubtedly drowned, and his shameful elation was pricked like a soggy balloon. Wretched, wretched. Dead. Two wasted lives. He felt he would be destined to trudge for evermore through a bog of heavy-heartedness. He was utterly exhausted, and the madly lurching trees, bending and whipping through unbelievable angles, began to daunt him considerably.

He came to the small bridge that spanned the stream. It was quite flooded with dark muddy water. Surprisingly the bridge had not carried away, probably because the weight of water on the wooden slats had protected them from the gale. He waded over, cautiously. The stream did not seem to be flowing at all, and this he found slightly curious – a fact to be stowed away in the back of his memory where something else seemed to be awaiting further thought as well. But his mind twitched away as he came in sight of the house.

It was still standing, anyway. The stoep had disappeared, leaving only the wooden supports and some tattered fragments. The boat shelter had gone without trace. Both could be replaced easily enough. But as he neared the front of the house he was shocked to see the whole aspect of the garden changed. The big palm that had shaded people since the house was built had been torn up. It lay diagonally across the garden like a fallen statue. It would take about eighty years to replace that palm.

No external damage to the house, it seemed. He surveyed it for a moment. Its old fabric had resisted remarkably well. Only a small window in the garret had been smashed, and the frame swung violently on its hinges, crack, crack, against the southern wall. That was the wall away from the direction of the wind, so it mattered little. They must have forgotten, or not been able, to close it.

He reached the side door to the kitchen, which he judged would be the most sheltered, and wrenched it open. Between opening the door and getting himself inside, the kitchen was transformed into a turmoil. Pots and pans, cupboards and their contents, fruit, vegetables, all were thrown into confusion, but God, what a relief to shut the door. There was a great peacefulness, and the silence almost hurt his eardrums. He crashed into things before he discovered he did not need to fight for every movement. It was like finally making a motorway after battling through the rush hour.

"Darling, I'm home."

Poor devastated kitchen. But home.

"Alice!"

She did not come running. The house was subdued except for the window-frame up in the garret: crack, crack, against the wall.

Not another disaster? God, I can't bear it.

He hurtled through the rooms. She was hunched up sideways on the bed, looking at him wordlessly, under great strain. Why was she holding her breath? In labour?

Yes. She couldn't speak. He couldn't touch her, or help her, or comfort her in any way. For a moment he flew round the room in desperation like a headless chicken. But stop – he must be steady; she needed his steadiness now more than ever before. His grim news could come later; everything could come later. She was about to have her baby and she needed help. He felt guilty. It must have been ghastly for her, all on her own for the past two hours. He realised with a shock of cold fright that he might well be unable to get a midwife or anyone to help in time. The responsibility of the birth would fall on him, inescapably. Yet it must be possible, he thought, for people to have babies without midwives. Probably half the world does. If only I knew more about it, if I'd read that childbirth book more carefully …

She screwed up her eyes and gasped. The pain left her and she could speak.

"Thank God you've come."

"Are you all right, darling?"

"W'y a-whay …" She tried again more slowly. "Why away so long?"

"It was the wind – very fierce. Lots of trees have been blown down."

"Hurts. It hurts having babies. I'm having a baby."

He put a firm hand on her shoulder. She sounded slightly deranged. He didn't know if that was a normal symptom. Perhaps it was nature's reaction against the cruelties fate had inflicted on her in the last nine months, an easing of the load so that the species would survive. Fate was certainly giving her a rough time. Frightened by a sham witchdoctor, left all alone by a pseudo-husband, paternity problems, no doctor, no midwife – mere human beings could not have devised such an unpropitious way of having babies. Crack, crack – the broken window above his head reminded him there was a hurricane, too.

"You'll be all right, darling. I'll look after you."

"You won't leave me again?"

"Never."

"Will you get the doctor?"

"I'll try. But we may have to manage on our own." This did not sink in.

"Doctor Meg," she said, trying to make him understand. "I need Doctor Meg. And midwife."

"I'll see what I can do."

He left the room and stood in the hall. There was not much he could do. The telephone would almost certainly be out of action, but he might as well try that first.

He picked up the receiver. No end-of-corridor noises, nothing. It was a lifeless piece of inanimate metal. The wires would be down all over the island.

Try the radio. He switched it on. There was a blurt of atmospherics, but nothing else.

So that's it, he thought. Incommunicado.

The nearest house is twenty minutes away on an ordinary day. It'll take half an hour now, even if the road's clear. An hour round trip. Even then I doubt if I'd be able to get one of the women – everyone will be wanting to protect their own families. If I managed to get to Meg's house – she would come, but I would be away an hour and a half, probably. Too long. Alice may have had it by then, and there should be someone here, even if it's only me. The midwife lives in Adventa Town, so that's no good. Inescapably, we've got to cope on our own.

God!

It was nearly dark now. Automatically he went to switch on the light in the hall. It did not work.

That adds a further complication, he thought. Why does all this have to happen to me? But we shall win through. Against all odds, dammit, we'll win somehow.

He went and had a wash and took off his foul shirt. Then he collected one of the Aladdin's lamps they used for barbecues. It was quite full of paraffin and would last several hours. He took it into the bedroom with some matches and lit it. It burned fitfully in the draughts but stayed alight, giving the room an unfamiliar soft yellow glow. Alice smiled at him from the bed.

"You're doing fine," he said. "There's no electricity but we'll manage. Lucky the shutters for this room really shut." He was putting on a clean shirt. "I think I'll drag the wardrobe in front of the windows even so – it will be further protection. Are you warm enough there, my love?"

She nodded, her hair in long streaks down the side of her face.

"I couldn't get Doctor Meg, I'm afraid. We'll have to manage together."

"Aagh …" It was a despairing wounded-rabbit whimper. And she held her breath. Another spasm.

The broken window had stopped its clattering – presumably wrenched off its hinges – but he had been listening to the ferocious noises of the hurricane which howled round the old house. Now he was aware that it was becoming quieter. Perhaps the worst was over. Alice's birth pangs were coming more frequently now, so if the hurricane was easing that was an untold blessing. He could sense in both of them the subdued wind lowering mental tensions. He went to the unshuttered drawing-room windows and looked outside.

Amazingly the sky was suddenly clearing. Stars were opening up on his right as the clouds scudded away. It was a very odd effect. He had the same vague feeling that he had had during the afternoon on the beach: something was not quite right. Undoubtedly the wind was dying away fast.

Try the back door.

He went there and opened it cautiously, and felt a mere gusty breeze. He stepped outside. The stars overhead were now visible, and there was a hint of diffused moonlight coming from somewhere. It was an incredible change. More incredible still was the noise of the sea breaking on the beach in a curious way – not the familiar rhythmic pattern of waves, but in irregular bursts like shots on a rifle range. It seemed very near.

His eyes, growing accustomed to the strange light, could now discern that the garret window had indeed been shattered on the south side, leaving a gaping black hole. No doubt there was chaos in the studio, and La Rue's pictures would certainly be ruined. But if that's all the damage, he thought, we've been in luck. I'm dead tired – but can't stop yet.

And then there rose from behind him a crescendo of sound that for an instant seemed like a crowd at a football match. It was the roar and havoc of the hurricane coming across the sugar cane – *from the south.*

He just had time to get inside the house before the wind arrived and shook it savagely. There was a tearing sound from the garret as the wind funnelled into the exposed studio. Something heavy thumped on to the roof.

Back in the bedroom the lamp was flickering wildly. Alice was sitting up on the bed, wide-eyed in the spooky light.

"What's that noise? What's happening?"

A deafening crash above their heads drowned his reply. Pieces of plaster were showered all over the room. The wind howled afresh, and heavy rain drummed onto the roof.

He tried again, almost shouting. "Wind's gone right round to the south. I think the garret's going. Get under the bed."

Another crash. The whole room rocked and all the glass in the windows shattered. She had hardly moved.

"Come on – we must get out of here."

He helped her to her feet, but a spasm began to take her and she sat down again.

"Come on," he shouted. "You absolutely *must come.*"

She tried but could not. As she writhed on the bed he covered her face as much as possible with his hands. The wind was whipping through the open window now, and the air seemed full of bits of plaster and glass and clothing. The light went out. Her spasm was going on and he must wait till it had finished. There were more cracking noises above them. A heavy beam thrust itself through the ceiling in the far corner of the room, and remained suspended at a crazy angle.

It would be much too dangerous to try to carry her. He must wait. "Hurry up!" he shouted at her, futilely. *Wait,* he told himself. Wait till this horrendous gust is over.

It was a severe one, but eventually it passed. He got her up and walked her to the door as one walks a drunkard home. The door was jammed. He leant her up against the wall, kicked out the bottom panel, scrambled through the hole, and with his shoulder broke the door open from the outside. Together they stumbled along the dark corridor to the other end of the house. Behind them was the din of the garret disintegrating and the roof falling in.

She was breathing heavily as he laid her on La Rue's bed. It could not be long now.

"I can't take another one like that," she sobbed, tearing at his heart.

"You must."

"I *can't.*"

He felt as though some skilful torturer was ripping his skin, tissue by tissue. She was at her extremity, but there was more to come. He could do nothing but watch. And a new hazard threatened them. Water started spilling in over the windowsill. He dashed to the window and looked out, and the sky was just perceptibly lightening with the dawn. But the garden – it had disappeared. The sea had risen right up to the walls of the house, and waves, pockmarked with rain, were slapping against the window.

This is it, he thought. I'm afraid there's no hope for us, all three of us. It seems a pity, but I don't think there is anything more I can do.

Alice heaved on the bed and he sat down beside her, heedless of the violent noises of the house. Perhaps he should pray. All kinds of wild memories faded in and out of his mind. He saw himself back in Churbridge, with the park stretching away from the windows of Upton House, and his Shetlands grazing under the great chestnut. And Alice was coming to tea, said his mother; she would make a sponge cake. And then he was back on the bridge of HMS *Wilton*, and Angus Swallow was storming around, slightly but significantly drunk.

"You crass idiot!" he kept shouting at James, while the signalman looked startled. "You insolent little puppy," he screamed. And then he was fishing on that stretch of the Itchen with Moraes, and Ishbel was reading her book on the bench beside the hut. "A couple of nice ones," said Moraes, taking the trout out of his landing net. Yes, you murderer, but I saw you leave them gasping on the bank to die in the afternoon sun. And then he was himself gasping, back in the muddy water of Santa Rosa river, equipped only with a knife and a torch, setting his wits against another murderer. Why was that torch flashing at him? He rose in alarm.

"That's all right, Jim-boy, it's only me, sunshine Spottiswoode. Ah just-come to see if Alice was okay and, man, Ah only just-made it one-time. A plague upon this howling! My, but the sea's a-coming flash in."

CHAPTER TWENTY-TWO

James stood a moment, dumbfounded by the arrival of Spottiswoode. Then, as hope returned, as a subtle part of the responsibility for the birth seemed to move naturally from him to her, he felt a great grinning happiness. They could still win! He would keep the seas back while she helped Alice. He put his arms round Spotto and kissed her flamboyantly. They *would* win.

What they needed most at that moment was some means of staunching the water coming through the window, and some kind of illumination. While Spottiswoode attended to Alice he left the room to see if he could deal with these things. The other end of the house was in a frenzy of devastation, for the wind had pierced their defences and was nagging away at the breach. The garret, it seemed, was completely demolished and parts of it had fallen into the bedroom. The old walls were resisting manfully but before long the hurricane would tear them apart and the sea come flooding in. Time, he thought, is what we need. A hurricane can't blow forever. We may have a good chance of lasting it out.

He found among the pile of beach gear he had cleared from the stoep the solid fuel burner that they used to cook with on the beach. And he gathered up an armful of towels and curtains to mop up the water. It was a start.

Back in La Rue's bedroom, Spottiswoode was in command.

"There, Alice, my love, that more comfortable? That just-fine. You got some way to go, Ah reckon, you just-relax and don't worry. We'll manage fine ourselves, why, one-time Ah had my Ramjohn during Carnival all on my own, and no one able to help, they were that drunk. You doing just-fine."

James lit the burner, and at last a little inadequate light was restored. It was a bizarre scene: Alice stretched on the bed, Spottiswoode with damp hair askew bustling round, and the floor covered in muddy water. He laid the curtains along the window-ledge and started mopping up with a towel. The windows were still rattling vigorously, but it seemed that less water was coming in. Amazing if he should find that the water was going down. You made a tiny gesture towards solving a problem and it sometimes disappeared. Like the butterfly that stamped. He looked out: the water *was* going down.

"Spottiswoode, I'm going to fetch Doctor Meg. I'm sure the water's going down now. I'll be as quick as humanly possible. Will you look after Alice?"

"My, man, you go wary. Me, Ah set off when the wind was all a-stop, but soon it blow again, all noisy-bruggadung, nearly lift me right off my own two feet. This is one destroyful hurricane. You go wary."

"Was the road clear?"

"Ah guess just-clear. You climb over fallen trees, but just-clear Ah guess."

"Look after her, won't you, Spotto."

"Yes, man. The very wind beshrew me if Ah fail."

He forced his way out of the house using brute strength against the front door, which crashed shut after him like a steel trap. Wind and noise were not abating much, but it was getting lighter, and the rain had moderated. He braced himself against the treacherous forces of the gale. Back to the old routine of fighting for every inch, but with less energy left to do it. He set off.

He turned round to look at the house. He could just distinguish the outline of the roof, straight-ruled along the skyline until you came to where the garret had been, and there the jagged edges merged into the background. Poor Brave Dolphin – it was dreadfully damaged.

Something hit him full in the face and wrapped itself round his head. He gasped and clawed it off; it was one of La Rue's canvasses, half-finished when she died. Poor La Rue.

But his only responsibility now was Alice, and he must get the doctor without delay. "The very wind beshrew me if I fail." It was a good theme song, a war-cry that would carry him through. The rhythm of the words marched along with him as he thrust himself forward against that very wind, over the broken trees and branches that lunged at him in the half-light. Beshrew me – if I fail – if I fail.

But he would not fail; not now. He was brim full of self-confidence once again and felt unstoppable. Besides, the wind was slackening, was it not? He faced it, and recalled the mnemonic that told him where the storm centre would be. As he did so he realised that the hurricane must have moved inland. That calm period when the sky cleared meant the eye of the storm was passing overhead, and the violent wind from the opposite direction was to be expected a little later. And now, with the centre over Green Mountain, the hurricane would presumably disperse itself in the land mass, and the wind die away.

The path led roughly parallel to the shore and he squelched along in thick mud. That was positive proof of the water level going down. The southerly wind must have piled up the water into the bay; and he remembered crossing the stream, which had already been obstructed by a rising sea. Thank God for that slope between house and beach. Another couple of feet and the sea would have burst the windows and poured through the rooms, sweeping away everything movable and possibly demolishing the walls themselves.

If I fail – if I fail. Sea's receding, wind's reducing, light's increasing –

the opposition is in full retreat. And we'll not fail! Fight on!

He fought on, as fast as he could through fallen trees and mud, and suddenly there was a flash of white and then all went black.

* * * * *

He felt dazed with tiredness but somehow in pain. He got the impression that it was broad daylight and he was lying in a tree. Then he closed his eyes again. It was puzzling. At least he could sleep now; after all he had been through he thought he deserved some sleep.

A sharp pain in his right arm jerked at him, and the pain spread all round till it was hammering on the inside of his brain.

Better wake up properly and see what the hell's going on.

He came to, and the pain hit him hard. It was indeed broad daylight, and he was lying in a tree. His right arm was pinned under him nastily. Everything hurt.

Damn it! *Damn* it! Something's gone very wrong, and there was something I had to do, something important.

But the pain stalked up behind him and caught him, in a fiery, steely half-nelson. For a moment he thought he could not bear it, then mercifully, sweetly, he passed out again for an unknown period of time.

This won't do, he then thought. I can't run away. Got to do something.

A black boy with his shirt covered in mud was peering down at him. The pain returned but was more manageable this time. Gradually he remembered things, working backwards. He was lying in a tree, and it was broad daylight. His arm was pinned underneath him. That much was certain.

The boy began helping him to his feet. God, it hurt!

The tree was lying across the muddy road. It must have been blown down, and would have hit him with one of the branches. Come to think of it, that's just what had happened. He remembered the noise and the confusion, and a great overpoweringness swirling out of shadows towards him. Knocked him down. No idea how long ago that was. The wind had stopped now and the sun was almost shining through a blanket of ground glass.

The boy helped him to inch his way out of the splintered branches. He could still stand, anyway. Might have broken an arm, but legs were still working. He hobbled along the road, the boy supporting him. The pain was excruciating and exhausting.

He recognised the road. It was near Doctor Meg's house. That was lucky – Meg would be able to look after him, patch up his arm. Some unresolved recollection nearly rose to the surface, then subsided under a new shockwave of pain.

Doctor Meg's house just round the corner. Can just make it, leaning on the boy.

But Meg was coming towards them, pushing a large wheelbarrow full of medical supplies.

"James! What have you been doing to yourself? That arm needs a lot of attention. Hello Ramjohn, just take this pan-cart, will you?"

Something clicked, and he remembered it all.

"Alice is having her baby," he said desperately. "Can you go straight down there, please. Quick!"

"I'll go as soon as I've dealt with you. Ramjohn, take the pan-cart down to the hospital, please. James, just stay still a moment."

All sorts of intolerable tensions, mental and physical, welled up inside James. "You must go," he burst out, "Alice is rolling around in agony, she needs you, she can't take it anymore, please go, *now*."

He thought he might be sobbing. For God's sake, a grown man sobbing. But a moment later he felt the morphine swill round his body and rinse out the pain neatly, like drawing a huge thorn from a septic foot. Aha! Sleep now.

* * * * *

He was sitting in the wheelbarrow and Ramjohn was pushing him along the deserted road. Every so often they would come to a fallen tree, and then James would have to climb out carefully and pick his way over or through, nursing his right arm, which was encased in plaster and resting in a sling. Ramjohn was a priceless aide. He had soon returned to Meg with his load of medical supplies saying there was no hospital; she had raised her eyebrows and left him in charge of the patient while she went off to Brave Dolphin. Meg's house, which was well sheltered by the hills, had lost a few windows and many tiles, but was otherwise more or less intact. Ramjohn had instructions to keep his patient in bed until further orders, but James, frantic with worry, had persuaded him to wheel him home. It was a slow, muddy business, but they would get there in the end. They might even meet Doctor Meg coming back with news that he would never forget.

James could not stop himself rehearsing in his mind what that news might be. Would he be able to deduce the outcome in Meg's face as he saw her approach? Perhaps she would say, "James, all's well, Alice is fine, and your baby is as fit as a flea." Or she might say, "James, my dear, you must sit down and rest. I'm deeply sorry to have to tell you ..." In spite of the heat he shivered. He was certain that he did not have sufficient reserves of endurance for that, and he might behave disgracefully. But it wouldn't matter; not then; nothing would matter. He would abandon everything, and possibly go mad.

And suddenly they rounded a corner and saw Meg walking slowly towards them, eyes down, and her ravaged face showed disaster clearly and bluntly, like a stone.

CHAPTER TWENTY-THREE

James clambered awkwardly out of the wheelbarrow. He felt slightly drunk, as when one knows it should be possible for one's limbs to perform certain straightforward tasks, and they will eventually manage, but in the meantime one has to be patient with them. He told himself, this is the *moment critique*; try to behave decently. He sat down in the mud by the roadside.

Meg's boulder-like face was suspended over him now, a white sculpture with a great mouth drooping at the corners, the apotheosis of grief. How clear that face was! How finely detailed! So this was how you confronted tragedy, by careful observation of your surroundings, thus depersonalising the instant of realisation, which would otherwise be too much to bear. Well, hold on, James, he told himself, there is plenty to come, and plenty of time. All the time in the world.

"James ..." said the white face, eyes down. His legs in front of him felt weak and undisciplined. He ought to say something, even if he had no way of knowing what it would become in the saying.

"Tell me what happened," he said. "What's happened? Is she ..." His words felt drunk too.

"Gone," said the face, and a horrible church bell started tolling in his head, reminding him of tear-stained Sunday evenings in the nursery: ding-dong-ding-dong! Madness is easy, ding-dong! Prepare for woe, ding-dong! Come and wail, weep mightily, ding-dong-dead!

Trees swung gently into the blue sky with an air of ordinariness. There was a powerful smell of mud drying out in the sun.

Meg's sad old mouth was speaking, and he caught the weight of sorrow and resignation rather than the words.

But *what in heaven ...?*

"I have no hope," she was saying. "It's inconceivable that she should still be alive. Apparently they went out beyond the reef in the ski-boat, and a small open boat could not possibly survive. It's ... heart-breaking. I have no relations left in the world now. She was so young, and attractive, and happy. I must learn to accept that she is gone ... but James, you are still suffering from shock, you should not have moved from my house. You must go to Brave Dolphin now and lie down, yes. Ramjohn, tell your mother to keep him quiet and not allow him to get too excited about the baby. Alice's well – they're both well. I've got to go into the town now. There must be hundreds of casualties and the hospital has been blown down. The problem is quite unmanageable, but I must do what I can. It will be a relief to be so completely occupied. I'll come and see you in a day or two, yes – as soon as possible."

"God bless you, Doctor Meg," said Ramjohn.

"Goodbye," said James weakly. It was all he could manage, and the strong, sad face turned away. He watched her walk up the road and disappear round the corner, a lonely woman with her sorrow and her gigantic task ahead. His thoughts were confused, but it didn't matter. Alice was well, the baby was well, the hurricane over – they'd won! Whatever else happened, this would be true. A great cauldron of mental suffering was drained away. It was like the morphine.

"Come on, Dad!" said Ramjohn with a grin. "Into your pan-cart, all a-spraddle." James got in and they started jolting down the road again.

Ha! thought James, I don't yet know if it's a boy or a girl. Nor even if it's mine! But she's all right. Everything will be all right. Not far now.

* * * * *

Brave Dolphin was a ruin. The right-hand end was completely demolished; beams, tiles and pieces of fabric were strewn all over the garden. A thick layer of mud was drying over everything. Apart from the big palm, there were at least a dozen other trees down. But the left-hand half of the house was still standing defiantly, more or less intact, and in there would be Alice and her baby.

Spottiswoode met him at the door. "Why, cuh-dear, Jim-boy, you gone a-breaking your arm. Doctor Meg, she say you not to move all day. Ah'll just-tell Alice …"

He interrupted, a thing he did not normally do. "Is it a boy or a girl?"

"Why, it's a boy-chile, and favours his Dad so!"

Alice was sitting up in bed looking radiant. Resisting the impulse to throw himself at her feet, he kissed her on the forehead. She was heroic, exhausted, the great earth mother. He loved her, loved her love for him, loved loving her, loved her utterly and infinitely. She was startlingly young and beautiful.

"How do you feel, my special love?" he said.

"Tired and happy. How do you feel?"

"Devoted."

"How do you like your son?"

"My son! Where is he?"

"In his cot, over there."

In the basket was a tiny scrap of dishevelled human, crumpled and squashed like a miniature Winston Churchill.

"Spottiswoode says he looks just like me," he said.

"Don't you think so?"

"Well …"

"He's yours all right. I know it. He's got blue eyes, just like yours and mine."

"You are a clever girl."

"Oh yes."

"You must get some rest now, darling. Try to sleep."

"So must you – your poor arm."

"That doesn't matter. Nothing matters now."

She smiled – that majestic smile – and relapsed into something close to sleep. He tiptoed out and closed the door.

He went into the drawing-room, and his steps left footmarks in the mud as though he was walking on wet sand. He took off his shoes and lay down on the sofa. Spottiswoode and Ramjohn were clearing up in another part of the house. Relax, he told himself; your responsibilities are over for the moment. Later you must go in to the town and see what you can do to help. At present nothing is as important as your getting some rest.

But in spite of a great feeling of relief he found it impossible to sleep. The sun streamed in through the window, and there were no curtains he could draw – he remembered tearing them down to mop up with. And his brain was turning round and round in circles. I have a *son*, he kept telling himself; a son, a son! It's ours, mine. Alice produced it for me. She's done marvellously well – her finest hour. She's fine; she's marvellous. But La Rue and Freddy are lost – must go and look for any wreckage as soon as I can. As for Angus Swallow, what was he up to? Peace, think about these things later, he told himself. But still the old prayer wheel went round and round: we have a son, we have a son, we have a son. Sound in wind and limb, ours, mine.

* * * * *

But he must have slept, he decided, because he seemed to be waking up now, and his tiredness had become sleepiness. Yet the sun was still shining high in the sky. Someone had thrown the kitchen curtains over him and tucked him in. The sofa felt sticky and somewhat scratchy and – bless my soul – there was Doctor Meg again. She must have come back.

"Had a good sleep, James?"

"Wonderful sleep."

"Arm?"

"Comfortable enough. How's Alice?"

"They're both pretty well, yes. No insoluble problems at the moment. This is no place to be having babies, but they are all right so far."

"Thanks for coming back so soon."

"It's not all that soon. You've slept the clock round."

"Good God!" He sat up.

"You needed it. Now listen, James. You must not exert yourself for several days and be especially careful, yes. I had to set your arm without an x-ray. That required more manipulation than I would have wished, and you must give it a good chance, a good rest, a chance to heal itself properly. If you overdo it you may develop complications and you'll be less use to Alice and the baby when they need you. I can't afford to spend much more time down here."

"What's the hospital like?"

"It doesn't exist anymore. I've been treating patients in the streets …"

"I must do something to help." He felt quite strong now.

"So you shall. Alice needs a clean dry blanket, and you can walk up to my house and get one off the spare bed. Also a packet of detergent you'll find in the kitchen. Then straight back here and rest. Take things easy for the next three days. Give your arm a chance to mend. I must go," she glanced at her watch. "Yes. Alice is asleep. What are you going to call him?"

"Sirius. Or Mark. Or Freddy. I don't know."

She left.

He decided to have another look at his son. Did he really have blue eyes? He went quietly into the bedroom. They were both asleep and he told himself again that he was the father of this particular family.

Out. To Meg's house.

On the road, still obstructed by fallen trees, he rearranged his thoughts a little. It was indeed no place to be having babies. Babies needed hot water, nappies, powdery things, elaborately clean food. If Meg was too busy, how on earth would they manage? No, at all costs they must get away from this island, back to a new world of disinfectants and neighbours, and health visitors; and soon. Surely there would be an organisation for dealing with medical evacuation. Hurricanes were, after all, a well-known hazard in the West Indies. They had happened many times before.

And Angus Swallow – that's a strange business. The corpse would still be down there, broken and dried up, buzzing with flies. What had been his game? Had he set out on a vengeance cruise, or perhaps to reclaim La Rue, or was he spying on Alice, or was it just coincidence that he was cruising off Adventa in the path of the hurricane? Because if it was not coincidence, how could he have known of their whereabouts? Perhaps Moraes had been with him.

But James thought it was too much to hope for, that both the villains of the piece should have been polished off so tidily.

The dry, grey mud crunched under his shoes. It was covered with cracks like the bottom of a dried-out reservoir.

He reached Meg's house and went inside. It was strewn with clothes and rubbish. Evidently the hurricane had done more damage than he had remembered. It was not until he looked on the spare bed for the blanket that he realised that the place had been looted. There were no blankets. No provisions. No ornaments, no silver, no radio. Everything portable and valuable had been stolen, and the residue was littering the floors.

James felt himself quiver with anger. The bastards! They had ransacked her house while she was out attending to the injured. Meg's possessions were gone; she had surely lost everything she valued. He felt a great revulsion against the island and its inhabitants, and a strong desire to get Alice away as soon as possible.

Let these swine stew in their own juice, he thought.

But hold on, he thought again, don't be unfair. I am a visitor; Meg is not. There are thieves of all colours in all countries, as she would be the first to point out. Abandon those juvenile colonial ideas – if you can. This is an unpleasant crime, not a racial issue.

Through his anger, which was still strong, he caught himself half wishing he could be a looter too, and with a just perceptible twinge of resentment he thought that if there was to be a wholesale rampage of looting he might be the only one not to profit by it. And that, he thought again, is presumably how these rampages gather momentum.

He walked away without the blanket or the detergent. He would have to try the town. He turned down the hill towards it. Perhaps someone would be able to spare a rug for a girl with a new baby. Perhaps he could also scrounge a hammer and some nails, and patch up Brave Dolphin a bit.

Round the next corner the whole town came into view. It was flattened.

He walked down towards it, slowly, appalled. The town was almost entirely flattened. Most of the buildings had been pulverised. One or two houses were recognisable as such, but had been blown over on their side like collapsed wine boxes, or tilted at crazy angles. Everything was caked with grey mud, and on the mud were black motionless objects. These were people he then realised – was it possible some of them were still alive? He walked more slowly. God, what an unholy mess.

He reached the debris that had once been Adventa Town, bare foundations of ex-houses, filthy clothing, crumpled furniture, and spillikin-piles of planks. There was a sofa, upside down with one leg sticking up into the air. There was a piece of matchboard covered with rather pretty flowered wallpaper. And a man propped up in the ruins of his house, watching him silently, motionless.

And that man must be dead. Indeed, quite dead.

Two women mumbled in low tones not ten yards from the body. Why had they not shut his eyes?

The sun streamed down on the ghost town, sharpening the colours and edges. It was an eerie scene.

There was a muddy piano on its back and a joyful tiny child thumping the keys. It made no sound.

But there was a sound. It was the noise of a Land Rover changing gear as it bumped over some wreckage and came towards him. James's taut stomach muscles relaxed a little with this reminder of civilisation. There were two white figures in the Land Rover, and it was slowing down.

It stopped, and Mark Hillier got out.

"Huwes, I presume." Mark held out his hand with mock formality. "I was just wondering what could possibly turn this surrealist scene into reality. But I hardly expected you. Well, well."

CHAPTER TWENTY-FOUR

He was telling Alice about it.

"Mark said he got here in the ship last night. He brought a lot of food and clothing and a party of sailors from the *Fowey*. The ship went off soon after landing them – apparently one of the other islands has been very badly hit also. Mark sent his love to you, but he was too busy to stop and talk much. He drove me to the commissariat, as they call it – the dump of blankets and rations – and told me to take what we needed."

James had brought two horse blankets that were clean but smelt vaguely of army stores, and a ration pack.

"Did you walk all the way back?"

"No, he offered to drive me. I asked him to come up this evening, and he was delighted to. We came to the first tree across the road and he said 'Ho, road's blocked, I'll get it cleared before tonight.' He seems to be organising things in a big way. He's coming up as soon as he can, about nine-ish."

"James, how could you? I haven't a thing to wear. And my hair needs washing."

He roared with laughter. "You are staying in bed, lady."

It was good to laugh again, but unfortunately it woke the baby and precipitated the routine for feeding. He watched, fascinated. She certainly looked charming and beautiful, and young Huwes played his part with gusto.

"Babies suit you," he said.

"It's nice to know I can have them. Lots of women can't."

"And such a fine specimen."

"What are we going to call him?"

"How about Felix?"

"That's my father's name."

"I know. I think it might oil the wheels a bit on our return."

"Our return …" The thought was longer than the sentence.

So he seemed to be called Felix, and they would settle other names for him later. But the future had loomed up momentarily, and both of them were preoccupied with it for a time. There will be problems, and difficulties, and possibly unpleasantness, thought James. She is actually married to someone else. But all that can wait, a little longer anyway.

"Don't worry, darling," he said. "I'm not going to lose you now. Either of you."

"Whatever happens?"

"Whatever happens. Though charcoal sprout and sailors turn to swine."

"You sound like Spottiswoode. But not quite as impressive."

* * * * *

Mark arrived very late, so that Alice and Felix were asleep when James saw the lights of the Land Rover flashing through the broken trees. He went out to greet him.

"Welcome, Mark."

"Hello there. Nice place you've got. Or it was. Much damage?"

"Yes, I'm afraid the house is pretty well past repair."

"It's a good deal better than any building in the town, except possibly the police station. Were you flooded?"

"Up to the windowsills."

"But nothing swept away and most of the roof intact. You were damned lucky."

"I suppose so, but it didn't much feel like it at the time. Come in. Excuse the mud."

"Wouldn't be home without it."

Mark said he had not eaten all day, so they unpacked some tins of army rations and heated them on the little burner. They had a glass of whisky while the soup was boiling.

"Tell me all," said James.

And Mark began to talk. He was a good talker.

"Well, we first heard of the hurricane about a week ago, when the ship was in Kingston. They can position these things pretty accurately by satellite these days, particularly if they are big ones – and Anthea, as they called her, was one of the biggest ever, 200-knot winds. So we plotted her on the chart for two days, and she seemed to be going straight for Guyana. There's a dump of hurricane relief stores in Kingston, and we loaded a vast quantity on to the upper deck and set off looking most extraordinary and feeling very top heavy. Fortunately we had fairly calm seas at that stage as we belted across the Caribbean, rolling slowly from side to side and wondering if the whole lot would slide. But they didn't. Then Anthea altered course for the Grenadines, and we prepared to land a disaster party at whichever island she should hit. It was an absolute tonic for the ship, I can tell you – we've spent so long swanning around quaffing jungle juice that it was a joy to be doing something tangibly useful for a change. As I fitted up and briefed my party I couldn't help wondering what on earth a place would look like after suffering 200-knot winds and the attendant tidal waves. I thought of my own village, and imagined what the effect would be there, with roofs lifting, walls falling, and the flood waters crashing down Blewburton Hill before a blinding wind – was it anything like that?"

"Something like it, but the water didn't crash, it just came silent flooding in. Here's your soup."

"Thanks. Anyway I read the Contingency Plan on disaster relief and it all seemed pretty tenuous. Then it became clear that Adventa would catch the worst of the hurricane, with possibly little Toriacao next door. So we slowed down a bit, to keep in the navigable quadrant in case it recurved, and when we were quite sure that the storm had passed we came in, and arrived off the reef late last night. It was hell coming through the reef – all the navigational marks had been swept away, and I had to take one or two risks I wouldn't have liked to answer for at the Navigation School. Anyway, we reached the harbour without mishap and anchored off. It was completely dark and quiet inshore – most unnerving when the Captain and I got into a boat and set off towards the loom of the land to see what was going on."

"How did you know where the jetty was?"

"We knew where the jetty should have been from the chart, but when we got close in there was nothing but a few piles and a plank or two. Complete silence everywhere. We decided to wade ashore. I jumped into about two feet of water, but the Captain wasn't so lucky – he stumbled in up to his chest and dropped his torch, so it was with a good deal of vigorous language that we splashed up the beach and got ashore. I had a rather puny pusser's torch of my own, and the Captain was swearing so much I gave it to him and immediately tripped over a sort of bundle of wet clothes. 'All right there, Mark?' said the Captain. 'No, bugger it, can't see what I've fallen onto, sir.' He flashed the torch at me and I was surrounded by dead bodies, lying all over the beach like jetsam. It was uncanny, swearing so healthily in the middle of all those drowned men ..."

"Appalling. This tin says Carrots (thin). Would you like it with your Stew (beef)?"

"I could eat anything with this splendid mess of potage."

But he was wrong, because the tin in fact contained a Mars Bar, neatly packed in paper shavings, and having been boiled it was more than Mark could take with his hash just then.

"Well, we tramped around a bit in the mud and the pitch dark," Mark continued, "and you've seen what it looks like, but I can assure you it was even more ghastly then. There were lots of bodies around, of course, but those who were alive didn't utter a sound, just sat there, so it was difficult to see who was alive or dead. They hardly looked at us, or if we shone the torch full into someone's face the reaction would be apathetic – a sort of pleading leave-me-to-die-in-peace. They were stupefied, and numb, and shocked. One young girl seemed to have a bit more life than the others, she got up when we approached, and the Captain said 'Are you all right? Have you got food and enough water? Can we help?' She just stopped and looked crazily at us as though we were men from the moon. We didn't get a single coherent word out of anyone. It was a town of zombies."

James remembered something of his own feelings during the hurricane. He could recall clearly enough giving up, as the water had spilled into the bedroom and all seemed lost. He had only just avoided becoming a zombie himself.

"Then we went back to the waiting boat with our own feelings. I felt that here was a job to do that I would remember all my life, but – how on earth to start? The Captain was almost speechless with depression, and kept muttering 'poor bastards' as we waded out to the boat. We went back aboard and had a little conference and decided what to do: nothing till sunrise, then I would land with my team and half the stores, and the ship would go off to have a look at Toriacao. I went to my comfortable bunk and thought of those unfortunates ashore, squatting helplessly in the muddy ruins of their homes. I lay awake for hours, visualising all too clearly what had happened – the hurricane heading suddenly for Adventa with little warning, the mountainous seas, the tidal wave swamping all the low-lying land, and those fearful 200-knot winds. I have a fertile imagination, and it's worse imagining details than living through them – you lived through them, so you wouldn't agree."

"Oh, but I do!" said James. Poor La Rue.

"Do you? Interesting. Anyway, eventually I dropped off, and just before daylight yesterday morning I was called to the bridge and told to go inshore with my party of armed sailors – I must say I would not have given them rifles if the Contingency Plan hadn't said so, but I'm glad I did – a man with a rifle radiates authority, and the locals were desperate for authority just then. There's nothing racial about this, it's just the state of affairs after a massive collective shock. We waded ashore amongst the dead bodies again, and there seemed to be somewhat fewer in daylight. The boat went back for its first load of stores and left me wondering what the blazes to do about landing them. A lad about three feet high emerged from somewhere and gave me a kind of comic salute. I said, feeling ridiculous, 'Are there any boats about?' and he said 'I've got a big boat,' and invited me to go with him. Feeling even more ridiculous, I followed him to the remains of a house literally lying on its side with a door facing skywards, and inside was a large flat-bottomed boat, miraculously more or less intact. The very thing! Twelve pairs of hands round, and we just managed to lift it and launch it, and with its help got all the stores ashore in an hour.

"As the boat went back after the last load, the ship weighed anchor and set off for Toriacao. I had twelve men, forty tons of stores, and a radio. It was up to me."

"This tin is called Apple Sweet, Mark. Try it?"

"Fine. Don't let me keep you up, will you."

"I had twenty-five hours sleep yesterday, so to speak. Shan't need any more for a while. Would you like some rum over your Apple Sweet?"

"Thanks. It tastes of pears. Not bad."

"What did you do then?"

"Well, it seemed to me that the locals were numb with the destruction of their town and we had to make a gesture of rebuilding. So I left a guard on the stores and we went around righting houses."

"You can't be serious!" said James.

"Indeed I am. Most of the houses are wood and were blown over and squashed and floated around in the flood. The technique is to find one that hasn't been crumpled, then get about six stalwarts to heave-ho and up she rises, rather lopsided and rhomboid, but at least the owner's got his own four walls on a new site, or perhaps someone else's four walls on his own site. More important, it's a morale booster to see something upright."

"Well done, Mark."

"No credit to me – they just needed a spark from outside to put a bit of hope into a situation that seemed literally hopeless. People at last began to see a connection with reality again. Then in the rubble we came across the church bell."

"So?"

"So I sets it up by the stores dump on a pole and rings the hours. I think that was a bit of a brainwave. It restored time. People began to stir. We gave out food as best we could. There was no mad rush, no disorder. That was yesterday."

"What about today?"

"Rather different," said Mark. "They're coming to life. And tomorrow more so, I expect. I've now got the full-scale administration of the town on my hands. They are discovering that they are very hungry. There have been some cases of looting – and that will get worse, no doubt at all. But people are beginning to rally round too. We are organising the men into teams, to bury bodies, clear the roads, try to patch up some buildings. My sailors will be less workers than sentries from now on. We were trying to get the main generator working this afternoon. That woman doctor-friend of yours has been doing great stuff amongst the casualties with no facilities at all. We found a Land Rover that works, as you saw. But by jove, there's a Herculean task ahead. Have you ever thought how much one takes for granted in the civilised world – shops, money, police, clothing, shelter, water, sewage? – you don't notice them till they suddenly aren't there. In Adventa everything, every single thing has stopped functioning and we've got to stoop and build 'em up with worn-out tools. It's exhausting. Fascinating. Like the day of judgement."

"How so, day of judgement?"

"James, I've never run a town before. No one's ever taught me how to distribute food or bury bodies. Suddenly I'm in the position of a rather shaky dictator, and decisions I make affect sixteen hundred people. But my father always says naval officers can do anything – he once had to arrest a lunatic axe-man in a sheikh's harem. So I keep trying."

"You remind me of my moment of reckoning, when the sea rose to the windowsill and Alice in labour. It was like a peep through the crack of doom. I'm afraid I more or less gave up."

"Hm. It must have been pretty desperate. The eye of the hurricane passed right over Adventa, or within a mile or so. As you know, the town's built on low-lying land; more accurately, a swamp. The highest point is about six feet above Mean High Water Springs. Tropical revolving storms always build up colossal tidal waves, and it seems that twelve feet of surging water went sweeping through the town. One wall of the Police Headquarters is still standing, and it shows a muddy high-water mark higher than I can reach. Of course this great mass of foaming sea effectively dammed the extremely swollen river, which then started spilling out towards the east, smashing houses, drowning the occupants, and sweeping all the gubbins out to sea."

"I can't describe how fearsome that sea was."

"You don't need to. I once made a small study of Turner's rough seas for a painting I was doing. I can imagine it – only too vividly."

"How many dead, do you know?"

"No, I don't. We've buried about sixty bodies – we had to, and not by any means all of them had been identified. That was a dictatorial decision, but three days in this heat ... there was really nothing else to be done. We are still finding corpses. Of course some people are thought to have evacuated the place at the last minute, and there's no means of knowing yet whether they're alive or dead. I expect the death toll will be about a hundred, maybe more."

"And what's the next move?"

"Well, we've got to get people working. I've got all the food, so I have the whip hand. Tomorrow we hold a kind of Both Watches of the Hands, and try to detail off parties of able-bodied citizens to start clearing up the shambles."

"Do you think that will work?"

"Yes, that bit'll work all right. I had two bits of luck. First someone found the seal of the Catholic church ..."

"I don't quite follow."

"... and then someone else found the mayor. The mayor has volunteered to pick out Leading Hands for these working parties, and when the job's done to my satisfaction I will give them a piece of signal pad with the church seal stamped on it. They then take this chitty along to the commissariat, and get some food in exchange."

"Sound scheme."

"It's a start. That's all they need – a start."

"Whisky?"

"Thanks. I've been talking too much. Tell me about your affairs."

"Alice and Felix …"

"Ah."

"Felix Mark – are both as well as can be expected, but I'm not too happy about them staying here. I wondered if there are any plans for evacuating the injured, that we could muscle in on."

"Your doctor friend was talking of this, but I haven't had a moment to think about it. What do you think we can do?"

"How about …"

"That's it, good idea – we'll divert a liner."

"You can't divert a liner!"

"James, after one full day's dictatorship there's nothing I can't do."

"I'll come and give you a hand tomorrow as soon as I can. I've got to look for two friends of mine who I think have been drowned."

"I'm sorry," said Mark dreamily. He was now lying back on the sofa and dropping off fast. He had perhaps done more in a day than most people do in a week.

"And, Mark, Angus Swallow's dead."

But he had not heard. James left him sprawled across the sofa and went into the bedroom. Alice was awake, Felix asleep.

"You've had a good natter," she whispered. "What's going on?"

"Mark's going to divert a liner to pick us up."

"You can't divert a liner just like that, can you?"

"Mark's in an unstoppable mood. At the moment he's sound asleep on the sofa."

The baby started crying. He seemed rather sensitive to whispering.

CHAPTER TWENTY-FIVE

It was three days later. James was having a bath. He poured in some warm water from a jerry-can Spottiswoode had filled. It was a glorious luxury.

Well, he thought, civilisation's gradually returning. Soon be back to something near normal, although it will be ten years before this island really recovers. And some people will never quite recover. Doctor Meg. My Aunt Katharine, who will be hearing of Freddy's death round about now. Me. When the sea reached the windowsill I more or less gave up; Mark was surprised when I told him.

But we weathered the storm. We did win. And most important of all Alice seems to be unscathed. Marvellous how having babies seems to be its own defence mechanism. The baby's got a bit of a sore bottom, but Alice couldn't be better. Those great folds of slack flabbiness are beginning to disappear into her normal figure. She always had rather a trim belly, and nice rounded hips, I remember. It will be good to see them again. I wonder if … no, perhaps it's too soon. She has been very cosy but rather shy and sexless since the baby. Childbirth is a curious thing.

Overarching everything is the fact that I am very much in love with her. She is, in practically all important respects, my wife, and has borne my child. I can see now that family love is bigger, more interesting, more subtle, than any other kind that has come my way. You don't choose it anyway; it just seems to happen. Trite, but true.

Herewith one faultless rosebud,
A symbol trite but true;
Accept it as a précis
Of the love I have for you.

Who wrote that ridiculous doggerel? Some introspective lover groping for words – just like me.

I am sincerely glad to have traded a bachelor's supposed freedom for the habits and conversation of marriage.

But what about La Rue, you hypocritical randy old goat?

Poor La Rue, of the water-skis and the singing piano and the wild dreams about the moon. A wasted, lost life.

He remembered the tiring search along the coast, investigating all the refuse thrown up by the sea. It had taken a long time, since much of the debris was scattered some way inland, and most of it was timber and planks of various sizes, which needed close scrutiny before you could decide it was not the wreckage of a boat. He had passed the spot where *Peccavi* had been dispersed to the winds. The body had presumably been removed by one of Mark's burial parties. Apart from the uprooted tree there was no sign of that particular drama. And if *Peccavi* left no trace, he had thought, what hope for the little speedboat? But he had searched thoroughly, as he knew he must, and was grateful for not finding anything.

So La Rue and Freddy had been transferred from the "Missing" to the "Dead" list, and their names had been tapped out by the Radio Operator back to the ship and the world at large. Angus Swallow too.

James put his broken arm, itching inside its plaster, on the side of the bath and stirred the water with his feet. Swallow – a strange business, that. Mark had been astounded when he had heard of it, and felt sure the visit had been intended as some kind of reprisal. "But it's an ill wind," he had said. "As I understand your extraordinary story, that disposes of all the baddies except one, doesn't it?"

Mark had stayed with them every night. Gradually the house was becoming more habitable, and they were now able to give him the bed in the spare room. Every evening he brought back news of the town and told of progress in the rescue work. The Army were moving in, flying four at a time in a tiny civil aircraft on to a grass strip behind one of the planter's houses. There were now about twenty soldiers in Adventa, headed by a lieutenant-colonel, and more were expected. Mark had turned over everything to the soldiery because the ship was running out of fuel and would soon have to leave the area; she was in fact in harbour that day and was due to go the following morning. Meanwhile about fifty sailors were rebuilding the jetty.

"It's fascinating," Mark had said, "seeing how these pongoes behave. The first planeload contained the colonel, a subaltern and two sergeants. They were magnificent – calm, level headed, very quick on the uptake. We got on famously. Of course they know much more about sentries and looting and patrols than I do, and they had some good ideas. More men arrived, and they put the ideas into swift action. But now typewriters are starting to appear, and a Transport Officer is demanding signatures and work-sheets, and a Joint Operations Centre vets all my snap decisions. The organisation's beginning to bureaucratise. There's a Disaster Committee meeting every evening, which is a drain on one's patience. Still, they've got to work much more with the locals, and gradually get the town to take over its own responsibilities. I've just scratched the surface of the problem."

But you haven't done too badly, thought James, lying back in the warm water. You made them realise they weren't bloody well finished, and you managed to stir them into action. You deterred most of the would-be looters without a shot being fired, and so far no fires, no epidemics, no actual starvation. Adventa has got a lot to thank you for.

The door behind him opened, and Spottiswoode came in, short of breath and shiny.

"Hello, Spotto."

"More matter for a May morning."

"What's happened?"

"My, James, you better just-get right out of that tub, there's a great big passenger-boat a-sailing right by your back door. Look, man."

She helped him out of the bath and led him to the window. Looking out over the prostrate palm and beyond the reef, they saw the stately mass of a liner gliding smoothly across their visible sector of blue sea. He watched, dripping, by the open window, and the ship seemed to lean back in the water like a swan.

"That's your ship, Jim-boy, you and Alice and baby Felix gotta be on that ship. My, didn't Mark just-say he go bring a boat, take you away? Ah'm sorry see you go, man. La Rue gone drowned, and Freddy, and Doctor Meg's house all mashiated. Now you all a-going, Ah'm just-sorry see you go."

She began to mop big tears with a red handkerchief. It was the first time she had mentioned La Rue.

He put his wet good arm round her shoulders.

"Never mind, Spotto, I'll be back some day. We won't forget each other. You saved us all, and I can never forget that. We'll come back sometime, you wait and see. What did Shakespeare say, 'Parting is such sweet sorrow'?"

"'Farewell, the gods with safety stand about thee.'" And she left him.

He dried himself. They could be ready in half an hour. Mark had told them not to waste any time in getting down to the jetty. No liner would wait for long.

It occurred to him that he might have found it difficult, with anyone but Spottiswoode, to converse quite so naturally without any clothes on. There was no one like Spottiswoode.

* * * * *

"Got everything, Alice my love?" They were in the wreck of the kitchen, nearly off.

"Everything that matters, I think."

"You don't seem to have much. Are you sure you haven't left anything behind?"

"Sure enough." That smile.

"Not taking the baby?"

"Oh, do you think we'll need it?"

"Might as well bring it, just in case. You never know when it mightn't come in 'andy."

Spottiswoode appeared carrying Felix, and placed him in a nest she had prepared in the wheelbarrow. He looked healthy enough but a bit red and sore in places, the result, James supposed, of not having all those powders and lotions showered upon him. But did babies from the backwoods of Borneo have powders and lotions? He thought not. And Borneo babies seemed to survive.

"He's got more luggage than both of us," said Alice. It was true. James had a bright red spare shirt, a toothbrush, a little money, some underclothing, and his razor. Alice had not much more.

"Have you got a bag to put our things in?"

"No. But better than a bag, I've got an idea."

He spread his red shirt out on the table, and put all their possessions onto it. Then he rolled them up into a ball, tied it by the sleeves to a piece of cane, and hoisted it on to his shoulder. It was the quintessence of a tramp's traditional bundle.

He couldn't stop himself bursting into song:

"Wi' me bundle on me shoulder,
Faith! There's no man could be bolder ..."

"Let's hit the road," he said, pleased with himself.

Spottiswoode wheeled the barrow out into the sun, and they followed her.

"Sad to be leaving Brave Dolphin," he said.

"Poor Brave battered Dolphin."

"Here was born Felix Mark Frederick Huwes ..."

"1968–2068."

"Scholar, poet, philanthropist ..."

"Cabinet Minister, Nobel Prize winner, First Baron Churbridge ..."

"Who gave of his millions for the alleviation of human suffering ..."

"And rebuilt this, his birthplace, as a world centre for the study of underdone mutton chops."

They looked back at the house, half of it habitable, half in ruins, wholly deserted.

"Our first home," he said. "We can never have another first home."

"Oh, James! What's to become of us?"

He could sense the panic not far away.

"First of all, we get ourselves home. Then we'll go and talk to my solicitors in London. I have great faith in them. They understand about these things in London. Then divorce, marriage, large family ..."

"Oh, I don't want any more. For the moment anyway."

The panic was averted, but he felt sad. There would be trials of love and patience ahead. Their desert island idyll was over. Back to the world of Moraes and what-would-people-think.

But he soon discovered the inherent jauntiness of a tramp's bundle, swinging on the end of a stick. It was impossible to be sad for more than a few yards. They smiled at each other and held hands, and the sadness was reduced to a slight background hum of wistfulness. She looked young and pretty.

"*In contenti e in allegria*" she quoted, "*solo amor può terminar.*"

"Translation?"

"Only love can end in contentment and happiness."

Nice girl, he thought. Clever mother. My wife. Proto-wife. Ultra-wife. Whatever. As near as dammit my wife.

* * * * *

They walked slowly into the town. The roads were fairly clear now. Planks had been stacked in piles, and most of the mud shovelled away. There were a few soldiers about. Makeshift houses were beginning to appear, the boards not straight or at right angles, but just about serviceable. Adventa was emerging from the rubbish.

And there was the *Fowey*, pointing out to sea, with the white ensign drooping from her stern. Beyond the reef they could see the liner at anchor, being either unable or unwilling to attempt the unbuoyed channel to the harbour. Down by the jetty a throng of sailors, stripped to the waist, were beavering away with planks and hammers. The little pier looked almost restored.

And it seemed that all the halt, lame and disabled were converging on the scene. Two men carried a bed like a stretcher; on it a woman was tossing restlessly under a sheet. A man hobbled along on crutches improvised from two paddles, one leg swathed in bandages. There were fathers with crying children, and children with crying smaller children. All those with serious injuries had been told to wait for the liner, which would take them to hospital in Bridgetown.

As he approached the jetty James saw that in fact most of the town seemed to have gathered to see everyone off. It was perhaps the first collective action since the hurricane, and everyone was talking excitedly. A kind of greeting, something between a cheer and an ooh of sympathy, went up as each casualty came on to the wharf. But James was not prepared for the reception they gave his party. Maybe it was sight of Spottiswoode, who had a large number of friends, or the tiny baby in the wheelbarrow, or the classic picture of young love and wounded hero; or maybe they identified James with the sources of food and assistance that they expected as a right but were no less extravagantly grateful for; but a loud rumble of acclamation arose and one or two whistles. People waved, and grinned, and discussed them volubly. They felt welcomed as well as bidden farewell.

Meg was there, checking off her patients on a list. She came up to them, grey and gaunt.

"I'm glad you managed to get down here so promptly," she said, ticking their names on her list. "That's just about all the evacuees now, yes. What a load off my mind when I see you all safely off for Bridgetown. Twenty adults and twelve children. All of them should have had proper medical attention a week ago."

"I feel a fraud amongst all these serious cases," said James.

"I don't think you need. This is no place for newborn babies, or broken arms for that matter. You need a proper convalescence."

"Meg, we've just left Brave Dolphin as we found it, that is …"

"That's all right, James, I'll think what to do about the house when I've got more time. I suppose it belongs to me now, yes."

Alice said: "Meg, I'll never forget how you helped me. Goodbye and God bless you."

"God bless, my dear. Take care of yourself and your beautiful baby."

James had noticed a profound emotional attachment between Meg and Alice before. Understandable. Alice could scarcely have had a more emotional situation than the one Meg had rescued her from.

"Meg looks tired," he said to Alice. "She's sorry to see us go. She has been a brick."

"Possibly a saint."

One of the liner's boats was approaching, and the crowd was becoming denser. "Stand back *please,* stand back *please,*" a Petty Officer was shouting. "All the injured this way, *please.*"

They said goodbye to Spottiswoode, who was quite cheerful now. They promised to write to each other, God spare life.

"All the injured *this* way."

"That doesn't apply to you," said Mark at their elbow. "The GI's a bit of a tyrant, he's used to drilling sailors on parade grounds. Don't believe I've ever heard him say please before. He's doing a good job. We should be able to get you all into one boat. It was a bit of luck there was a British ship so close. The *Orpheus* will have at least one doctor on board, and apparently she's got room for all of you. Bridgetown has been warned you're coming. I must say I think you are well out of it here. They tell me the fire danger gets worse every day. Also the pongoes say the dogs are getting out of hand and they plan a dog-shoot at dusk this evening. Sounds highly dangerous to me, and I shall hide. I hope you have a good voyage. I've never discovered what passengers do at sea – we must have dinner in London sometime and you shall tell me. Here's your boat now."

"Thank you, Mark, for everything you've done for us – all three of us – and everybody else in this wonderful place." Alice was good at thanking people, with her steady-eyed smile. She always sounded a hundred per cent sincere.

The boat came alongside the rebuilt jetty. Someone in the sternsheets started waving.

It *can't* be.

But it was.

Oz.

CHAPTER TWENTY-SIX

Oz was first out of the boat, and came bounding along the jetty waving both hands in the air above his head. There was no mistaking that face which hung in folds like a bloodhound, or that zestful enthusiasm.

"Stiffen the lizards!" were his first words.

"Good morning, sir," said James, offering a left-handed handshake.

Oz was cheerfully flabbergasted. It was an appealing sight. "Jumping cuttlefish," he said.

James was enjoying the situation too.

"Alice, I think you will remember Commander Hodges – Alice Moraes."

"Of course," said Oz, remembering a little but understanding nothing.

"And this is Felix," said James.

"Felix? ..."

"Felix Huwes. He's got some other names too, but we haven't quite decided on them yet. Have we, darling?"

"Not altogether," said Alice.

"I see," said Oz, talking slowly but thinking fast. He did not like being at a loss, and James thought he would by now have deduced most of the facts.

"Very good to see you again, sir. Are you on your way home in the *Orpheus*?"

"I am. And are you – all of you – being evacuated with the wounded?"

"Yes, we are."

"Astounding coincidence."

"Lots to tell you."

"Well, I came ashore to assist with embarking the casualties. The Master's insisting on getting away before noon, so let me help you aboard. We can talk later. I've got some news for you, too. We were expecting to have to wade ashore. Someone's done good work getting this jetty rebuilt."

He pronounced it "rebeelt". Unmistakably Oz-speak.

They stepped carefully down into the boat. Alice was helped by a large, grinning sailor, and for a moment her slim forearm was gripped by his strong, red hand. The baby was passed down in a bundle of clothing. "Don't drop it, Jimmy!" said someone from around Glasgow. It was strange and exhilarating to be back amongst one's own countrymen again.

James felt vulnerable with one arm in plaster. Boats are designed on the assumption that their occupants have two hands. But Nelson must have managed somehow, uncomplainingly.

Eventually all the injured were embarked, and the boat drew away from the pier. It seemed the whole world was waving them goodbye. Meg, Mark, Spottiswoode, all the sailors, all the people waved. Alice waved back vigorously and James copied her. He felt a great affection towards the little island that had hosted them for six weeks. They would never forget their island in the sun, with its friendly folk, and its catastrophe.

I hope Adventa revives, he thought. I hope to come back one day to find her prospering.

People were still waving, but as individuals had become indistinct. They merged back into their own lives, and the boat from the *Orpheus* headed out to sea.

Oz was beside them, in high spirits.

"What a fantastic piece of luck," he was saying. "All through the business of the last two months I've been wondering where you could have got to. I've managed to repatriate all the crew except Framley, who still isn't allowed to travel by air. So I'm bringing him home. We picked up this ship in Panama, and were a few hours out of Port of Spain when we diverted to Adventa to rescue the casualties. How did you break your arm?"

"I was hit by a falling tree."

"That hurricane must have been ferocious. Was the baby born before or after?"

"More or less during."

"Hm. You must tell me everything very soon. You and Framley are the only residual casualties of the whole ghastly *Mozart* saga. Rod Trumper turned up all right, and he's flown home. Some money came through, mercifully. Nothing more happened about the wreck. Santa Rosa was pretty well back to normal when we left. There's a new British Consul."

"Any news of Moraes?" asked James.

"None."

They were passing HMS *Fowey* now, a gleaming grey piece of abstract art. They all three watched her. James surreptitiously stroked the fair hairs on Alice's forearm. It was difficult to believe that so many different emotions could have been packed into the last half hour.

* * * * *

So James found himself taking passage once again. It was his third ship in three months, and with each change, he reflected, his dependants had increased in number.

The trip to Bridgetown was only half a day, and the ship turned over one anteroom for the exclusive use of the Adventa people. The ship's doctor bustled to and fro busily; he had never before found his professional services so much in demand. His patients strewed themselves round the padded benches and the armchairs, or sat on the deck with their backs against the bar, and mostly slept. They were more comfortable than they had been for a week.

Oz swiftly arranged for a passage in the *Orpheus* all the way home for James and Alice. "I tried to get you a first-class berth," he said. "Winter said I was to come home first-class, so I don't see why you shouldn't too. But surprisingly they haven't any first-class billets left. So you'll have to slum it way down on D deck. Not a bad double cabin, as a matter of fact. There'll be room for Felix."

A steward appeared and addressed himself to James.

"Would you check in with the Assistant Purser on B deck, sir," he said. "And I can't find your baggage – was it labelled?"

James gave him the red bundle. "This is all there is. Please show my wife down to the cabin while I see the purser."

It was the first time he had ever said "my wife" in public, and it gave him a good deal of pleasure. He was indeed back in the world again. And the steward, naturally enough, did not doubt that they were properly married. But would the purser ask some awkward questions, or demand passports?

In fact he said:

"Welcome aboard, sir. I'm glad to hear you're going to come with us back to Southampton. I'm afraid I haven't a first-class cabin available right now, but I'll have one free after Bermuda. Your cabin will be D52, your steward Steward Harting. Now let me just get my list up to date – what name did you say, sir?"

"Huwes." He spelt it. He always had to spell it.

"Initials, sir?"

"Just J."

"And the wife, sir?"

"A."

"Thank you, sir. I hope you enjoy the passage."

First, no one would know they were not married until they reached Immigration in Southampton. Secondly, Oz asking for a first-class passage had ensured that they would be treated like lords, even in second-class accommodation. But thirdly – dreaded Bermuda again.

He found their cabin. It was small, but entirely adequate, with light blue bulkheads and a large brass-rimmed porthole. Alice was bedding down the baby in a ship's cot provided by Steward Harting. They were not air-conditioned, but there was plenty of air. There was a large inviting double bed. They would be comfortable here. He grinned at Alice and went over to the open porthole, and putting his head and shoulders out saw the vast smooth sweep of the ship's side, and the sea crawling below. They were just beginning to move.

"Somewhat different from our last voyage," she said. The steward had left them.

"Slightly more room, slightly cooler."

"Slightly more legal."

He paused.

"Don't let future uncertainties spoil things for the present, my love," he said. "The future is always unknowable. Be happy. Now."

"Oh, but I am – exuberantly."

The word cheered him. Conversation with Alice would never be dull. How had he ever thought so? She was much more articulate than he was.

"Let's go and have a drink with Oz. He's absolutely eaten with curiosity."

He kissed her thoroughly. Ah, but she was good to kiss, with her warm breath like clear air. And that first gin-and-tonic – tall, icy, tinged with blue, and with a neat slice of lemon – that would be good too.

* * * * *

The days galloped by. Three of them passed in the lazy sunshine-cruise routine of too much food, drink and sleep. But as he leant on the rail and watched the gently-tinted landscape of Bermuda slip past, he had time to recall all kinds of memories: *Mozart's* maiden voyage; Lady Steyne's arrival; the first Swallow party; La Rue; that dramatic gamble when he had, with La Rue's and Freddy's help, kidnapped Alice – near this very spot, he thought, looking out towards Spanish Point. There was the house where she had spent six miserable months, almost a prisoner. And Grand-Piano Island slid into view. It was an odd business. She was below now, feeding Felix, and he would join her soon. Neither of them cared to go ashore during the half day they were to spend in Bermuda.

He put his elbows on the rail. The ship's doctor had renewed the plaster, and many of the passengers had autographed it. He smiled as he thought how the whole ship had lionised them, the young couple with the baby and the broken arm, who had so bravely withstood that dreadful hurricane and lost all their possessions. It made a good story, which he had not discouraged. The plaster was a magnificent souvenir and, although sometimes itchy, he would be half sorry to lose it.

Oz joined him.

"I remember when this dockyard was alive with ships," said Oz. "Look at it now. Damn shame."

"Sic transit ..."

"Lots of things are a damn shame. Do you remember that joiner?"

"The one who hanged himself at Cowes?"

"He. Do you know, I think he must have surprised Moraes tinkering with the safe and got done in in consequence."

"But how could Moraes have fixed that safe, with all those wheels and things?"

"I think he did. I've been enquiring about those safes. Each wheel has a slot, and when all the slots are aligned by setting the combination, the locking bar drops home. But, if you cut another set of slots in the wheels – not impossible to do carefully with a small hacksaw – the safe will open on *that* combination as well as the proper one. And, if you remember, you said you saw 'slots' in the wheels. You should have been able to see only one."

"Good grief."

"Never underestimate your enemy. Moraes is a clever, evil, vicious bastard, and his mother probably mated with a many-banded krait."

For Oz this was pretty strong.

He went on, "He's been fooling us for a year. Long enough, don't you think?"

"Entirely too long."

"I'm going ashore this afternoon to reconnoitre that Swallow house. I'll probably draw a blank, but you never know."

"Do you think that's wise?"

"We'll see."

* * * * *

Oz did draw a blank, or nearly so. He had found the house looking empty, but not long empty. He had knocked on the door, and receiving no answer looked around. There were curtains in the windows and rubbish in the dustbin. The garden was not neglected. Short of breaking in there was nothing more he could find out. But going back along the drive he suddenly saw a ferocious face looking at him over the hedge. It belonged to a very tall black man.

"You looking for someone?" said the face.

"Yes … Commander Swallow?"

"They're not here."

"Mr Moraes?"

"I told ya, they're not here."

"Can you tell me when they left?"

"You some kind of reporter?" said the man. "Listen, there's no one here, like I said. And Mr Moraes, he don't like people nosing around his place. He told me to keep an eye open for reporters, and he hates reporters real bad. You want some advice, you beat it, okay?"

Moraes was clearly not far away. And, true to form, he had enrolled some dubious allies.

But that night at sea, after Oz had told James of this incident in the bar, they tended to forget about everything except their return home. Oz was talking about Marie-Claire, and the girls – they would all be that interesting bit older; had they remembered to wind the clocks? Would he find the car unscathed, and the "bomb" still able to jolt around the orchard? And the money: the Steyne estate presumably would not refuse to pay what had been originally agreed. It would be a good thing to have that money firmly in the bank; it was, after all, the chief reason he had embarked on the whole extraordinary affair.

And James, listening, thought of his mother; high summer at Churbridge; hot tiring trips to London in dark suits to see solicitors; explanations to friends and relations. How would his mother have reacted to his telegram ARRIVING SOUTHAMPTON 25TH IN ORPHEUS LOVE JAMES? It must be reaching her just about now. Would she move out of Upton House when they were married? No, she would find some reason for not doing that. So where to live?

And what about Alice's parents? Alice had cabled them too. They would be enormously relieved to have heard from her, but scarcely happy with the situation, at least at first. That problem would have to be faced.

However, surrounded as he was by after-dinner conversation, tobacco smoke, and a most attentive barman, their return home still seemed a hypothetical matter. He kept reminding himself that in three days it would be real; but Oz did not help him concentrate.

"Have this one on me, James. One for the broken arm." Oz of course was drinking beer.

Tomorrow, he thought, I really must do some thinking. Tomorrow, I really will.

It was late when they decided to turn in. James went on deck, and the thick warm air fuddled him. An absurd green-grey moon was swaying low over the water. What a glorious night! Pity La Rue, I mean Alice, can't be up here to enjoy it. Perfect, romantic night at sea. Well, to bed. I'll tiptoe in quietly. I'm not really drunk, just a bit light-headed.

He groped his way to the main stairway and found the right deck. In the passage he passed a fellow he knew just coming out of the heads, and said goodnight. But when he reached the cabin door he realised his mistake: of course, we've changed cabins now, we've got a first-class cabin up on B deck. Silly me. There's something else wrong too.

Christ Almighty! Was that fellow Moraes?

Couldn't have been. Moraes on board – ridiculous! You've got the shriekers, boy; too much whisky. It may have looked like Moraes, but it couldn't be, could it? Just check that Alice is all right though, just in case.

He reached the cabin, the right one this time, and burst open the door.

"Alice! Are you all right?"

She sat up in bed with a start and switched on the light.

"Oh, it's you. Do be a bit quieter, or you'll wake up the baby."

"I'm very pleased you're all right," he said.

"Of course I'm all right. What's the matter?"

It was difficult to know what to say. He bolted the door carefully. "Oh not tonight, darling," she said. "I'm very tired and you're a little bit drunk."

"All right, all right," he said tersely. It wasn't that anyway, he thought, as he pulled off his shoes. And she might have left the light on. It's not easy undressing with one hand in the dark when your head is spinning.

But he didn't sleep long. His stomach roused him an hour or two later, and his first thought was that the ship must be rolling heavily. He got up and went to the porthole, feeling awful. The horizon was silvery and steady. It was his stomach that was moving, not the ship. What a balls-up, he thought, hunched over the basin, I'm going to be sick. Our first few days of married life in a civilised community, and I have to get drunk and disgrace myself. Idiot.

Suddenly there was a faint noise at the porthole, and a rope's end swung across his horizon. An instant later the moonlit sea was blotted out by some dark shape. As he leapt for the glass and banged it shut in automatic self-defence, he felt something hit it from the outside.

Quick. On clips. Oh quickly!

His left hand was all thumbs. But he got the brass butterfly nuts over the frame, and screwed down tight. Really tight.

Alice was waking up.

"Do be quiet, darling," she said sleepily.

But he knew what had to be done now, and at all costs he must get there first.

"Bolt the door behind me," he shouted.

"What's going on?"

"Don't argue. Bolt the door." And he was out in the passage.

Don't panic, he told himself fiercely. The man's got to climb back up that rope. If I can only find the place I'm sure to get there before him.

He clattered up two ladders and came out on deck. He rushed to the rail. Eighty foot of ship's side dropped away vertically into the sea like a smooth cliff. The rope was nowhere to be seen.

He looked behind him. He was just below the bridge. The deck was unlit and in deep shadow. It seemed deserted.

A noise at his feet made him jump violently, like treading on a snake. His eyes, now more accustomed to the darkness, picked out a slight movement at the base of a stanchion. It was the rope, secured to itself with a round turn and two half hitches, almost invisible in the moonlight. He peered over the rail again. A dark shape was just becoming distinct against the unbroken sweep of the ship's side.

He positioned himself where his right arm in plaster could have a free swing at anyone climbing up the rope. No holds barred now, he told himself. The man's a murderer. He's killed at least twice, and he's certainly out to get me and Alice.

But have I the right to murder him? Is it fair to knock him off the rope? Will they accuse me of manslaughter? Does he really want to murder me? And why?

Because you have his wife and the evidence that can convict him of murder. Be your age. *Kill him.*

And there at the top of the rope James waited to do murder. Time seemed to drag. He looked at his new watch; it was ten minutes to four. He looked over the side: he could now see a face looking up.

An age later, when his watch showed nine minutes to four, it had become obvious that Moraes was unable to climb the rope. For some reason he was stuck, dangling over the sea.

What the hell do I do now, thought James? What on earth can I do? *Cut the rope.*

At that moment a white figure appeared, saw James in his pyjamas, and checked his stride.

"Good morning. Is all well? Can't sleep?"

The forces of ordinary reason returned. He could not murder Moraes now. Catch him alive if possible, but not kill him in cold blood.

"No, I need help. There's a man on the end of a rope here."

"Is there, indeed?" It was the First Officer, on his way to the bridge to take over the watch. He had been at sea for more years than he had spent ashore. It was not the first lunatic who had gone over the side. He had a look.

"Yes. Cordage stopper and six hands. I'll get the watch-on-deck. Stay here please, and watch him."

But James did not stay. He dashed away to give Oz a shake. It was an automatic reaction, and he got the old automatic reply: "Coming up." By the time he had returned to the deck there were sailors everywhere. He joined them in pulling with his one good arm. The First Officer was giving orders.

"Haul away. You've got the weight now. Easy does it. Pull him up handsomely. There she comes. *Vast heaving*. Buggeration."

The rope was slack.

"What's up, what's the problem?" said a number of voices.

"He seemed to let go of the rope. He scraped down the ship's side and hit the sea hard."

"Silly bastard," said someone. "Doesn't deserve to be pulled up."

"Man overboard!" shouted the First Officer.

The cry was taken up on the bridge. The siren bellowed, unspeakably loud in their ears. A flare was thrown into the water. Very slowly the ship began to turn.

Oz appeared out of the darkness.

"Are you sure it was Moraes?"

"Wait – I'm just going to see Alice."

"I'll come too."

As they ran together down the corridor Oz said: "I saw him hit the water, *splat*. I don't reckon he could've survived it."

"Alice, it's me. Open up!" He banged on the door.

She was in her nightdress, rocking the baby in her arms. She looked tense and frightened.

"What happened?" said James.

"Peter was hanging on the rope, and he had the front of his shirt caught in the porthole. He tried to struggle out of it, and then someone started pulling the rope out of his hands. He tried frantically to hold on but he couldn't, then the shirt tore and he disappeared."

She took a deep breath. "I could have freed him but I didn't."

She inclined her head over her baby like a Madonna and continued to rock. But she was crying now, soundlessly and despairingly.

James went towards her but she did not respond.

"Just leave me tonight," she said. "I'll be a good wife tomorrow, but please, just leave me alone till the morning."

Oz was opening the porthole and removing a piece of silk material. They left without looking at each other.

CHAPTER TWENTY-SEVEN

Back on deck, there was a good deal happening. A party of sailors were getting a boat ready for lowering. The ship was heeling over slightly and still turning. She seemed to be going much slower. Far out there was a tiny flare that flickered irregularly. They were using searchlights that cut brilliant circles of light on the surface of the sea.

Oz said: "I saw it fairly clearly. He was pinned to the porthole by his shirt, and the rope just pulled through his fingers. And when there was no more rope, of course the shirt couldn't hold his whole weight. He tried to push off from the ship's side as he fell, and he hit the water with a hideous belly-flop, spread-eagled. It must have knocked him unconscious, at least. And then he might well have been drawn into the propellers. They may find the body, but I doubt it. Dead bodies sink for several days. So do unconscious ones."

James said nothing. He was remembering his thoughts at the top of the rope towards the man at the bottom. He had already killed the cousin, and now Moraes was dead. And who would carry the can?

"How do you feel, old boy?" said Oz.

"Shaken." The nervous energy was wearing off, and he began to feel sick again.

"You'd better go down to my cabin. I'll go and tell the Bridge what I know. We can't do any more."

James found his way to Oz's cabin and locked the door. He was shivering. The back of his mind was framing legal questions against himself:

"And you therefore admit abducting the dead man's wife?"

"Well, I ..."

"And committing adultery with her under his very nose?"

"Yes, but ..."

"And are we to understand that you closed the porthole on his clothing, and assisted to drag the rope from his hands while your mistress looked on from inside? Take your time, Mr Huwes; the jury will wait for your answer."

Oz banged on the door, and James let him in. "The Master agrees there's no chance. But he's going to search till dawn – another hour. There'll be a police investigation back home, of course."

"What should I tell the police?" said James shakily.

"Why, tell them the truth, of course," said Oz. "Don't try to hide anything. Nothing on earth to worry about if you tell the truth."

Oz's gift for sounding reassuring had never been more appreciated.

"This will be Exhibit A, I suppose," he said, taking the piece of shirt material out of his pocket. "And, conveniently enough, it's got his monogram embroidered on the silk."

He pronounced it "seelk". All was well. Oz would see them through.

"I've often wondered what was the use of a monogrammed shirt," said Oz.

* * * * *

The ship remained searching in the area until daylight showed that the sea was positively empty, and then she proceeded on her course at best speed.

So Moraes is really dead, thought James. That simplifies things. No divorce, no delay, explanations easier all round – some of the explanations, anyway. And good riddance to a thoroughly evil man. God moves in a mysterious way.

He managed to shake off his feelings of guilt. But Alice was subdued.

"I killed him," she said.

"You didn't really. And I would have done. And he would have killed us."

"He was my husband."

"Yes, but you mustn't blame yourself. You hated him. He was ruthless and wicked and a murderer. We have our lives ahead of us now. The whole ugly drama is over."

"What should I tell the police?"

"Tell them the truth. Don't try to hide anything. Nothing on earth to worry about if you tell the truth."

* * * * *

The Master made a signal to shore asking for a police investigation on arrival. He also told his First Officer to conduct a preliminary enquiry.

"Did you know the dead man?" the First Officer asked Alice.

"I was married to him."

"Good. That solves one problem. He joined the ship in Bermuda under a false name and we've not been able, until now, to trace his next of kin."

* * * * *

"So this is it," said Alice.

"Home from sea," said Oz. "The most memorable moment in a sailor's life."

The end of an epic adventure, thought James. A decisive end. From now on it's a new world for James and Alice. The past stops here, and the present begins.

They were on deck watching Southampton Docks materialise through a thin mist. The air was cool and easy to breathe; English air must be like this always. There on the passenger wharf was a knot of people waiting to welcome them. A police car was parked a little way away, but still uncomfortably conspicuous. The Law would doubtless swarm aboard like a pack of dogs as soon as the gangway was down.

The ship slid nearer. Tugs churned her into position, puffing and blowing.

There was his mother. Dear old ma, he thought, just the same as always – a thought that I may not be the first to have hit upon, but it is absurdly comforting all the same. Trite but true. What will she say when she finds she has a grandson, born out of wedlock?

Marie-Claire was there, and, it seemed, most if not all the girls. They were unfolding a large banner that read "Welcome Home" in a cartouche that included clocks, chinoiseries, sheep and bees. Oz was grinning from ear to ear.

Mr and Mrs Cullerby were there, looking anxious and well dressed. Alice glanced at James for reassurance. He said: "You're looking beautiful and very young again. I like it. But don't forget you're a proper widow with a family and a perfectly respectable lover. *Nil carborundum.*"

And he thought, perhaps nobody is entirely self-reliant. I needed Oz. She needs me.

Mr Winter was there. He would be able to sort out the financial shambles. There would be quite a lot of sorting necessary.

And Ishbel was standing by herself, waiting patiently. Has anyone told her, thought James? What will become of her?

"Do you see all I see, darling?" he asked.

She nodded.

"There'll be mayhem when that lot converges on our cabin," he went on. "Or perhaps they will all cancel each other out. I'm afraid there's a lot of explanations going to be required of us. Let's go below and lie in wait for them. It may be a bit of a joke really."

They went down to the cabin. Felix was gurgling happily in his cot. He was a cheerful, noisy creature, and had a particularly rapt blue stare.

"Darling, as soon as we decently can, let's get away from everything and everyone, and go off somewhere together," she said. "Somewhere remote and private and just be ourselves. All these people frighten me."

He laughed. "Good idea. There was a splendid little cottage in Argyll I once borrowed, very private and very comfortable, bit of fishing, and a boat. I'll see if I can fix it."

They sat on the bed and held hands.

"Who will be the first to find us, do you think?" she said.

"My mother."

"I think the police."

"I have a great admiration for the pertinacity of the police, but I still think my mother."

In fact it was neither. The first person to reach their cabin had a camera and a notebook and a red moustache, and appeared to be a newspaper reporter. It seemed he had already talked to some of the crew.

"Señora Moraes," he said, "I hear you lost your husband under tragic circumstances during the voyage, while he was trying to enter your cabin by the porthole at the end of a rope. Was it this very porthole perhaps? Not very big, is it? Was it open at the time? What time was it? You weren't sharing a cabin with him, I believe, were you?"

The reporter was scribbling furiously in a notebook, although so far no one had spoken except him.

"May I ask," he went on, "whether you were on good terms with your billionaire husband? Or whether you had arranged a separation by mutual consent? And could you say what your feelings were ..."

"Get out," said James. "Now ... immediately. Just get out. I don't know what you are talking about. Go away and leave us alone."

"One last question, Señora Moraes. What do you intend to do with all that money?"

"Hrrrr ..." James produced a fine aggressive growl, and the reporter backed out of the door, still scribbling.

"What money?" said Alice.

"It's just occurred to me, my darling, you were his legal wife, so you'll presumably inherit all the Steyne money."

"Oh my God."

"Wow! I'm going to marry a billionairess! Thank you lucky star ... thank you guardian angel ... yoohoo!"

He did a little hop and skip over to the cot.

"Felix!" he cried. "What's it feel like to be the heir to a fortune, eh? Heir to a fair, fat fortune that you've done nothing to earn? Pretty good?"

Felix gurgled happily, gripped James's little finger and, surely, almost winked.